The Enchanted Kingdoms

Haunting Fairytales Series

R. L. Weeks

Praise for the Haunting Fairytales Series

Amazon reviews

One of the best fairytales I have ever read! Page turning suspense! Fairytales gone wild!

This is the BEST fairytale book with new twists on classic characters I have ever read!

I absolutely loved this book! If you loved Fairytales as a child, you will love them as an adult. Truly twisted! Definitely a must read!

Dark and suspenseful, very fast paced and hard to put down. Fairytale and dark fantasy lovers won't want to miss this!

Its a rollercoaster ride that you'll want to get on over and over again and each time you will feel something different!

The evil gets better and better and the teams are changing. The story is getting better and better as you go. I couldn't put the book down!

* * *

R. L. Weeks always puts such a unique and dark twist on the classics, but she outdid herself with this one. The way each classic fairytale flows through this book is flawless and original in an unexpected way.
Bewitched Reader Review Blog

Enchanting!! I fell in love with this Collection of Fairytales!! Suspenseful, Dramatic and Unexpected!
Fractured Fairy Tales Book Blog

The fairytale atmosphere was definitely present here, and though none of the tales were particularly happy, they were written in a manner which created a nice balance between the lighthearted wonder I was familiar with as a child, and the dark roots of the original tales.
Claire Kavanaugh Blog

This book is sold subject to the condition that it shall not, by way of trade or otherwise, be lent, re-sold, duplicated, hired out, or otherwise circulated without the publisher's prior written consent in any form of binding or cover other than that in which it is published and without similar condition including this condition being imposed on the subsequent purchaser.

This is a work of fiction. All characters and events portrayed in this novel are fictitious and are products of the author's imagination and any resemblance to actual events, or locales or persons, living or dead are entirely coincidental.

Cover designer: Custom Cover Designs
Edited by Editing4Indies
Published by Vamptasy Publishing

R. l. Weeks © 2016
All rights reserved
Second Edition
2017

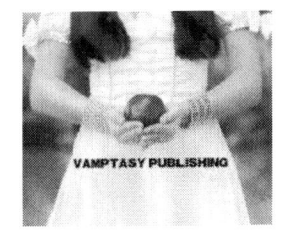

Haunting Fairytales Series

INTRODUCTION

The world of Cantata has ten enchanted kingdoms.
Northmanni, Colomorgh, Milborn, Forosh, Sirani, Agrabah, Dolorom, Fainland, Santeria, and Tilan.

To the east, Santeria was once the largest land. Vikings lived there, and they knew nothing but violence. Santeria, however, turned into Neverland due to an enchanted fountain found deep within the forest.

The second largest is Dolorom, a rich and powerful country. Bordering Dolorom is its poorer yet greener land, Fainland.

To the west is Northmanni, a cultured and proud land. Bordering Northmanni is Colomorgh, a poor land, and Milborn, known for its beautiful statues and delicious shellfish.

At the south of Cantata is Agrabah and Tilan, which have the hottest climates.

To the north are the two coldest lands; Forosh, named after the delicious fish that swam in its waters, and Sirani.

Cantata is an enchanted world filled with sorcerers, witchcraft, shapeshifters, mermaids, and fairies. It once had eight founders, who controlled the magic in the world. The only founder left in Cantata now is Merlin. He holds an object called the moral compass, which all sorcerers must use. It prevents them from using their powers to cause harm. However, some sorcerers have found loopholes and manage to use their powers for evil. Those sorcerers were quickly drained of their magic and must find more every few years.

The only exceptions to Merlin's rule are Neverland, which is governed by its own power, and witches. Witchcraft is taught and uses the five elements. It doesn't come from the natural powers that sorcerers have, so they can do whatever they like. Although, it is extremely difficult to master and can age a person greatly.

Many years ago, Edward, the prince and only heir to the Queen, was cursed by his former lover, Lori. Edward and Lori were both sorcerers. Edward was selfish and vain and broke her heart. Out of anger, Lori cursed him into a frog. With every curse, there must be a loophole.

Edward must find someone who will kiss him so he can become a man once more. Only one problem with that; the kiss must come from a princess, and we all know that no princess would want to kiss a frog.

Haunting Fairytales Series

FROG PRINCE

Edward croaked and looked down at his disgusting slimy feet. Soon, he hoped, he would be a prince again and no longer a frog. He sat on the palace wall in the fine Kingdom of Colomorgh. King Stefan of Colomorgh was widely known for being the most ruthless king of them all and that was possibly why Edward admired him the most.

The princess, Rapunzel, was in the palace gardens, playing with a small dog. Her hair reached down to her ankles, and she spun around, throwing a small red ball to the fluffy dog. It jumped into the pond, splashing the princess, who just laughed. Edward groaned and hopped down the groves in the wall until he was among the grass. The dog was called back inside by an old woman. Rapunzel started to walk inside too.

This was possibly his only chance to get his freedom back; at least, in this decade. Who else would kiss him more easily than a princess with a secret she wanted to keep hidden?

'Wait,' Edward called out. The princess turned and looked around in confusion. 'Down here,' he shouted as he hopped over to her feet.

The Princess kneeled, blinking repeatedly. 'You can talk,' she said, stating the improbable fact. 'Frogs can't talk. Yet here you are, talking.'

If he could roll his eyes, he would. 'Yes, yes. Look, I have a deal to strike with you. I have been watching you.'

The Enchanted Kingdoms

Her eyebrows shot up. 'You've been doing what?'

'Sorry,' he mumbled. 'I had to work out what you would want in exchange for'—he paused and croaked— 'well, for a kiss.'

Her big, blue eyes widened. 'You want me to kiss you? Why?'

'I'm cursed,' he admitted. 'I know you don't want to marry a prince. I saw you with your true love, the one you can't be with.'

'You saw? You mustn't tell a soul,' she gasped. 'Please, if Father found that I am ...'

'I won't tell,' he interrupted. 'I understand, in fact, I think it's sweet. However, you must marry a prince, yes?'

She nodded and frowned. 'Unfortunately, I must. If not, I will never become Queen. Father will choose my cousin, who is just as horrible as him. The kingdom will never know a fair ruler.'

He nodded. 'Daddy issues, I get it. So here is what I have to offer,' he said. 'If you kiss me, I will turn back into a prince. I am also in love with someone else,' he lied. 'So we can have just a mutually beneficial relationship,' he continued. 'I must marry a princess to appease my mother and stepfather. We can both be with who we love and remain married to unite our kingdoms. We can talk about the details later. So are you in, princess?' he asked. 'Also, Rapunzel,' he said before she could answer, 'if you do accept, we should probably provide just one heir,' he said, trying to sound convincing.

He had chosen this opportune moment to offer her this deal. Now that her lover had left, he could finally get her at her most naïve.

Rapunzel leaned forwards and placed her hand on the grass. Edward hopped onto her hand. She brought him up to her face. 'You'd better be telling me the truth,' she warned.

Edward laughed. 'Why would I lie? Do you not want to see your true love again?'

She took a deep breath and brought him closer to her lips. 'I would do anything. Okay, so just one kiss, right?'

He nodded. 'Right.'

Her expression twisted into one of disgust as she felt the slimy feel of his skin against her soft, thin lips. He croaked one final time and jumped off her hand, landing on the grass just in time.

Green mist swirled in hypnotising patterns as the shape of the frog grew larger, morphing into the shape of a handsome, athletic man.

As he grew taller, Rapunzel grew smaller. She looked down at her hands and screamed. She had turned into a frog. She looked up at the prince distraught. 'What have you done?'

He shrugged. 'Sorry, love, better you than me. I needed a princess to kiss me, and you were the perfect target. You'll probably need to find a prince to kiss you now, so yeah, good luck. It took me years to get that kiss.'

She hopped after him as he turned to walk away. 'I will tell my parents! They will hunt you down!' Edward turned and scratched his neat beard.

The Enchanted Kingdoms

He pondered as Rapunzel hopped around pathetically, trying to shout for the guards. 'You're right,' he said and swiped his hand through the air. She felt her voice leave her throat and when she tried to talk, nothing came out but croaks. 'You'll get your voice back once you turn into a human again, which will probably never happen,' he admitted, pressing his lips together. 'Well, I have my kingdom to go back to. I haven't seen it for so long.' He looked down at his naked body and conjured up some riding boots, black trousers, a white and gold jacket, and a sword in its scabbard.

He felt the warmth run back up his arm as the magic faded, and he was dressed as a prince once more. He didn't have a lot of magic left and would need to be careful with it until he could find a way to get more.

The annoying thing about being a sorcerer is, unless you're Merlin, you only have a certain amount of power. Edward didn't go by the rules, which meant his powers drained fast.

He stretched out his legs, feeling the wonder of being able to walk again as a man and strutted off, leaving poor Rapunzel hopping desperately after him.

He lost her as he hurried outside the palace, heading for the nearest inn so he could find some poor soul and con them into helping him get home. Edward decided to sail home instead of using magic to transport himself there so he could save what magic he had left to find more once back in Dolorom.

***

Three days passed as Edward enjoyed his newfound freedom, drinking until late. He had managed to secure a horse and cart to take him down to the docks early in the morning. He was lucky to find a man who would help him, an old merchant called Thomas, who fortunately had his own ship.

Thomas brought Edward another drink and sat down at the wooden table.

Everyone in the room was rowdy, sloshing ale down their throats. 'Thanks,' Edward said and took the drink. 'I will give you fifty gold coins when I return to Dolorom.'

Thomas ran his hand through his thick grey hair and drank some of his ale.

'I do not want gold. However, my daughter is single and lonely. I was hoping you could perhaps find her a good suitor in your fine kingdom?'

Edward pressed his lips together. 'Is she attractive?'

'Beautiful,' Thomas replied.

Edward smirked and drank the last of his drink. Of course, the old man would say his daughter is beautiful. He examined the man's wrinkled complexion. He wasn't bad looking for his age, but he wasn't conventionally handsome either. If she looked like anything like him, then it would be hard for him to find her a husband. In Dolorom, far too many exceedingly attractive or filthy rich women were looking for husbands.

'If,' Edward pointed out, 'she is not as beautiful as the ladies in my kingdom, then it is unlikely I would find a wealthy man with a title to wed her. Especially with being the daughter of a merchant with no title too,' Edward admitted.

The Enchanted Kingdoms

The old man leant forwards. 'She is called Griselda.' He showed Edward a picture of his daughter. As he thought, she was average, nothing special.

'I have four daughters, yet I worry about Griselda the most. My other daughters, especially Belle, would have no problem finding a husband. So can you help me? This is the condition in which I help you get back to your kingdom.'

'I will find her a husband,' Edward lied. 'You have my word.' He shook the old man's hand and left to go to bed. It would be a long day tomorrow, and he was excited to return home after all this time.

Since his former partner, Lori, cursed him, he had wandered the forests trying to find a way to become human once more. Then he found a witch, Gertrude, who tampered with the curse so any kiss could turn him back into a prince after Lori had left him with the '*only true love's kiss can break the curse*' out of spite.

After all, he had said he loved her. Lori, Princess of Forosh. He could not see how it was his fault. After all, Lori was beautiful in her own right, but one of her ladies was much more beautiful and that was what mattered. He had wondered all this time how she could stay so angry? Did Lori honestly expect him, the most handsome prince in all the lands, to stay loyal to someone as average as her?

***

The following morning, Edward awoke to a most peculiar yet horrifyingly familiar feeling.

He was surrounded by darkness and felt strangely cold. He moved and felt the sheet under his slimy webbed hands.

He had somehow turned back into a frog.

Cheers erupted from the hallway. 'The princess has returned,' one man shouted cheerily. Edward gulped.

Another man spoke outside Edward's room. 'She's telling everyone that she was turned into a frog. Can you believe it? Wherever she disappeared to clearly made her loopy.'

Edward hopped off the bed. If anyone did believe Rapunzel's unlikely story, then there would be a hunt for him.

Not caring for his magic supply, which would be useless if he were dead, he made himself vanish just as Thomas opened the door to take Edward down to the docks.

Edward reappeared outside of Gertrude's candy cottage and hopped onto the gingerbread windowsill. The haggard woman he had dealt with before was sat in front of a pile of small bones and a roaring fire.

'Come in,' she said, noticing his presence. He hopped through the open window.

'I need your help,' he admitted.

She smirked. 'After all this time, you still can't find anyone to kiss you?'

'I did,' he said. 'A princess. It didn't work. You promised it would work!'

She scraped the rest of the meat from one of the small bones and stood up. 'You obviously didn't do it properly.'

'How can anyone get a kiss wrong?' he asked, feeling frustrated. 'We had a deal. I led those kids to you,' he said, feeling a little sick to his stomach. 'Killing isn't beneath me, but they were just children.'

She cackled. 'They were delicious. Thank you.'

He hopped onto her oak table. 'Make this right!'

She rolled her eyes, grabbed her cane, and made her way over to the bubbling cauldron.

'Fine, I will. I may have left out some important ingredients. I will try something new,' she said, hunching over the cauldron.

Edward laid out on the table, stretching his legs and basking in the warm glow of the sun that shined through the window.

He could hear clanking from the kitchen followed by a smash. 'Clumsy fool!' Gertrude said to the closed door. Edward figured it must a servant and laid back down.

Green and orange smoke swirled up from the cauldron where she worked. Gertrude wiped the sweat from her forehead with her tattered sleeve. 'It is done,' she exclaimed, filling a tiny vial with orange liquid. She handed the vial to the Edward who gulped it down in one.

Gertrude grinned. 'The next time you kiss a princess, you will turn back into a man permanently.'

He looked up at her annoyed. 'I've heard that before.'

She slammed her fist down on the table. 'It will work,' she promised. 'I always fulfil my deals.'

'You'd better,' he warned. 'I will be leaving then. I have another princess to find and trick, which will take me another year at the least. Thanks a lot.'

Gertrude huffed and walked toward the kitchen. 'Wait here. I have someone who can help you.' When she returned, she was accompanied by a handsome man with a wide jaw and small brown eyes.

'This is Henry,' she said. 'He is my servant, and now, he is yours.' She looked at Henry. 'Henry, the talking frog is called Edward. He is a prince. You will help him to find a princess to kiss. You are free from my charm binding you here.'

Henry arched his tangled eyebrow and looked at Edward. 'You don't eat kids too, do you?'

Edward glanced at Gertrude with disgust then looked back at Henry. 'No, I'm not that sick.'

'Thank God,' Henry breathed.

Edward hopped onto the windowsill and turned to Gertrude. 'How do I know he will help me?'

She cackled. 'I'd hoped you'd ask that.' She took a dusty vial from one of the rickety shelves and handed it to Henry. 'Be a dear and take this. If you wish to be free from me, that is.'

Henry begrudgingly took the potion and clutched at his chest as if he were having a heart attack. 'Now,' Gertrude said, 'he has a sadness coiled around his heart for you. It will only break once your curse is permanently broken. I have been waiting to use that potion for a long time.'

'Interesting potion,' Edward said.

She grinned, loving the acknowledgment of how powerful she is. 'It takes a lot of skill to make one, but it was easy for me.'

Henry walked over to the door and grabbed Edward from the windowsill, setting him on his hand. 'Let's go,' Edward said.

'Oh,' Gertrude called after them, 'before I forget.'
Edward turned. 'What?'

Gertrude sat back in front of the fire. 'You must kill the girl you kiss when she turns into a frog.'

'You left that part out!' he snapped.

She cackled. 'We both know that killing innocents isn't beneath you.'

'Suppose,' he replied.

She laughed. 'Were you trying to turn over a new leaf?' she asked. 'Get it, frogs, lily pads?'

Henry opened the door, and Edward looked back at Gertrude for hopefully the last time. 'Worst. Joke. Ever,' he replied, annoyed.

'Good luck, little prince,' she called out before Henry slammed the gingerbread door behind them, making crumbs fall onto the sticky candy mat below.

MAGIC HAIR

Rapunzel was brought into the throne room. King Stefan lowered his gaze down to his daughter. 'I know you have always been a free spirit,' he spat. 'I have had that burden since the day you were pushed into this world!' He stood up from his throne and walked down to Rapunzel and Rapunzel's mother, Marie, who held a stiff upper lip and crossed her hands in front of her green velvet dress.

Rapunzel stepped forward. 'Father, I—'

'Majesty,' he corrected. 'It's Your Majesty.' Rapunzel nodded and stepped backwards. Her father towered over her. His barrel chest and muscular arms were intimidating enough.

He often liked to display his strength against anyone he could. Unlike Rapunzel, he had a wide jaw and eyes the colour of the deepest ocean; a blue so dark they were almost black.

'This is a step too far. Half the kingdom thinks you're crazy!' he boomed.

'Telling everyone you were turned into a frog? That's just ridiculous. Magic may do many things, but there is not much magic in this kingdom, let alone enough to turn anyone into a frog.' He slammed his fist down on the table.

'The ones who do believe you think that you're a witch. So many rumours are attached to your name. I cannot have you in line to be the next queen. The kingdom will do better under the rule of your cousin—'

'No,' Rapunzel shouted.

Her father ground his teeth and looked over at an expressionless Marie. 'She will need to be locked up!' he shouted. 'Guards,' he said, and the guards stepped forward. 'Lock my daughter in her chambers. Do not let anyone in and do not let her out.'

'Please, Father,' she cried. 'I mean Your Majesty.' She sniffed. 'Please don't. I'm telling the truth.'

He looked his daughter up and down. His expression faltered as he saw nothing but honesty in her eyes. 'Maybe we could have a trial.'

She knelt, thanking him, but as she cried, her hair began to glow. She wished to be free to live her life when suddenly she was lifted from the ground and her father was pushed backwards.

He fell onto his throne as Rapunzel swept through the air to the door, looking around, confused at what was happening. 'Magic hair,' her father gasped. 'Witch!' he shouted. 'Grab her.' The guards ran to her. She dropped to the floor, but her magic put a barrier between them and her. King Stefan shouted, 'Jacqueline Malasini.'

A witch appeared in the room. Her greasy black hair and muddy brown eyes suited her dirty ragged brown dress. 'What?' she asked, bored. She sat down on the throne.

King Stefan rolled his eyes. 'Did I pull you away from doing nothing?'

'Actually,' she said, 'I've been struggling to keep my home.'

'Too lazy to actually keep the magic up?' Stefan asked. 'As always. Anyway, I have proposition for you that won't require much work.'

She stood up. 'I'm listening,' she said and looked over at Rapunzel who was sobbing by the door behind a barrier spell. King Stefan looked at Rapunzel. 'My daughter has lost her mind. I will give more than enough gold coins and a tower I own deep in the forest. All you need is to put a strong spell up around the tower to keep her in there and look after her. She's sixteen, so she wouldn't require much caring for.'

Jackie nodded. 'She is magical,' Jackie said, sensing Rapunzel's magic. 'From a leftover curse, it seems. It seems to have trapped itself into her hair.'

Stefan ground his teeth. 'I don't care. Use her magic. Just take her.'

Jackie nodded. 'Of course, Your Majesty. I know the tower you mean.'

Jackie walked over to Rapunzel and grabbed her arm. Rapunzel screamed as she was transported by Jackie to the tower. Betrayal rippled through Rapunzel's mind as she was thrown to the stone floor.

Jackie smiled. Gold coins, a home, and a girl with magic hair that she could use to channel the magic and keep the barrier spell up. One day, she could even take Rapunzel's hair when there was enough magic.

Magic left over from a curse is powerful, powerful enough that in ten, maybe fifteen years she could syphon enough magic to be able to build the home she always wanted. She could turn so many men into her servants. She would never have to lift a finger again.

Jackie put up the barrier spell, unknowingly to Rapunzel, channeling the magic from her hair.

Rapunzel tried to use magic again to escape, but it didn't work, due to the channeling. She looked out of the arched window and wept. She was now locked away with a lazy witch. She was trapped in the tower for all the time. She would never see her love again and her dream of being queen was as lost as her freedom.

DOPEY

Henry looked around in the dead forest. 'I'm freezing.'

'As am I,' Edward replied from the satchel where Henry was carrying him.

'We can take the shortcut,' Henry offered, pointing at a path that wound around the trees. The path was covered with overgrown ivy and brambles. 'Not many have gone down it.'

'Great,' Edward replied. 'More reason why I don't want to take the shortc- OW!' Edward fell out of the satchel and frowned at Henry. 'You fool!'

'Sorry,' Henry replied and picked up the satchel. 'I have always been a little ...'

'Dopey?' Edward asked smarmily. 'Take better care!'

Henry nodded. 'Of course. I am so sorry. Are you hurt?'

'No.'

Henry smiled. 'Good. I really do think we should take the shortcut.'

Edward sighed. 'Fine, get on with it. I want to get this over and done with.' Henry carried the satchel and proceeded down the winding, uneven path. The dead trees creaked in the wind as the light faded until Henry and Edward were showered in the moonlight.

They avoided the small frozen pools that littered the path; winter had come, leaving the woods looking as depressing as Edward's life had become.

Henry's stomach rumbled loudly.

The Enchanted Kingdoms

'I'm starving,' Henry said and huffed. It was getting darker by the second, and he hadn't eaten all day. To distract himself from the hunger, he opened the satchel slightly and looked down at the frog. 'So you told me that you are looking for a princess to kiss and turn into a frog, but you didn't tell me the whole story. You know what they say—time passes quicker with good conversation.'

Edward grumbled. 'Ugh, fine.' Henry took Edward out of the satchel and almost dropped him but caught him just in time and placed him onto his hand. 'Careful,' Edward shouted. 'Right, Dopey ...' he started. 'It was some years back now. I was with a woman I loved, Lori, but she wasn't all that. So I cheated on her with one of her ladies. Beautiful, she was, but Lori got jealous of her and killed her. To punish me, she turned me into a frog. I'd promised her marriage, and she had devoted her life to me, so she saw it as a fitting punishment to add in that I could only turn back into a man with a true love's kiss. If a princess could love me despite looking like a frog. It had to be a princess too because she knew princesses could be vain. She knew I'd never find a princess to fall for me while I looked like this.'

Henry pressed his lips together. 'I can see why she was hurt.'

Edward nodded. 'Guess so, but I think she acted irrationally. I mean she wasn't the nicest person to begin with. She was jealous of everyone, all the time. It was annoying.' Edward looked out through the dark trees and sighed. 'I expected her to turn me back once she had moved on from it, but she never did. Anyway, Gertrude changed the spell so I could kiss any princess; it didn't have to be a true love. The problem was the spell didn't work properly, but then Gertrude changed it so ...'

'Yes,' Henry said. 'So you have to kill the princess once she is a frog. Isn't there any other way? I mean couldn't you just leave her as a frog?'

Edward sighed. 'I wish. No, I have to kill the princess once she is a frog.'

Henry almost dropped Edward again. 'Sorry. Look, I don't think I can assist you with murder!'

Edward tilted his head. 'You have no choice.'

The sadness around Henry's heart tightened as he battled with his morality. 'I guess I don't,' Henry said sadly.

They reached a clearing in the woods where they found a small cottage, and outside the cottage stood the most glorious apple tree either of them had ever seen. 'They look delicious.'

'No,' Edward whispered. 'Look around you, every tree is dead except that one. I sense magic, bad magic. Do not—' Henry pushed Edward back into the satchel and ran over to the tree.

He picked the reddest apple he could see and held it in his hand. It made him feel warm inside, and the smell coming from the tree was glorious. He bit into the apple and let the sweet taste run down his throat. As he enjoyed his apple, he didn't notice he was shrinking until he was four foot tall. 'What the ...?'

Edward climbed out of the satchel and looked at Henry. 'Crikey, you're ugly!'

Henry ran over to the cottage and looked in the window at his reflection. 'It's taken my looks,' he said then gasped as a face of a woman smiling evilly looked through the window back at him. He jumped backwards and sent Edward flying. Edward only caught a glimpse of the door opening before pulling the satchel over to Henry and making them both vanish and reappear in the main town of Northmanni. 'Why didn't you do that to begin with?' Henry asked.

Edward jumped back into the satchel and poked his head out. 'I have little magic left. I must save it, and thanks to you, it's almost gone! You're even dopier than I first thought.'

Henry looked around at the dimly lit town, quaint shops, and glorious inns and smiled. 'Pretty town.'

'We need to go to an inn!' Edward barked.

Henry laughed. 'I don't have any money ... And you don't unless you're storing them in hidden frog pockets.'

'Funny.' Edward snorted. 'I'll do what I always do, at least until I return home. Trick them into letting me stay!'

They passed the shimmering river that ran through the centre of town and headed over to an inn. Edward grinned. He was finally going to get his kiss and get to go home.

He was finally going to get his happy ending.

***

The following morning, Henry and Edward walked through the picturesque town and stopped by the river.

Edward poked his head out of the satchel, careful not draw any attention to himself, and looked up at Henry. 'Henry,' he whispered. 'We can't just waltz right into the palace and demand the princess kiss me. We must find out her weaknesses before we make our move.'

Henry bit the inside of his lip. His morals were being twisted in a way he hated, but when he thought of saying no, the sadness around his heart tightened.

He had no choice but to help Edward kill a woman. He couldn't wait until he was free again. So he could finally fall in love, have children, and live happily ever after.

Some would have called Henry lucky—he had snuck into the witch's cottage as a child to eat the candy. Gertrude caught him and his friends. She cooked two of them, and luckily, she was full so made him run errands for her under a spell until she felt hungry again.

However, over the next few days, she realised that having him as her servant made her life a lot easier, so he was spared his life in return for his eternal service.

He would have rather died.

He was forced to lure children to the cottage for the witch to eat, and then clean up after she had finished. He had tried to help the children, but her spell on him was too powerful.

But now, he had a chance at freedom. He may be ugly and small, but looks had never mattered much to him anyway. Henry had one simple dream; to fall in love.

He looked across the river dreamily and squinted. He ignored Edward as he droned on about a drawn-out plan, and instead focused on the beautiful woman who was feeding swans by the river. Her hair was jet black, reaching down to her shoulders, and her smile was so contagious that Henry found himself smiling just watching her from afar.

'Henry,' Edward hissed. 'Pay attention!' Edward looked over at what was distracting the man who was supposed to be helping him. 'She is quite beautiful,' he admitted. 'But no time! We must find the princess.'

Henry pushed the prince back in the satchel. 'Give me a minute.'

He walked over the wooden bridge and hurried toward the bench where she was sat. She looked at him as he approached with the kindest gaze he had ever had the pleasure of seeing. 'Do you mind?' he asked, gesturing to the spot on the bench next to her.

'Not at all,' she replied. Her voice was soft and lulling so he couldn't help but smile.

He sat down and breathed in the beautiful, floral scent. 'Sorry, it's just I have never seen such a beautiful woman in my life. I know that's forward, but I just had to come and say hello.'

Her smiled widened, and her cheeks flushed. 'Thank you, but I know you're just saying that because I'm a princess. They all do.'

'You're the princess?' His eyebrows shot up.

'Princess Mary.'

'I'm Henry.' He shuffled uncomfortably as he felt the prince try to get out of the satchel. 'Well, it was nice to meet you, your highness,' he said, jumping to his feet.

She stood up too. 'Wait,' she said. 'You're leaving?'

He nodded sadly. 'I have some things to take care of.'

She looked down at the small, ugly man yet felt warm inside. She hadn't had anyone look at her in such a genuine way since her husband died. 'I'm actually having a ball tonight to celebrate my daughter's fourteenth birthday. Would you like to come?'

'Uh.' He hesitated as he pinched the top of the satchel, making sure that the prince couldn't come out. 'I–'

'Here,' she said, handing him an invitation from her bag. 'It'll be good to see you again.' She walked off, leaving Henry and Edward alone. Edward climbed up, and Henry finally let go of the top of the satchel once the princess was out of sight. 'You really are dopey! That's our princess, and you declined to spend more time with her?'

Edward would have struck him down with his sword, if he still had his sword, and you know, he wasn't a frog. 'We are going to that ball, and that's that!'

'No,' Henry protested, but the sadness coiled around his heart pushed hard.

The urge to help the prince was the same urge a parent had to protect their child. The potion was strong. He couldn't hurt the prince, and as much as he didn't want to do this, he had no choice. 'If we go and you do what you have to do,' he said, annoyed, 'then I go free?'

'Yes,' Edward said. 'Go a million miles from here—the farther the better. Now, come on Dopey, we have a ball to get ready for. Well, you need to anyway.'

Edward had to conjure a suit up for Henry. Due to his height, there just weren't any suits that fit him.

Not only was Henry the size of a child, but he was muscular, which meant the children's dress clothes just didn't look right on him, and if Edward cared about anything, it was people looking their best. They walked up the long winding road to the palace. The sounds of carriage wheels going along the gritty road were mixed with the sound of drunken cheers as people made their way to the

The Enchanted Kingdoms

princess's ball. Henry walked over with the frog in his pocket and handed the invitation to the guard. He nodded and allowed Henry to enter. He gasped as he walked in.

He had never seen such a beautiful place. Huge chandeliers hung from the ceiling, glistening against the white stone roof. The room was so big that Henry had to squint just to see to the other side of the ballroom. Along the side of the room were several tables decorated with ice sculptures.

Bowls of delicious foods, including the finest oysters shipped in from Forosh, juicy venison from Dolorom, and spiced foods from Agrabah.

On the balcony, overlooking the room, the king and queen sat on red velvet thrones. The flag of their kingdom hung down the front of the balcony.

A band stood on a small stage, overlooking the crowd of people dressed in their finest garments. They continued to play the beautiful music from their brass instruments. Henry spotted the princess by the table holding the hand of a miniature version of her; he guessed that must be her daughter. Snow lived up to her name; her skin was as white as snow, but her lips were the colour of blood, and they looked striking. Her eyes were as green as the emeralds on her necklace, and her hair, which fell to the small of her back, was as black as ebony. Although only fourteen, she looked older. She walked with such grace and spoke quickly yet clearly. Her eyes sparkled with wonder as she looked around the room decorated in silver, white, and red. Henry gulped and took a deep breath. His hands were clammy. He held onto the gift he had managed to get for Snow.

Edward had encased a snowflake in some strange, see-through substance, so it looked like an ornament, then shaped into a circle. It was small, the size of a gold coin. Edward had helped him turn it into a necklace. He peeked into the black box to look at the beautifully encased snowflake on the sparkling, white gold chain and smiled.

He walked over to the princess and bowed. 'Majesty,' he said.

Princess Mary smiled widely. 'I'd hoped you come! This is my daughter, Snow,' she said, gesturing to her beautiful daughter.

Henry bowed then handed her the box. 'For you, Princess. Happy birthday.'

Snow opened the box and gasped. 'It's beautiful! Thank you so much!'

Henry smiled sadly. 'I would offer to put it on, but I wouldn't reach,' he admitted, embarrassed.

Snow giggled. 'Here,' she said and knelt so Henry could reach her neck. He moved her hair out of the way, which he noticed was perfectly straight, and hung the necklace around her neck. She stood up and examined it. 'It's so beautiful.'

Her mother looked down at her. 'Like you. Beautiful and unique.' Since Snow's father had died, her mother was all she had left. They were close and happy, and they meant everything to each other.

Fortunately, Snow also had amazing grandparents, so she never felt unloved. However, she felt such immense pressure to marry. She knew her mother didn't want to marry again.

The Enchanted Kingdoms

She said love would be the only reason she would marry, and being a princess meant that men only wanted one thing; to be king. Love had nothing to do with it. Mary had stopped the king from sending in suitor after suitor for Snow, explaining that she is just fourteen and needs to live a little first.

However, Snow knew that her future was decided for her. As soon as she reached sixteen, not even her mother would be able to stop the king from marrying her off. She would enter a loveless marriage then probably soon after become queen. Snow loved her birthday. It took her mind off everything. Her days were filled with lessons, greetings, meetings, more lessons, and appearances around Northmanni. She was always travelling too. This would be the only time in the next year when she could be free from her tasks and hoped that she and her mother could spend some time together in the evening.

Mary looked down at Snow and looked over at the Duke of Carlin, the largest town in Northmanni. 'Snow,' she whispered. 'I believe the duke wants another dance.'

Snow sighed. 'Last time, he stomped on my foot!'

Mary laughed. 'He's just a little clumsy. Go on.' As Snow walked away begrudgingly to dance with the duke, Mary turned her attention to Henry. 'Thank you for Snow's beautiful gift. It really is one of a kind.'

Henry blushed. 'My pleasure.'

'Would you like to dance?' Mary asked, biting her lip. She didn't understand it, but she felt a warmth when she was around Henry.

Henry frowned. 'I'm too small. Everyone will look at you, and we won't be able to dance properly.'

Mary looked around. 'I do not care what people think, but if you would rather, we can go into the gardens and dance away from everyone. I can be quite clumsy, so I don't like to dance in a crowd.'

He laughed. 'My nickname is Dopey. I'm ... well, a bit dopey.'

Mary smiled, making her cheeks ball up as they flushed red. 'Guess we make the perfect pair.'

***

The clouds swept together, slowly moving past the full moon. The sound of water trickling from the palace pond and frogs croaking were all that could be heard.

'It's beautiful,' Henry said.

Mary smiled but didn't reply. He noticed every little detail about her; her cute dimples, the way her lips didn't lose their colour when she smiled, her little freckle above her top lip, how one eyebrow arched more than the other did. He was falling for her. Their dance had been perfect. They both fell over, Henry accidentally stood on her toe, and they walked over to a hill, not far from the palace pond.

Henry pondered about Mary's husband and hesitated to bring it up all night, but now it seemed like the right time. 'What happened to your husband, if you don't mind me asking?'

She sighed. 'He was ambushed and stabbed for his jewels when returning to his kingdom. It was some time ago now. I just get upset for little Snow, growing up without a daddy.' She gulped and wiped a tear from her cheek.

'I may have to marry again, probably to someone I won't love. Someone picked by my father. I guess I have to just settle for a loveless marriage; it means Snow won't be pressured into one, and it'll be for the good of the kingdom, I guess.'

Henry placed his hand on top of hers. 'We all settle for so much in life. Mostly everything is mundane, but love shouldn't be. It is one of the few things that can change us. We should feel as if we are being swept up in a hurricane. It's hard to breathe; it's scary yet so exhilarating. You'd die smiling because of that feeling—even if only felt for a millisecond, it's a million times better than an eternity of just being content. I'd die happily if I could feel that feeling; that is what life is about.'

He paused as she looked at him, but something was different in her gaze. Something he couldn't quite put his finger on. He slowed his breathing and continued. 'I guess I'm just a hopeless romantic. A fool.'

'Actually,' she interrupted. 'I think you're one of the wisest men I have ever met.'

He blushed. 'Don't give up on love, sweetheart. Don't settle for a loveless marriage. There's someone for everyone. Fight for it.'

'I did give up on love,' she admitted, 'until I met you.'

His heart skipped a beat, but the croak of the prince coming from his pocket brought him crashing back down to reality. The sadness he felt for the prince was much more consuming than the love, yet it was tearing him in separate directions. He was stuck between two people, two emotions—both strong, both deadly.

'But like hurricanes, it can cause uncontrollable amounts of destruction. And on that thought, I must bid you goodbye. Thank you for your hospitality. I hope you find what you're looking for.'

She stood up, lifted the bottom of her dress off the grass, and turned away from him. 'If that's how it must be, then goodbye. I thought you said love is worth fighting for?'

Henry peered into his pocket to see an angry looking frog. 'It is.' His heart sunk as he chose to lie. He had to save her, even if going against Edward's wishes was crushing his heart. 'Mary, we met for all of a few hours. This, this was never anything more than a friendship,' he lied. He walked away, leaving a disappointed Mary behind.

Edward poked his head out of the pocket. 'That love rubbish was perfect! She was perfect! What were you thinking, leaving like that?' he asked.

Henry looked at the prince and closed his pocket after whispering, 'I was in no way going to let you hurt her.'

Edward forced his way back out of the pocket. 'You would have; that sadness wrapped around your heart would have meant you would have stood aside, and you know it!'

'Yes. That's exactly why we are leaving!' Henry said and walked back to the inn; his thoughts focused on Mary. 'You'll always be the one who got away,' he whispered to the sky before taking a deep breath.

***

Edward waited for Henry to fall asleep. 'Your snores are loud enough to wake a dragon,' he said as he hopped out of the neat little bed that Henry had made him earlier. He jumped out of the little room in the inn and went down the stairs. After what felt like an hour, he reached the bottom. 'Damn door,' he mumbled and looked up at the closed, heavy oak door. A slight breeze swept the room, just enough for the prince to feel. He found his way up to an open window and leapt out into the cool night. He made his way to the palace. The ball was finishing, and everyone was leaving. He avoided everyone's feet as he hopped around the palace to the gardens. He spotted Mary on the bank, still sat in the same place. 'Surely, it can't be this easy?' he muttered under his breath. He hopped over to her and croaked. Tears fell down Mary's porcelain like cheeks and into her hair as she laid back. As she heard the croak, she sat up.

She tilted her head. 'Hello, little frog.'

'Hi,' he replied.

She jumped and scrambled to her feet. 'You're not supposed to talk. You're a frog!'

He sighed exasperatedly. 'Magic, love. I'm cursed and need a princess to break it.'

She furrowed her eyebrows and knelt. 'Break it, how?'

He puckered his green lips. 'With a kiss.'

Her eyes widened. 'Oh, uh, I don't really know what this means or why you have come to me, but I have had my heart broken already tonight. I can't help you.'

He hopped closer to her. 'Henry cannot love you or be with you as he is cursed with me, you see. He is cursed with an eternal sadness that coils his heart for me, so being with anyone else would be torture for him as he could never put them before me.'

She sat back down and wiped her eyes. 'Oh, it makes sense.' She looked down at the grass and then at the palace. 'No wonder he left so suddenly. I was hoping he and I could be together. I know it's quick, and I am usually cautious, and yes, he is a dwarf, but I get this sense of beautiful kindness from him. He's different, and he liked me for me, without even knowing I was a princess. It would be good for Snow to have a father figure. Do you think he feels the same?'

Edward waited patiently and hid his irritability. She could talk for Northmanni. 'Yes, he does.'

'He told you this?' she asked, her cheeks flaring pink.

'Yes,' he snapped. 'Anyway, he wouldn't ask you to do such a thing, but I would. Kiss me, break my curse. I turn back into a prince, his sadness is broken, and bam, you two can go on your merry way,' he said and watched as she pondered the thought.

She looked down at him suspiciously. 'Why wouldn't he ask if it's only a kiss?'

He hopped onto her hand. 'Because his sadness prevents him. He wants only a true love to kiss me ... old-fashioned type. I'm happy to find someone when I am a man.'

She smiled. 'Just one kiss?'

He nodded. 'Just a peck, really.'

She bent over and just as her lips touched his, a loud scream shattered the silence. Henry ran at them from the edge of the palace gardens. The princess shrunk into a frog and hopped around aimlessly. Just before Henry got to them, Edward stomped on her, leaving her splattered remains across the grass. Henry felt the sadness around his heart shatter, leaving him free of Edward. However, a new emotion replaced it; anger.

Inside the palace, the duke wrapped his arm around her and placed his hand on her back then twirled her around. The duke was ten years her senior, but it didn't matter when you were royal or noble. 'Beautiful party,' the duke said as they danced. He smiled, showing off his dazzling white teeth. His eyes were bluer than the royal drapes and lips were paler than Snow's skin. Still, he was a handsome man and seemed nice enough.

Snow caught her grandparents' gazes and smiled at them. The music faded and her grandfather, the king, stepped out, looking over the balcony. 'I want to thank everyone for coming to our kingdom on this most gracious evening to celebrate the fifteenth birthday of my granddaughter, Princess Snow.'

Snow beamed at him. He looked down at her with doting eyes. 'Happy birthday, sweetheart. You'll be a fine queen one day.'

The last part cut through her. *Queen.* The duke took her hand and kneeled onto the marble floor. 'Snow, happy birthday. When you turn sixteen, I would find it most gracious if you would accept a marriage proposal from myself.'

Unorthodox, indeed. Dukes didn't propose so personally. Snow half-smiled. 'If the king wishes it, then I will graciously accept.'

The duke nodded, seeming pleased with the offer. Everyone in the room clapped and returned to dancing and stroking each other's egos; the two things they did best.

Snow watched as everyone poured out of the room, leaving behind a trail of half-eaten food, streamers lying on the floor, and half empty champagne glasses littering the long tables. 'Where is my mother?' she asked one of the guards who was making sure everyone was leaving the palace. Snow heard a fight break out outside the doors of the palace. Clearly, some men had drunk far too much.

'She was last seen in the gardens.'

'Thank you.'

Snow walked out of the room with grace, thanking people as she left and offering a smile to the king and queen. As soon as she was out of sight, she ran to find her mother. Her white dress flew out behind her as she pattered down the dark corridors until she reached the back doors. Opening them, she furrowed her brows at the strange sight.

A flash of magic danced in the air—leftover from some curse. Snow looked around but couldn't see her mother anywhere.

'Mama?' she called out.

Snow walked down the hill and stepped on something slimy. 'Eww, what the ...' She inspected it. It was a frog, a dead frog. 'Did I kill you? I ...' She noticed her mother's necklace next to the frog, and the frog's eyes were exactly the same colour as her mother's ...

Snow gasped.

The magic must have been from a curse that had turned her into a frog, which means ...

She must have killed her own mother.

ENCHANTRESS

Edward reappeared in the kingdom of Milborn, where Gertrude had told him he could find more magic when they had made their first deal. He'd heard of the Castle of Hearts before. Apparently, it was hidden in the confines of Milborn forest, surrounded by enchanted gates, tall trees, brambles, and snowy mountains. There, he heard, lived an enchantress who took care of the castle.

The villagers looked at him cautiously. The town had an air of mystery hanging over the small market stalls and wooden shops. A man fell out of a tavern across the road. He stumbled down the steps, followed by the door slamming shut behind him, with a lot of insults being shouted as the door shut. The man tried to throw his bottle at the tavern door but missed by at least four feet. 'Idiots,' the man grumbled and walked down the path, swaying from one side to the other, almost getting knocked over. 'If they knew what I'm capable of! Who I am!'

'Sir,' Edward called. The drunk man looked back and waved his hand dismissively. Edward ran across the road. 'Sorry to bother you,' Edward said to the man who had now turned, looking annoyed.

'Do you know where I can find a horse? I need to venture into the enchanted woods, up to the mountains.'

The man laughed wheezily. 'You'll die in there. You're mental!'

Edward bit the inside of his lip and forced a half-smile. 'Can you help me or not, sir?'

The man sighed and started walking away. He looked back at Edward. 'Come on then!'

Edward smiled genuinely and ran after the man. He followed him for two miles. Silence hung between them. The drunk man was taller than Edward and twice as wide. He was handsome, though, and his muscles looked like they would rip his tight t-shirt at any second. Edward looked around at the run-down houses surrounding the winding path they were walking. Snowflakes began to fall, floating down from the white sky and landing on Edward's dark hair and the drunken man's black hair, which was tied in a little ponytail at the back of his head. 'Why do you want to go into the forest?'

Edward noticed that there was a slight feminine edge to the man's voice. 'Um,' Edward hesitated. 'It's complicated. I need something from a castle in there.'

The man gasped. 'You're going to the castle? Impossible! Do you know how many times I've tried to get into that castle?' The man looked down at Edward and smirked. 'If I couldn't, you won't be able to!'

'You underestimate me.' Edward smirked back.

They reached the edge of the woods. 'If you make it in there,' the man said, 'you must promise to share your riches with me.'

'Why would I promise that?'

'Because,' the man looked at Edward with menacing eyes, 'I won't tell you where it is. Promise you will share your fate with me with a magic bond.'

Edward raised an eyebrow. 'You possess magic?'

'No,' he admitted. 'But you do.'

Begrudgingly, Edward made a magical pact with the man then took the directions to the castle. The man waved as Edward walked into the forest. The snow was falling harder, and soon, it was up to his ankles. He looked at the lucid snowflakes with annoyance. It was blistering cold, and the castle was still nowhere to be seen.

Hours passed as Edward ventured deeper into the depths of the never-ending forest. The blistering wind swept over his face. Edward tried to block the heavy snowfall with his hands. He tried using magic to reach the castle. He did not care about his limited amount of magic as he feared for his life. Yet no matter how hard he tried, he didn't transport. The further he went into the forest, the more his magic seemed unreachable.

The forest was a winter wasteland, even the trees looked like they had died a long, long time ago and were preserved by nothing more than a memory. The wind hurt his ears as it howled louder than any wolves could. Close to giving up, he fell to his knees. His hands fell into the inches of snow, and thorns rose from the ground, reaching into the sky to form a wall. Tears froze almost instantly on his cheek.

'Please,' he begged. 'Please let me in.' He could sense the magic pulsating from behind the thorny wall. 'I need magic.'

On the word magic, the thorns sunk rapidly back into the ground, and a gothic castle appeared, surrounded by meadows of frosty grass. It stood hauntingly against the grey, stormy sky. Several broad towers dominated the skyline, forming a protective barrier around the castle. Two semi-circle staircases mirrored each other. They wound their way up to the gated entrance. In front of the staircases stood a fountain which Edward imagined would have looked glorious in its prime. The weathered, grey fountain now matched the rest of the castle. Edward walked up the steps, and the snowflakes drifted down, landing around him. He reached the heavy, wooden doors that arched into a point.

The gate was up, its fatal spikes pointing down at Edward as a warning. The black metal knocker was the snarling face of a beast. Edward knocked once, but the door creaked open, pushing against the skeletons of leaves that littered the cold ground.

His steps echoed eerily on the white marble floor. Stone arches lined either side of him, leading off into other rooms and corridors. Cream-coloured stone pillars stood central to the room, branching off into ivory beams on the curved ceiling. He walked past the arches, each darker than the previous. He couldn't shake the unnerving feeling of being watched. The castle was quiet; too quiet.

He continued to walk until he reached a black door, surrounded by gold patterns. He heard a twinkling sound and looked up. Above him was a large silver and black chandelier, and hanging from it were hundreds of small diamonds, all different to each other, like snowflakes. He took a deep breath and pushed open the door. The room was magnificent; obviously, it was once a ballroom, the main room for entertaining.

On the walls were grand paintings of former kings and queens, of what once must have been a separate kingdom to Milborn. As he looked at the pictures closer, he noticed each of them were marked by violence and death.

Dried blood splatters stained the plaster frames. He turned on hearing footsteps and saw a woman dressed in an emerald velvet dress walking down the central staircase.

There were three, all leading up to the balcony he bet this mystery woman had seen him from. She stopped at the bottom of the staircase and strode over to Edward. Her silky black hair was twisted into a knot, held up by a silver comb, decorated with emeralds to match her dress. As she walked over to him, he noticed her expression change. A smirk hung on her lips, and a mischievous glint danced in her green eyes.

She said nothing; instead, she beckoned for him to follow her, and for some reason, he did. She led Edward up to the first floor. They closed in on a spiralling staircase which twisted upwards, consumed by darkness. 'You're Edward,' she stated while looking up into the twisted darkness.

Edward nodded slowly. 'How do you know my name?'

She smirked. 'They always want to know the hows and the whys ...' She raised her hand, twisting it up in a royal fashion. Edward felt the spark of magic before he saw it.

The power surged through the castle then the stairs creaked and the spiral staircase twisted down from the ceiling until it ground to a halt by their feet.

She stepped onto the black metal steps and beckoned for Edward to follow her, and he did. They walked up the staircase. Edward looked around confused; it stopped by the ceiling, but the enchanting woman stopped halfway up and extended her hand again, and with another surge of magic, a door appeared and so did a metal bridge between the stairs and the door. 'Follow me,' she ordered and walked across the bridge to the door. The door was wooden, arched, and plain. It swung open on her touch. He could see flickering candlelight inside and followed the stranger into the dimly lit room.

A spell made the ceiling look like a starry sky. It was done so well that he couldn't see where it ended. It spilt into the walls which then turned to stone, like the rest of the castle walls. No pictures hung, only candlesticks that were already alight. He hovered his hand above the flame; it did not burn, and when he blew, it did not dance then disappear. In the middle of the room was the most enchanting thing. On top of a small solid gold table engraved with beautiful black swirls was a glistening rich red rose, which hovered slightly above it with magic.

It was not covered with anything, it was not in a vase, but it looked more vibrant, more beautiful than any rose he had ever seen. The enchantress ran her hand around it as if there was an invisible wall, and turned to Edward with longing in her eyes. 'Beautiful, isn't it?'

'Yes, it is,' he admitted. He drew closer to it and reached out, then, 'Ouch!' she had batted away his hand.

'You don't want it,' she said and winked. 'Trust me.'

He cleared his throat and faced her. 'Why did you bring me up here?'

'And here come the 'whys'.'

He ground his teeth. 'Tell me what you know, witch, or I will remove your head from your shoulders!' He grabbed his sword and pointed it at her.

She laughed and touched the end. It turned to pure gold and heated up until it dropped. The end broke off. 'What have you done?'

She waggled her finger. 'Now, now. Don't make threats then.'

He huffed. 'You owe me a sword.'

'You could buy hundreds of swords with the gold from that sword, now,' she said simply and stood by the wall. 'Why are you here, Edward?'

'You know my name, so you probably know why I'm here, so why ask?'

She shrugged. 'It's more fun this way.'

'That's my line.' He looked around. 'I need magic.'

'Ah.' She stepped forward and took the amulet from around her neck, dangling it in front of him. 'So you're after this?'

He could feel the magic beating through it. Eternal magic. He reached out for it, but she pulled it back. 'With great power comes great responsibility.'

'Yeah, yeah,' he said dismissively. 'Give it to me.'

She seemed to consider it but then placed it back around her neck. 'It's my burden, not yours.'

'I will gladly relieve you of your burden,' he said.

'The only way you could get your hands on all of this,' she said sweetly, 'is by kissing me. I wouldn't recommend it. You don't want any of this. Consider this a warning. Do not try to either.' With a daring, mischievous grin, she turned and left the room, leaving Edward staring longingly at the rose.

He turned away and headed down the stairs. When he reached the bottom, the staircase creaked and rose back up to the ceiling. He growled and headed to the room. He would get that kiss; no woman could get resist him!

Edward walked back into the ballroom and noticed the scurry of maids, chattering and hurrying to ready the table for dinner. They were short, most around five-foot tall, all carrying silver platters of food, some covered, some not, and silver goblets. The enchantress walked in dressed in blue and smiled at Edward. He strutted over to the table, not caring to look at the maids. He looked at her with his best smoulder. 'So,' he said silkily, 'may I join you for dinner, um ... what's your name, by the way? I forgot to ask.'

She grinned. 'Felicity.'

'Beautiful,' he replied and took the seat next to her. 'Big table yet no guests?'

She looked down at her plate and sighed. 'Never any guests, but I do have my maids.'

'You let them eat with you?' he couldn't hide the look of disgust on his face.

'Of course,' she said and looked over at the doorway. 'However, they are eating separately tonight.'

His forehead creased. 'Because of me?'

She smiled widely. 'You're my first guest in a long time. Well, the first I have let in.'

He raised both eyebrows and bit his lip while grinning. 'Thought I was special enough to let in then?'

'Something like that,' she said, sounding bored.

He gulped at the delicious wine and bit into a crab cake. 'Compliments to the cooks,' he said and continued to stuff his face.

She looked at him sideways and played with her food with a fork, moving the shrimp and other seafood around her plate. 'Do you have any children? A wife?'

'No,' he replied smoothly. 'Hard to believe, isn't it?'

She scoffed and pretended to just choke a little on her wine. 'Truly hard to believe.' Thanks to his ego, he didn't detect the sarcasm lacing her words.

'You look beautiful tonight,' he said and wiped his mouth with the gold embroidered napkin before dumping it down on the empty plate. 'Would you like to dance?'

She looked around at the ballroom and clicked her fingers. Music boomed throughout the room—classical and elegant.

She took his hand and followed him to the centre of the room. He wrapped his hand around her waist and twirled her around.

To anyone else, they would look like two beautiful swans, carefree, maybe even in love. But to them, they were in a dangerous waltz. He wanted to use her, to take her power, and she was having trouble pretending to like him. They finished the waltz, but the music continued to play. They danced more, and Felicity took a deep breath and looked at Edward with flirtatious eyes. She sunk down on his arm as the final dance ended. She bit her lip, and he took the opportunity. Leaning in towards her lips, he could feel the magic calling to him. He pressed his lips against hers and then, everything changed.

***

Edward blinked his eyes open and looked around at the old ballroom. Felicity stood over him, laughing. 'I knew you were the type of man who if told not to do something, would want it even more, and I was right.'

She dropped the amulet onto his stomach. 'You're a spoiled, snobby, selfish man, and now, your ugly personality shows on the outside. Thank you, though'—she smiled—'for taking the curse from me.'

He furrowed his brows. 'You're … ugly,' he said, disgusted that he had kissed the haggard woman who now stood in front of him.

She laughed harder. 'I looked how I am on the inside when I was cursed, and now, I am back to the way I looked before the curse. I may be ugly, but I have nothing on you.' She laughed more. 'I showed you the rose, hoping you would want it. It's the power of this castle. Hundreds of cursed hearts live here—mad, dangerous—and now, you're their master. You can never leave here unless you can find someone to kiss you.'

Edward sat up, and his head was throbbing. One minute, he was kissing, and the next, he was waking up. He felt more powerful than he had ever felt yet horribly different. He recognised the same tingly feeling that he had when he was a frog; when he was cursed.

He jumped up and looked down at his body. His arms and stomach were covered in thick, long scars. His fingernails were tinged yellow. He turned and ran to the table, grasping for a silver goblet.

He gasped when he saw the strange man reflected at him. His handsome features were barely noticeable under the wrinkled, scarred skin. His eyes, once a handsome warm brown, were now the colour of grey slush. His nose was longer and more pointed, like a beak. Dark circles and crow's feet made his beady eyes look even smaller. His hair, his beautiful hair looked like grey bristle.

'What have you done to me?'

'You did this to yourself,' she stated and walked away. As she left, the man who had helped him find his way to the castle walked in.

'You ...' the man started, squinting. 'You almost look like him, yet you look so ... ugly.'

'I'm a beast,' Edward cried.

The man raised an eyebrow. 'Yet I am not?'

Edward shrugged. 'I have been cursed,' he admitted, feeling sick.

'Our promise ... we share the same fate. I was pulled toward the castle less than a half hour ago. I tried to stay in the town, but I couldn't. I see now, however, that thankfully we do not share the same fate.'

Edward looked at his hands, following each putrid crease. 'I guess you're a nicer person than I am.'

The man looked at the door. 'I should leave,' he said. 'I, uh, hope it all works out.' He left the castle door but returned less than fifteen minutes later, looking pale. 'I cannot leave the grounds.'

'Same fate.' Edward smirked. 'Guess you're stuck here too.'

The man gasped. 'I must leave.'

Edward growled and turned. 'As do I, but I cannot!'

'Well,' the man said, looking around, 'how do we break the curse?'

Edward pressed his lips together. 'I must be kissed.'

The man's eyebrows shot up. 'Only a kiss?'

'From a woman ... before you get any ideas.' Edward sat on one the chairs and lowered his head.

His eyed widened. 'I know that.' He blushed. 'I meant ... well, it's not hard to find a woman.'

Edward laughed patronisingly. 'Because plenty of women go this deep into the forest.'

'Best make sure you're ready for when one does,' the man said, looking solemn. 'I'm not being stuck here!'

'I never asked, but what is your name?' Edward asked.

'Caleb.'

Edward sighed. 'Well, seeing as neither of us can leave, you will help me.'

Caleb nodded. 'Guess I have no choice.'

'Neither of us do,' Edward said snidely. 'We just need to find a woman who is willing to kiss a man as beastly as me.'

LOST

Belle's father smiled as she waved goodbye to him. 'I'm going to the library. James is coming with me,' Belle said sweetly. James looked up at him with warm brown eyes, just like hers. She looked more like her mother than her sisters did. They held that against her, though. In fact, they held a lot against her. They hated that she was happier than they were, that she settled into their new life better than they did, and that Belle was, of course, extremely beautiful.

Griselda looked over at her and smirked. 'No wonder you can't find another husband with your nose always stuck in a book.'

Thomas scowled. 'Enough. Be nice to your sister,' he scorned then looked up at Belle. 'Of course, take your time.' He watched her and James leave and sighed. It had been two years since her husband died. Belle was only sixteen when she had James, and now, he was fourteen, which made Thomas feel older than he was.

He knew Belle was beautiful enough to find another husband, yet she didn't seem to care much about marriage anymore. He turned and looked at his youngest, Griselda. Since the man in the inn, Edward, had broken his promise and disappeared without a trace, his hope at finding Griselda a husband was growing harder by the day.

Griselda might not be striking, but she was beautiful. All his daughters were in his eyes. However, all except Belle had such spiteful tempers, which was the ugliest thing of all.

Thomas checked his pocket watch. Only five hours until he had to leave for Milborn. Having lost all three of his ships, Thomas was anxious more than ever about the fate of his daughters. So finding out earlier that morning that one of his ships had made it back with the shipment still intact had brightened all their spirits. All except Belle's. She was happy that the family was close again. After losing her husband, she had moved back in with her father and younger sisters. For most of her life, she had lived in a grand mansion where her spoilt sisters took everything for granted while spending Father's hard-earned money.

Now they were in their small house, and Belle was happy that the family was back together again with the promise of a closer family.

That evening, Thomas's bags were packed for his trip to Milborn, and Belle and James had made it back just in time. 'Be safe, Papa.' Belle said and hugged him tightly.

Griselda ran in from the kitchen, handing him a list. 'Everything I want is on this list. Pearl necklaces, dresses, lace, and perfume,' she said and gave him a short hug. 'I will never find a husband while dressed like a peasant.' She looked down at her cloth dress and frowned.

'No matter, you came through for us, Father. Don't let me down.' With that, she walked away.

The twins, Diana and Demira, who were just one year older than Griselda, handed their father a similar list. 'Finally, we can go back to our old lives,' Diana said.

Demira chirped in. 'I want silk, for my dresses.'

He nodded and smiled. 'Of course, darlings.' He turned to Belle. 'What do you want, my dear Belle?'

The twins ground their teeth and mumbled, 'All he cares about is her,' as they left the room.

Belle pretended not to hear them and looked out onto the garden. 'A rose,' she said and smiled warmly. 'It was Mother's favourite flower, and we don't have any here.'

Thomas nodded and smiled back. 'You can have a whole garden of roses once we move back into our old home.'

Belle's smile faltered. 'Where we won't spend any time together? You will be working all the time, and my sisters will be out every night, like before, trying to find husbands and attending elaborate parties.'

Thomas took Belle's hands. 'We will make it work. This will be good, for all of us.' He turned to James. 'What would you like, James?'

James pressed his lips together. 'A sword.'

'What?' Belle barked. 'What would you need a sword for?'

James bit his lip. 'I've always wanted to be a knight. I want to learn how to sword fight.'

Belle sighed. 'Fine, get him a sword. But he will only be using it under my watchful eye!' Thomas hugged them both before walking out the door and rode off with his horse and cart.

***

Thomas slammed his hand down on Charles's shoulder and laughed. They hugged and looked at the glorious, wooden ship that had somehow made it through the storm. 'Glad we got her back.'

Charles's smile faltered as he turned and looked up at Thomas dismally. 'I called you here because I thought it was only fair, but ...'

'Yes?' Thomas said, feeling uneasy.

'Your debts,' Charles admitted. 'They've taken the cargo to pay off the debts from the other two ships that sunk. I'm so sorry, Thomas.'

Thomas ground his teeth then sighed. 'It's not your fault. Thanks for telling me. At least, we still have the ship.'

Charles pressed his lips together and looked down at the road. 'I'm afraid that's been seized too.'

'No!' Thomas shouted so loudly that a few passers-by turned and looked at them. 'They cannot! Who can I talk to? This is a travesty, this is—'

'Life,' Charles said. 'I managed to get this before they took everything.' He handed Thomas a ruby. 'It fell from one of the chests when they carried them away.'

Thomas took it and rolled it around in his palm. 'This isn't enough.'

'It's all I could get.'

Thomas nodded. 'I need a drink.'

'Inn?'

They headed to an inn and drank until darkness fell over the small town. Thomas staggered outside and looked around, furious. 'They've taken my cart!' he screamed.

'I ... I don't know what to suggest,' Charles admitted, saddened by his friend's bad luck.

'Belle, James, my family. I must get home, but how can I face them empty handed?' Thomas lowered his head and sighed.

The Enchanted Kingdoms

'You still have that ruby,' Charles offered.

Thomas growled. 'Yes, and now, I must use that to get home,' he grumbled. 'Thanks again, Charles, but I must go.'

Thomas walked off with his head hung low and headed to the stables. There, he saw a stable boy and offered him the ruby in exchange for a stallion. The stable boy got his masters and they agreed to sell Thomas their black stallion.

The fur around the bottom of its legs hung down to its hooves, and his mane was raven black and glorious. The horse was strong—strong enough to take his weight. *Perhaps, he could sell it once home*, he wondered and jumped on its back. He headed for the road that led out of town but stumbled into a forest covered in a sheet of snow. Looking around the icy paradise, the trees seemed to merge into one.

He continued, looking for a way out of the forest, but as he headed forwards, he ended up venturing further into the depths.

The horse neighed as it reached a steep drop. He and the horse tumbled down, leaving Thomas shivering at the bottom, dusted with snow. He looked sadly at his steed, which clearly had a broken leg. 'I don't even have a gun to end your misery,' Thomas admitted and looked around. His legs felt like jelly and the cold seeped through his clothes. He knelt on all fours and tried to get up. He wished for warmth, for food, when a wall of thorns appeared. They quickly sunk back into the ground, showing off a beautifully haunting castle.

Thomas's hair froze around the top of his ears. Shivers slithered down his spine as he crawled through the frostbitten meadow. He reached an old fountain which stood in front of mirrored steps leading up to a solid door. He pushed himself to stand, but his knees felt weak. He held onto the side of the steps and pulled himself up to the door. He reached the door and looked up at the spikes then ran his hand over the doorknocker, which was the face of a snarling beast.

Thomas did a mental check as to where he had seen that beast before. A memory fogged in his mind that he remembered, just, on one of his travels. A curse, one that shows the inner beauty or ugliness. The beast was the symbol for that. He hesitated and turned around, looking out at meadow and then the endless sea of trees and gulped. It was the castle of death.

The knock was louder than he expected, creating an echo inside. The door creaked open. Thomas was confronted by a long corridor, walled by symmetrical archways leading into dark rooms. He looked down at the marble floor, which was cracked and littered with dead leaves and small stones.

He slowly made his way up the corridor, glancing behind him every minute. Paranoia set in. Questions crossed his mind. Who was here?

How did that door open on its own? Finally, he reached the door. His leg was dodgy, so it was painful to walk. His kneecaps felt as if they were grinding together.

He bit the inside of his cheek until it bled. He breathed a sigh of relief as he pushed open the heavy door and was presented with a long table filled with delicious food. 'Hello?' Thomas called out, waiting for a reply. The ballroom was huge. At the back were three staircases and a balcony, which reached around the room. Portraits of royalty hung on the walls, but none that he had ever heard of, though. The walls were cracked, and all the corners covered in spider webs. Beautiful 17th-century art decorated the ceiling, yet it was dull, not preserved at all.

The smell of beef, lamb, gravy, and potatoes wafted in the air, pulling him to the table with an invisible string. He looked down at the food and looked around. It felt wrong; this was clearly someone's meal, but he thought that this was a lot of food, and they wouldn't miss a plateful.

He grabbed slices of meat, potatoes, carrots, cabbage, and gravy and ate. When he was finished, he ate a couple of handfuls of grapes and cut himself a nice sized piece of fruitcake. He washed it all down with red wine and relaxed back into the cushioned chair.

He walked up the middle staircase and down a dark corridor, which was only lit dimly with a few candlesticks. He looked up and saw a black staircase, which oddly started five feet up. He shrugged and turned right into a darker corridor. The door creaked as he closed it. Hundreds of doors ran up the seemingly never-ending corridor.

Thomas stopped in front of one door and looked at the metallic heart, which also served as a peephole, it seemed. The more he looked, he realised that it was tinged blue. In fact, each door had a heart on it. Most of them were blue. He continued down the corridor and came across a couple of red ones. The door at the end of the corridor opened on its own. Thomas froze and looked around cautiously but could see nothing but the gentle flicker from the candles. He took a deep breath and walked through the door.

Shelves reached up to the high ceiling, circling around the entirety of the rounded room. All the shelves were packed with dusty books. Hanging from the centre of the ceiling was a beautiful black and red chandelier, which matched the drapes on the one window in the room. The stone floor offered little warmth, so Thomas walked over to the wine-red armchairs. In front of them was a magnificent stone fireplace. On the mantelpiece were small yet expensive looking ornaments of roses, snowflakes, and trees. He lit the fire and poked the coal with the poker then rubbed his hands together. The room heated quickly and he sat back into his armchair.

How could his family manage? How could any of them survive?

He fell into guilt ridden dreams and tossed and turned.

A gust of wind swept over the room, and Thomas awoke abruptly.

He began to relax as he looked around at the bookshelves. In here, at least, he felt closer to Belle. He imagined his sweet Belle's face were she to see all of this. She would surely make better use of being in the castle than he was.

He groaned when he saw that the fire had gone out. He sat up and rubbed his eyes. Through the drapes, the first rays of morning crept through the gaps.

He walked back to the ballroom slowly. He tried to form a plan of action. As he walked down the corridor and through the wood door, though, he noticed the spiral staircase, previously halfway up in the air, was now touching the floor.

Curious, he began to climb the staircase until he reached a small metal bridge which took him to a small, half-open door. He looked down over the side of the thin bridge and gulped. He hated heights. Carefully, he crept through the door into a dimly lit room.

A rose, hovering in mid-air above a small table, shone brighter than anything else in the castle. Entranced, he drew closer and reached out his hand. Edward watched from behind a red and gold screen.

Shame of his appearance had prevented him from showing himself to his guest.

Offering the man food and shelter, he hoped, would have helped him become handsome again. The words *as ugly as you are on the inside* rang in his head.

Thomas managed to touch the rose to Edward's surprise. Edward ran out from behind the screen and toward a startled Thomas. He tackled Thomas to the floor and punched him in the side of the head. 'After I gave you food,' Edward yelled. 'You attempt to steal from me.'

Thomas tried to shield his face as Edward landed another punch on his head. 'Sorry,' he spluttered.

Thomas expected another blow, but no more came. Instead, Edward stood up and helped Thomas to his feet. 'You're the man who offered me safe passage at the inn,' Edward stated.

Thomas squinted. The man he met looked a different, yet there was something recognisable beneath the ugly. 'Possibly.'

'You told me you had daughters.'

Thomas nodded. 'I was taking the rose for my eldest daughter, Belle.'

'Bring her to me,' Edward commanded. 'And I will let you leave with your life.' He grabbed Thomas's hand and an inked rose appeared engraved into his skin. 'You have until tomorrow. If your daughter does not come to the forest before the sun sets, then you will die a most painful death.'

Thomas looked down at the rose and gulped. His heart raced. He looked at Edward with panic in his tired eyes. 'Not my Belle, please. I am sorry about your rose. I appreciate your help. Please—'

'No,' Edward interrupted. 'Your daughter or your life. It's your choice. Now leave.'

'I cannot get home that fast. My horse was injured,' Thomas said.

'Your horse,' Edward said, 'is outside the castle waiting for you. While you were sleeping, Caleb and I lowered the barriers so your horse could be accessed and saved.'

'It broke its leg? You could not have fixed it that quickly,' Thomas protested, confused.

'Magic. Now, leave. You don't have much time,' Edward said. Thomas walked out of the castle and looked up at the moonlit, starry sky and sighed. He didn't have much time.

Thomas galloped toward the house with a flurry of emotions circling in his stomach. The wind swept through his hair, and it made him feel alive. A sudden appreciation for the life he had taken for granted coursed through him. He had less than a day to somehow make sure his family would be okay. Although he did not want to die, no way would he hand Belle over to the beastly man. Goodness knows what he would do to her, and Thomas couldn't live with himself if anything happened to her because of his own selfishness. It wouldn't be as bad if she didn't have James. He was all she had and vice versa. He would see that no harm came to them, even if it meant his untimely death.

The little house came into view, and Thomas sighed. The quaint little windows were lit up and hanging baskets were hung around the door. *Probably from Belle*, he thought. He stopped in front of the house, and the front door clicked open. As soon as he jumped off the horse, Belle ran from the door into his arms. 'I was so worried when you didn't return,' she admitted. A smile spread across her dark pink lips. James stepped outside and hugged his grandfather, smiling.

Griselda ran out smiling with the twins, Diana and Demira. Their smiles were quickly replaced with shock. 'Where is the lace, the dresses, the pearls?' Griselda cried, looking around for a cart filled with treasure.

'Yes, where is our stuff?' Diana and Demira demanded in unison.

Thomas swallowed and looked at the floor. Belle stood in front of him protectively. 'You should just be happy that he is home ...' She looked around at her sisters and scowled, 'That he is safe!'

Diana's brown eyes bored into Belle's. She itched underneath her pearly blond tight bun and scowled back. 'I am!'

Belle scoffed. 'Seems like your more interested in *dresses* than you are about *him*.'

Griselda looked at Belle hard and then up at her father. 'Father, we are happy that you are back safely, but what happened to the ship? We were supposed to get our lives back.'

Thomas sighed and brushed the snow out of his grey hair. 'They took it all to pay the debt.'

The twins screamed, 'That's not fair!' Belle almost laughed and expected them to start stomping their feet. They didn't, but they did fold their arms over their chests and huff. The twins turned and stomped back into the house, followed by Griselda. Belle couldn't take their anger seriously. They had their hair pulled back so tight that they looked constantly surprised.

James ran his hand through his honey-brown hair, which flopped down to the top of his ears, and frowned. 'No sword then?'

Belle looked at James sternly. 'You're just as bad as they are.'

'Was just curious.' James shrugged. 'I would rather have Grandpa back safely.' And with that, he walked inside.

'Teenagers, eh?' Thomas laughed and linked arms with Belle.

'You must be starving. What happened to you?' Belle asked as they walked into the small kitchen.

Thomas hesitated. 'I, uh, got lost on the way home and found a castle to stay in.' He put a pot of water on the boil and forced a smile. 'I had some food, and then I left for here.'

Belle raised an eyebrow. 'You're hiding something. I can always tell with you.'

She looked at him with the same knowing, stern look that her mother had. He shrugged and made them both cocoa. 'I'm not lying.'

'Hmm.' She drank her cocoa and looked at him suspiciously. 'So that's it. You went to a castle and what? Food was just there? Who lives in this castle? Where is it?'

He gulped and sat down, shifting uncomfortably on the wooden chair. 'Milborn forest, umm, just a man.'

'Really?' Belle furrowed her brows and finished her cocoa. 'So he lives in a castle, alone, in the middle of a forest, and just happened to have food?'

Thomas shrugged. 'That's what I'm saying.'

Belle groaned. 'You're lying.'

'I'm not.'

She bit her lip and looked at the cooker. She walked over to heat up the soup she had made the previous night. It wasn't exactly breakfast food, but it was better than nothing. 'So ...' Belle said, trying to fill the awkward silence. 'Did you see Charles?'

Thomas nodded but didn't elaborate. She placed a bowl of leek soup in front of him and sat down. 'I'm sorry about your ship. Things will get better, you'll see. We have everything we need right here, and Griselda and the twins will come a- uh, what's that?' She pointed at his hand.

Panicked, he pulled down his sleeve. He'd forgotten about the mark that the curse had left. 'Nothing.'

'That's not nothing!' Belle grabbed his hand and pulled the sleeve up. The rose looked like it had been drawn under a thin layer of skin, and it moved slightly, wriggled even. A petal on the rose faded then disappeared altogether. Belle examined it then pushed his hand away from her. 'You've been marked by magic? How? What's going on? If you don't tell me, I'll drag my sisters down. I'm sure they'll go on at you enough until they get it out of you.'

'Okay, okay,' he said, giving up. He huffed and ate the last of the soup. 'It's a ... well, it's a curse, Bells.'

A knot appeared in her stomach. He only called her Bells when he was feeling overly affectionate or he was going to give her bad news. He had called her that when he sat her down to tell her that her mother had died. 'What will it do?' she whispered.

He blinked back tears. 'It's true about the castle, the man, the food, and getting lost. But as I went to leave the castle, I saw an enchanted rose, and I remember you saying you wanted a rose...'

Belle gasped. 'Is this my fault?'

'No,' he said quickly and placed his hands over hers. 'It is mine. I shouldn't have tried to take it.'

Belle ground her teeth and tried to hold back tears. 'What does the curse do, Father?'

He sighed and felt a tear trickle down his face as he saw Belle's expression. Guilt, anger, and concern. He couldn't lie to her. The least he could do was to be honest, all except the part about her. 'He saw me try to take it and cursed me to death. I have until sundown this evening.'

Tears instantly ran down her cheeks. She gripped her father's hands, fearing to ever let go. 'There must be something we can do.'

'Calm down, Bells. Everything will be fine. The house will be in your name as you're the eldest.'

'No,' she cried. 'You can't die.' She stood up and went over to his chair, wrapping her arms around him. He held her as she sunk her head on his shoulder, patted her back, and cried with her. Belle eventually let go, but when she turned, she saw James stood in the doorway.

Sadness filled his warm brown eyes. 'I heard everything.' James walked over to his grandpa and hugged him tightly. Belle had expected him to run off, unable to deal with the news, like he had done when he found out his grandma died. Belle saw the strength in him. James let go and hugged her. He did not cry; instead, he comforted. 'Let's spend what time we have left together,' James suggested. 'Mother.' He looked up at her, but there was a knowing behind his eyes. 'Let's go into the garden and pick some apples. We can have some of your famous apple crumble.'

Thomas smiled. 'That would be nice. I will talk to your sisters.'

Belle nodded and took James's hand. They walked out into the brisk cold. James headed for the stables instead of the apple tree. 'Where are you going?' Belle asked.

James walked in and led out the horse that Thomas had taken. 'We're going to that castle. When Grandpa was talking about it, something didn't feel right. We must do something. We can strike some sort of deal, I'm sure.'

Belle breathed heavily and jumped on the horse. 'I must go alone. It's not safe. I won't risk your life.'

James jumped on the horse anyway. 'I'm going with you. I can't stay here with Aunt Griselda and the twins, anyway. I promise that whatever happens, it'll be better than being stuck here with them.'

Belle tried to protest but instead looked up at the sky. It was late morning, which meant they had little time left, and Milborn was far. 'Fine, let's go.'

Thomas walked over to the window and saw Belle and James riding away. He ran outside, but they were already disappearing from view. He dropped to the frost covered ground and watched another petal fade away, hoping they wouldn't find the castle.

CASTLE OF HEARTS

The cold wind kissed their cheeks as they rode through the cobbled streets of Milborn toward the forest. Darkness pinched the horizon as the sun set dangerously low. Belle's heart thumped loudly as they reached the forest's edge.

They rode through the tree line and into the wintry, isolate paradise. Snow fell from the branches as they galloped, disturbing the wildlife.

The last dewy glow of orange disappeared as they reached a clearing. They stopped and jumped off the horse. Though beautiful, the snow was sharp as it bit at their fingers. 'We're too late,' Belle cried as the darkness spread, etching the world in black. It strangled their last hope of saving Thomas, and Belle couldn't take the grief. She fell to the ground, powdered white covered her faded yellow dress. Her hair fell out of the lazy ponytail that she had quickly put it in before leaving. Satin chocolate strands tumbled down her back, capturing the unique snowflakes that fell through the dead branches above.

James placed his hand on her shoulder, trying to think of the words to say, but nothing came. They sat in silence, allowing the cold to bite at their skin when thorns pushed through the inches of snow, reaching up to the sky. Belle looked up, mesmerized. As quickly as they came, they sunk back into the ground and a castle appeared from nowhere. James backed away, dragging Belle with him. 'What is this witchcraft?' James asked, poising himself in front of his mother defensively. Belle felt as if a blizzard had begun in her mind. Her father, her family, the castle—everything buzzed like a swarm of bees. Then, the castle, her son, and the forest faded grey until there was nothing.

***

Yellow light seeped through the gap in the drapes. Belle could feel warmth on her face and something soft on her skin. She could hear muffled talking as she stretched. Then the pool of memories, the forest and the castle, crashed into her mind, and she sat up. She kicked off a white fur throw and looked around. She was in a bed, one big enough for five people. Four posts coiled up to the roof of the bed, which was carved with patterns of leaves and roses. The talking, it seemed, was coming from the other side of the door. 'James,' Belle gasped and jumped off the bed. She threw open the door and realised that the talking was coming from a room which was directly across from hers. She walked into the light study. James stood up when she entered and so did another man with muscles that looked like they would burst at any moment and dark hair pulled back into a short ponytail. 'What happened?'

James placed his drink down on the table and gestured to this muscular man. 'This is Caleb. He lives here. He helped you. You fainted.'

'Oh.' Belle looked around the study. A thick layer of dust covered almost everything. The walls were white, and the window looked out onto a wintry meadow. 'My father was here ... he is probably already dead, but in case he isn't, I wish to make a trade!'

'Your father is fine,' Caleb reassured. 'My master has lifted the curse. The agreement was a trade for you, and your father delivered, well, just in time.'

'The deal was to trade me for his life?' she asked but didn't need him to answer, though he did anyway. She just needed to say it aloud. She supposed it made sense.

'Yes,' Caleb stated.

James frowned. 'We're trapped here.'

Belle opened her mouth and looked around. 'Prisoners?'

Caleb bit his lip. 'Kind of, yes. But the master is kind, he will feed you and—'

'Kind?' Belle scoffed and put her hands on her hips. 'He cursed my father and has now imprisoned me for no reason at all! He is not kind.' Caleb went to protest but stayed quiet. Edward wasn't kind; even he couldn't lie that well. Belle grimaced and walked over to the door. 'Where is this *master* of yours? I'd like to say a few words to him!'

Caleb jumped up. 'Don't.' He pressed his lips together. 'He's uncomfortable with how he looks. Look, he will let you go eventually. He's just upset that someone tried to steal from him when he tried to help them.'

Belle sighed. She couldn't condone her father's actions, but then, he probably didn't even realise that taking a rose could be stealing. 'What's there to do around here then?'

James piped up. 'Any swords around here?'

Belle scowled. 'What's with the sudden sword fascination?'

He shrugged. 'Just want to learn to fight.'

Caleb grinned. 'We have swords, and I can teach you.' He raised his head proudly. 'I'm an excellent sword fighter.'

'We'll see,' James challenged.

Caleb laughed throatily. 'Come on then. Show me what you got.'

They headed for the door. 'Please be careful,' she called after them. James turned and nodded then followed Caleb out of the door. Belle walked over to a mahogany cabinet and looked through the bottles of drink. 'Only whiskey and wine,' she grumbled. She walked out and down the stone steps, looking for a kitchen. She passed a beautiful tapestry and marvelled at the craftsmanship. It was of three men all fighting over one piece of bread, and one man was in the background offering out his bread to little children. She continued to walk while looking at the paintings and tapestries and almost walked right into a woman. 'Sorry,' Belle spluttered. The mousy woman looked up at her and half-smiled. 'Is okay.' The woman spoke slowly and Belle guessed that she must have been from a far-off land. She couldn't place her accent, but the only thing she noticed was that her voice was squeaky.

'Can you direct me to the kitchen, please?' Belle asked. The woman looked at her confused. Belle rubbed her stomach. 'Kitchen? Food?'

'Yes.' The woman turned and scurried off. Belle followed swiftly, hurrying down the winding, narrow stone corridors. They walked through a doorway and into a large kitchen that housed three oversized cookers and three long work surfaces. Belle reached up to the cupboard and fumbled for a cup. A small teacup fell out onto the side. Belle picked it up and examined it. It had chipped. 'Oops.'

The Enchanted Kingdoms

The maid scurried over. 'Is okay.' She tried to take the cup, but Belle held it.

'I'll use it,' Belle said sweetly and smiled. The woman smiled back. She filled it with water and decided to explore her new prison. She walked back up the same way she came but turned left instead of right. She stumbled into a corridor that seemed darker than the rest and noticed that the rows of doors all had coloured hearts on them. Some red, some blue, and some green. She could hear muttering inside and listened harder. She pressed her ear against the door when a loud bang shook her away. 'Who's there?' a man boomed from inside.

'Uh,' Belle hesitated. 'A maid,' she lied.

'Don't sound like one,' the man replied.

Belle shifted uncomfortably. Who were these people? Guests? 'I'm new,' she lied.

There was a pause. Her heart pounded as she looked down at the lock. 'Get me some food, maid,' the man spat.

Belle breathed a sigh of relief. 'Sure.' But as she walked away she felt something churn in her stomach and walked back to the door. 'No, actually. I will not get you food. You are being rude.'

There was another pause. 'It's your job!'

Belle ground her teeth. 'No, you can go without until you learn some manners.'

The man started shouting, and Belle walked off, folding her arms in front of her chest. She stopped by the last door and heard cackling from inside.

A man spoke. 'You're no maid.'

She froze. 'I am.'

'A liar too.'

Belle pressed her lips together. 'Am not.'

'We shall see,' the man said. Belle backed away, not liking the edge of madness that laced his words. The man shouted after her, and she could just make out the words through the thick wooden door and the distance between them. 'You're going to get a lot more than you bargained for being here.'

***

Caleb finished his sword fighting lesson with James and headed to the study. James was surprisingly good, which he didn't expect. He was a natural. Caleb walked into the study, ready to kick off his boots and have a drink in front of the fire but was surprised to see Edward sitting in his arm chair.

'She has a son?' Edward asked.

Caleb nodded. 'Yes. He is clever and great at sword fighting.'

Edward waved his hand dismissively. 'Yes, yes. I saw you both in the garden. I'm interested in her. Is she beautiful?'

'Yes,' Caleb admitted. 'She is a sweet person.'

Edward rolled his eyes. 'Your version of beautiful is probably different from mine. Her father showed me a picture of one his daughters when I was in Northmanni. Trust me, she was nothing special. However, this one is another daughter of his, so maybe she doesn't have his unfortunate genes. If she wants to be with me, she would have to be very beautiful.'

Caleb scowled. 'You are such a vain …'

'No matter,' Edward interrupted. 'It's only a kiss I require. Ask Stilt to make some dresses for the lady. Treat her like a princess and remember,' he looked at Caleb with heavy eyes, 'tell her that everything is from the master of the castle, me.'

Caleb raised an eyebrow. 'She doesn't seem the type to be interested in material possessions. I doubt you'll get her to kiss you this way.'

Edward smirked. 'You don't know women like I do. Now, leave. We are both relying on this kiss. You want to free, don't you?'

Caleb sighed. 'Yes.' He walked over to the door and turned before leaving. 'One question ...'

Edward raised his eyebrows with impatience. 'Yes?'

'Will Belle be imprisoned here like us if she kisses you?'

Edward stared back blankly. 'Obviously.'

'Right,' Caleb said and left the room with a heavy heart.

***

Belle sat down for dinner with Caleb and James. 'Looks wonderful,' Belle praised, looking down at the plates of turkey and potatoes. She looked at Caleb and sighed. 'I would like to return to my family.'

'Sorry,' Caleb replied. He didn't elaborate. He didn't need to. The look on his face told Belle everything she needed to know. That the castle master was intent on them staying. Caleb forced a smile and tried to brighten the mood. 'James.' James looked up from his plate and put his fork of turkey down. Caleb raised an eyebrow. 'Would you like to practice fighting again tomorrow? Perhaps, we can go the far side of the meadow? There are some hills, so we can practice footing.'

James grinned, showing off his straight, pearly white teeth. 'Sounds good to me!'

Belle rolled her eyes and smiled. 'You're growing up too fast.'

James scowled. 'Not that you'll ever see me as anything but a kid.'

Belle laughed. 'You'll always be my little brown-eyed boy.'

He groaned. 'Great.'

'Sit up straight,' she ordered. James sat up from his slump and ate the rest of his food.

Once he'd finished his last mouthful, he looked at the door. 'I'm gonna go exploring.'

Belle nodded. 'Be careful.'

They watched James leave, and Belle turned to Caleb. 'Is this some sort of weird magical hotel then? I walked down a corridor in the left wing yesterday and some guy spoke to me through the door. He thought I was a maid. He was very rude, so I told him off.'

Caleb couldn't help but laugh. 'Sorry, it's not funny, but I can just imagine you telling off a prisoner.'

'Prisoner?' she gasped. 'Like me?'

Caleb bit his lip and looked up at Belle. 'Well, they're here because they are all cursed, and some of them are dangerous—some, not all.'

Her eyes widened. 'What?! Well, I definitely do not want to stay here anymore!'

'Wait,' he said quickly. 'They're not really dangerous to us. The ones who are cursed with a love spell are only cursed to hurt the ones they love. If they have a sleeping curse, then they, well, are asleep and can't hurt anyone. The ones changed into an animal or object are no danger really.

There are only a few that we know would probably hurt one of us.'

Belle frowned. 'And they're locked in their rooms all the time? Those poor souls.'

Caleb shrugged. 'Master's decision.'

'We shall see.' She smirked and drank the rest of her wine. She didn't particularly like wine, but seeing as it was the only drink that was readily available, aside from whiskey, she had developed a taste for it. 'Why are you here?'

'Cursed,' he admitted. 'Along with Edward.'

'Edward ...' She pondered his name. 'He is the master here then?'

Caleb nodded. 'He's not a bad guy. He just has a lot of demons.'

'Don't we all,' she replied. 'What are you both cursed with?'

'Inner beauty,' Caleb replied and grinned. 'As you can see, I'm quite the nice guy.' He winked, and Belle laughed. 'Edward, on the other hand,' he continued. 'Well, he was a handsome man, but now ... not so much.'

Belle picked at her cherry cake and looked at Caleb properly. He was conventionally handsome. His eyebrows were thick, and his eyes were deep set. The pale blue shone against his olive skin. His hair was slicked back into a small ponytail. He looked a little feminine even but extremely butch. It didn't make sense, but it suited him. His teeth were a little crooked, but nothing noticeable. On his lips, he had a few small scars and a long one his cheek. 'How did you get those scars?'

Caleb instinctively placed his hand over them and looked down. 'Fighting.'

'Why?' Belle asked.

Caleb pressed his lips together. His hands were clammy, and he felt beads of sweat push through the skin on his forehead. 'Protecting myself. I'm ...'

Belle could see the nervousness and smiled as kindly as she could. 'It's okay, you can tell me. I promise I won't ... well, I don't know until you tell me, but I'm going to go for I won't judge.'

Caleb moved the hand from his scars and took a deep breath. 'I like men.'

'Oh.' Belle's eyebrows shot up, but she continued to smile. The more she thought about it, the more she guessed it made sense. She was unsure how she hadn't detected it earlier. 'Do you have a partner?'

The question caught him by surprise. This was around the time when most people would spit at him, poke fun, start a fight, or at the very least make a quick excuse to leave. 'No. Milborn isn't the most accepting kingdom.'

Belle bit the inside of her cheek. 'Oh.' She perked up. 'Northmanni is quite accepting actually. I have a lot of friends from there who like the same sex. Most are in relationships. You should go there, you know, once you leave here. Can you leave here? I mean all curses can be broken, right?'

Caleb shifted uncomfortably. 'Well, sort of. It kind of requires someone else taking the curse... I just have to accept I will be stuck here.'

Belle reached across the table and squeezed his hand. 'Looks like I will be too.'

Caleb squeezed back. 'Oh dear Belle, I sincerely hope not.'

MEETING BELLE

The next morning, Caleb met James outside, wearing a thick woollen jumper. James laughed. 'Morning, Grandad.'

'Funny,' Caleb said and laughed. 'It's cold.' He looked at James's attire. A thin white shirt, brown trousers, and brown riding boots. 'You should put a jumper on too. It's chilly out.'

'I'm fine,' James replied.

'Now,' Caleb ordered. 'Or I won't take you sword fighting.'

James sighed. 'You sound like my mother!' He skulked back inside to get a jumper. Caleb grinned. He had always wanted a son, but it wasn't possible. Now, at least he had someone who he could guide as best he could. At least while James was at the castle. Caleb had skirted around the subject of James's father since they came here. Finally, James ran back outside, out of breath. 'Ready.'

'Let's go then.' Caleb handed James a sword and scabbard. James put it on and walked toward the foggy edge of the meadow. Caleb glanced to his side and looked at James. 'Shouldn't your father be teaching you this?' He had to ask. He found it odd that since their arrival neither of them had mentioned James's father.

James's expression changed to one that Caleb hadn't seen yet. Hurt. 'He died some time ago.'

'I'm so sorry,' Caleb said, wishing that he hadn't said anything. 'I'm sure he'd be proud of you. You're an excellent fighter.'

James shrugged. 'Doubt it. He was an artist.'

Caleb felt his heart thud with each, crackled cold step. 'Do you paint?'

James shook his head. 'No. I wouldn't mind painting, but I must learn to fight.'

'Why?'

James glanced back at the castle. 'To protect my mother. She only has me now. My grandpa is old and frail, and my aunties are reckless, selfish, and stupid. It will only be a short time until they get themselves into sticky situations. I'd like to be strong enough to help them out of it.'

'Oh.' Caleb gulped. That wasn't what he was expecting at all. 'You're mature for your age.'

James nodded stiffly. 'Thanks. Mother doesn't think so.'

Caleb laughed and stopped. James stopped and looked at Caleb oddly. 'What?'

'Your mother,' Caleb said, laughing still, 'does think you're mature. She just wants you to be her baby forever. That's all. You're taking it literally.'

James scowled. 'Maybe. It just aggravates me. Soon, I will be a man, and I want to get into trade. Lots of money in that.'

'Ah,' Caleb said and smirked. 'So you want to be a businessman too?'

'Or a knight,' James admitted.

Caleb nodded. 'Well, I can give you some advice and help you train. That way when you leave, you'll be a couple of steps ahead.'

James, in a rare moment, smiled. 'Thanks.'

***

Caleb took his seat in the study and watched Edward walk in. Edward slumped into a red armchair and sulked. 'I've been thinking.'

'Uh-oh,' Caleb teased.

Edward rolled his eyes. 'Why didn't I become handsome again? I helped the old man. I mean, yes, after I did curse him, but he was going to take my rose. Either way, I should have at least looked a bit better than I am now. I seem to become uglier by the day.'

Caleb sighed. 'It didn't make you handsome again because you helped the old man for your own gain. Selfishness won't earn you any points. If you want to be as beautiful on the outside, then you need to do a selfless act.'

'No act is truly selfless!' Edward stated. 'Everyone wants something, even if it is self-satisfaction. I'm fed up of all this 'good verses evil, true love, love at first sight, and happily ever afters.' It doesn't exist. We live in the real world.'

Caleb looked at Edward wide-eyed. 'You don't believe in happily ever afters?'

Edward exhaled heavily and looked down at the floor. 'It's unrealistic.' Caleb watched Edward leave with sadness. For the most part, he couldn't stand the ignorant prince, but for the first time, he saw a glimmer of vulnerability.

Edward stormed down the corridor. No longer would he try to be a good person, no, this was time for action. Despite how he looked, he would walk in to Belle's room and show himself to her. She would be disgusted by his looks, of course, he knew that. In fact, it was the only thing he was sure of. However, he had his wit, charisma, and charm. He'd never had a problem with the ladies, and he wasn't about to let a load of scars get in the way. He was ready to leave—so ready he could taste the freedom and even felt a smile spread across his face.

He reached the door to the guest room and hoped she would be inside. He pushed down the handle and threw open the door. A startled Belle who was reading on the futon sat up straight and looked at him.

Everything slowed down. Edward opened his mouth, waiting to stay something charming, but words failed him. It appeared he had forgotten how to speak. He must have looked confused because Belle smiled broadly at him and walked over to the door. Her quick footsteps matched his heart beats. He could see his scared reflection in her silky brown eyes and felt ashamed. Her heart-shaped face was petite and perfectly symmetrical. Her big eyes and small button nose looked perfect. Her skin was so smooth and clear, it looked like porcelain. Her hair was pushed to one side, tumbling down past her chest in warm ringlets. Her voice brought him back to reality. 'You must be Edward.' Her voice was so unique. Incredibly well-spoken yet she did not sound snobby like the women he was used to meeting. There was a unique softness to her words. Her smile was dazzling. He could understand why his staff seemed to be so taken with her. Her cupid bow lips formed the perfect princess smile. He opened his mouth again, but nothing came out. 'Are you mute?' she asked. He ground his teeth and stormed out of the room, leaving behind a confused Belle.

'Edward,' Caleb called. He had followed Edward and watched the moment with Edward and Belle with amusement. He shouldn't have found it funny, but to see Edward speechless was an unlikely event he was sure he'd never see again. He followed Edward into one of the castle's many living rooms.

Edward poured himself a drink and stood in front of a fire, lighting it with his magic. 'Shut the door,' he ordered without looking at Caleb. He continued to look into the fire, the flames dancing in his grey eyes. 'I don't know what happened,' he admitted.

'I do,' Caleb teased, feeling his lips curl into a smirk. 'You liked her.'

Edward scoffed. 'She's attractive, but I do not know her. I do not like her.'

'Denial,' Caleb said and laughed. 'Wait, does this mean that you're experiencing love at first sight?'

Caleb jumped as Edward shattered the glass onto the marble floor. He watched the broken pieces of glass skid toward him and moved over to the door. Edward looked at him with eyes colder than snow and growled. 'Do not mock me! It was a hiccup and will not happen again.'

Caleb gulped and nodded. 'Of course.'

'We need a plan,' Edward said, absentmindedly sweeping the glass with magic. It fused back together, forming back into the glass again as if nothing had happened. 'Invite her to dinner tonight.'

Caleb nodded and hurried out of the room. Edward sat in the stretched-out leather armchair and sighed. Why couldn't he get those honey brown eyes out of his mind?

***

Edward dressed in a black tux and scowled at his reflection in the long oval mirror. He traced his fingers along the deep scars and over his pointy nose. The grey slush colour of his eyes was made to look worse by the dark circles and crow's feet. The tux was slightly too big. His muscles now sagged and he could vomit looking at himself. Pushing back his grey hair, which made him look older than his twenty-nine years, he decided this was the best it was going to get. He strutted out of the room and down to dinner. Yet as he drew closer to the ballroom, a strange, unexperienced feeling crept into his stomach. Like a million moths were flapping their wings. He felt incredibly nauseous, clammy, yet weirdly excited. 'Hope I'm not getting ill,' he said under his breath.

When he walked into the ballroom, the feeling in his stomach exploded to the point where he was unsure to how he was still standing up. Belle was dressed in a champagne-coloured dress. He had told Caleb to give Belle the dresses that he had ordered Stilt to make, yet never did he expect the dress to look so exquisite. Or was it her? *No, it had to be the dress*, he decided and sat down at the head of the table. Belle's mouth formed into a perfect smile. Edward felt his mouth go dry. Why was she smiling at him? Could she not see how ugly he was? He pondered these thoughts while remaining fixated on her smile. He noticed how she had a slight scar on her top lip. It wasn't noticeable when she smiled, but he could see it when her smile dropped. There was a certain sadness in her expression masked by sweetness that to anyone, it wouldn't have been apparent. He shook himself out of his trance-like state when he saw that she was talking and to him. 'So do you?'

Edward furrowed his brows and grunted. He must have missed half of what she had said. 'Oh,' she continued, 'I forgot. You're mute. I'm so insensitive!' She looked down at her plate and mentally kicked herself.

Edward cleared his throat. 'Sorry, not mute. What were you saying?' His voice sounded different, soft even. He cleared his throat again and looked at her shocked expression.

'Sorry.' She blushed and dabbed at her lips with a napkin. 'I thought you were. I was just asking about the castle. How long have you lived here?'

He smiled. She sounded genuinely interested. He wasn't sure if that was through practice, or if she genuinely did just take an interest in other people. 'I have been here for a little over a year.'

Her eyes widened. 'I see. Do you want to leave?' she asked, even though she knew he couldn't.

Edward chose his words carefully. 'I guess. Please, excuse me.' He stood up and walked away from the table, leaving his food untouched. He left the room and walked up to the corridor where the prisoners were in their rooms. He pulled out the small gold master key and unlocked one of the doors. On the door was a green metallic heart. He looked around the corner. The man who had been here since he took over still lay asleep on the bed. He had never woken and probably never would. A green heart meant a sleeping curse, and true love's kiss would never find him here. From what he could gather from the books that the haggard woman had left behind, the man's family had taken him to the castle so he could be safe while they tried to find his true love. Clearly, they never had.

He walked up the corridor some more and almost tripped over a mop. After realising he and Caleb were alone, he knew that he would need some help. He had Caleb do the cooking for them both and had turned a candlestick into a servant. They called him Bronze, and he delivered the meals to the prisoners. Edward then turned a couple of mice that were hiding in the castle into two small mousy women. They cooked the meals for the prisoners and cleaned out the rooms, as well as made his bed each day and cleaned the bathrooms.

He unlocked each door as he went and checked they were all in there. He hesitated as he reached the last door. On it was a red metallic heart. The love curse. In the room was a man who made Edward feel unintelligent and aggravated, but he was good spinster. He put the key in the door and heard the familiar click then let himself in.

Inside, the short, pale man with golden straw-like hair that reached down to the bottom of his ears sat at his spinning wheel. Gold straw littered the stony ground. Through the barred window, moonlight seeped in. Stilt always blew the candles out when they maids lit them. He preferred to sit in the dark, alone. 'Just doing the weekly check,' Edward said. 'The dresses were beautiful, thank you.'

Stilt laughed, maddeningly, and smiled a menacing grin. 'Oh, I am so glad. So you have a lady friend here. Tell me ...' He walked over to the bed and propped his head onto his hands. Edward noticed that Stilt would be around the same height as Belle's five-foot-nothing stature. Stilt looked directly at Edward with amber eyes. 'Does she like you? Will I be getting a new castle master?' He cackled and glanced over at the spinning wheel. 'I can make you more dresses. You would never find such beautiful garments, but I would need something from you.'

Edward scoffed. 'I will never make a deal with you, and to answer your question, I don't think she likes me in that way. I don't care anyway. I only need a kiss.'

Stilt laughed louder. 'Oh Eddie, I think you're lying to me,' he said snidely. 'Something has changed already in you. It's your eyes. I think you like her.' Stilt's eyes lit up, but Edward looked away.

'Good night,' Edward managed and walked out the door, locking it behind him. The way Stilt always looked through him almost felt intrusive.

Edward walked off to his favourite place. The Rose room.

THE DANCE

He watched out the window as Belle ran around in the meadow with James and Caleb. They were having a snowball fight. Even the two maids and his servant, Bronze, had joined them. A sadness clutched at his chest. Why hadn't he been invited? He shook it off. He would not, could not, get jealous. He tried to turn, but he couldn't take his eyes from them. Off her. His heart pounded in his throat, and his cheeks flushed with warmth.

Belle laughed as the powdered snow dissipated over her red cloak. Under it, her pink dress was slightly damp. She glanced up at the castle windows and noticed Edward looking out. He quickly moved away from the window. 'I'll be back soon,' Belle said and ran off to the castle doors.

Edward jumped as his door was thrown open minutes later. Belle stood in the doorway, showing off a mischievous smile. 'Any good at snowball fights?'

Edward almost smirked, but then his face dropped. 'I was when I was a man.'

Belle furrowed her brows and walked over to him, placing her hand on his forearm. 'What do you mean when you were a man? You are a man.'

Edward looked down solemnly. 'I am a beast.'

Belle tilted his chin with her hand and looked into his cold eyes. 'You are only a beast to those who can't see below the surface. I am not a liar, nor am I delusional. So I won't pretend to find you attractive.' The knot in his stomach twisted uncomfortably, but Belle continued to gaze into his eyes. 'But I will tell you that how you look is not the most important thing to some people. What I don't like is that you seem like a kind man yet you also seem to be grumpy and selfish. What annoys me the most is that you mope around, feeling sorry for yourself because of how you look, and it's infuriating.' She pointed a finger at his chest. 'There are far worse things that can happen to a person than how they look! I suggest you stop skulking around in this castle and come outside with us!'

She placed her hands on her hips, and he swallowed hard. A huge part of him wanted to shout, scream at Belle for daring to talk to him like that. Talk to a prince like that. She had no idea how he felt. Yet a small, nagging part of him knew she was right. He hated that part. 'You know nothing about me!'

She rolled her eyes. 'Fine. Sulk.' She walked out and slammed the door behind her.

Edward slumped back into his chair and huffed. He couldn't understand what he said that was so wrong? And he was perfectly within his rights to feel sorry for himself! After all, hadn't he been cursed by some hysterical woman, which had ruined his chances to get his crown? After spending many years as a frog, he finally becomes free, and then is tricked by *another* woman and cursed to stay in this forsaken castle, taking care of cursed commoners. He felt rage bubble up. She *didn't* know him! She knew *nothing*! He threw his glass of whiskey at the wall, and this time, he didn't bother fixing it. He thought of his life back home, back at the palace, and growled. He tipped over the desk in the corner, breaking it into pieces. With each punch, he felt his rage dissipate. The splinters sunk into his knuckles. 'I am alone!' he screamed, feeling a whirlwind of sadness. Eventually, he stopped breaking the desk. He did not heal his cuts. The pain was the only reminder he was alive. That he had somehow survived all the obstacles blocking his way to success.

Belle's heart thumped loudly on the other side of the door as she listened to his anguished cries. Her stomach twisted as she heard him hit and break things. The words 'I am alone' fell on her ears uncomfortably. They had one thing in common. She too, although surrounded by her family for years, always felt alone.

***

That evening, Belle looked down at her bed and opened the white box. Inside lay a golden folded gown. On top of it was a small bit of parchment. On it read *Sorry for earlier. I hope you come to dinner – Edward.* She read over the note a few times and sighed. He hadn't realised that she had heard his anger after their conversation, only that he was a little rude beforehand. She decided not to being up that she had heard him and pulled the dress out of the box, shaking it off. She held it up and looked at it in all its glory. The pearl beaded fabric of the dress glinted in the light from the chandelier above. Flecks of champagne shined from the lustrous gold. The corset-style bodice was strapless and looked like it had been spun with real gold. The arms were gold lace that reached down to the elbows.

One of the maids entered the room to help her dress. She had learned that her name was Lola. She wore a white pinny and a pale blue dress that reached down to her knees. It seemed that the maids had even dressed up. Lola squeaked with excitement when she finished dressing in Belle.

Belle couldn't help but smile at her excitement and couldn't wait to look in the mirror. She was never one for fashion but loved a beautiful dress. Belle gasped when she looked at the mirror. Her hair was half up, half down in silky chocolate curls. A glistening white gold hairpiece held part of hair up and shone as brightly as her dress. The silk band wrapped around the top of the bodice. The arms didn't start until the bottom of her petite shoulders and reached down just past her elbows. Her nails had been buffed and covered with a shiny, clear liquid. The dress showed off her collarbone and slender neck. The corset cinched in at her already small waist and flared out at the bottom. It was the most beautiful dress she had ever seen. She lifted the skirt and looked at her shoes. Champagne coloured with pearls on them to match the dress. Smiling, she walked over to the door but stopped before opening it. She felt strange flutters in her stomach and was oddly a little nervous about dinner.

Shrugging off the feeling, she walked down the steps with the help of Lola and entered the ballroom. The table stood centred, and she swore it was twice the length than usual. It was covered with a glistening silver tablecloth, gold runners, gold and silver candlesticks, and gold embroidered cloth napkins. Shock pulsated through her as she saw around twenty guests heading down the three staircases. Caleb walked in with James and Edward. Edward stopped and looked Belle up and down. She was *breathtaking*. Caleb grinned as Belle and Edward looked each other, and James looked cautious.

The guests all took their seats at the table. Caleb, Edward, and James reached Belle. Belle smiled her princess smile. 'The dress is beautiful, thank you.'

Edward opened his mouth to speak, but it was another strange voice from the table that answered. The same voice with madness attached to the words as a warning.

'Thank you.' Stilt smiled broadly and did a little dance before returning to his seat.

Belle looked at him, unsure of how to take him. She guessed he was the man who had spoken to her through the door, yet for some reason, she had expected him to look more threatening. She curtseyed to Caleb, James, and Edward and walked over to the table. Everyone looked at her with sagging faces, yet they all looked pleased to be there. She addressed Stilt. 'You have quite the talent.'

Stilt giggled, which sounded forced. 'You have quite the infectious smile, sweet lady. What is your name?'

'Belle,' she replied.

He laughed again. 'Sit with me.' He gestured to seat next to him and smiled, showing off his blackened teeth. She nodded and took the seat. Edward ground his teeth and took the seat at the head of the table. Caleb sat next to him and James sat across from his mother.

Edward knocked his fork against his glass and cleared his throat. Everyone looked up at him. 'Thank you for being here.' He had invited everyone—all except the few known to be dangerous and those with the sleeping curse.

One guest, a man with green eyes, auburn long hair, and a thick moustache, stood up. 'Why tonight? This is the first time we have left our rooms for a long time.' The man's voice was hoarse. Belle guessed he would be from a northern kingdom.

Edward smiled in return and glanced at Belle. 'You can thank Belle, our guest. She felt sorry for you all being stuck in your rooms like prisoners. I spoke to Caleb this morning, and we decided that you should be allowed to leave your rooms. You are not a danger to anyone here, and I am powerful enough to stop anything from happening if you were.'

The guests raised their glasses which magically filled with red wine. They all cheered and toasted to Belle. She blushed and looked at Edward. He looked at her with his glass raised and grinned. She felt warmth flush her face and quickly looked away and at James. Even James was smiling, for once. The castle seemed to be good for him.

Stilt glugged down his wine quicker than anyone else, and it refilled straight away. Belle guessed that Edward was using his magic.

Once the maids and Bronze had finished bringing the food, they sat at the table too. Bronze was flirting with one of the maids, Lola. He pushed back his auburn hair and smiled, showing off his white teeth. His skin was a luscious shade of mahogany, and Lola kept blushing. Belle looked at them and smiled.

Edward looked out at the table. Everyone was smiling, laughing, and just generally enjoying themselves, and that was infectious. This was, of course, just an elaborate plan to get Belle to kiss him after getting some helpful pointers given begrudgingly by Caleb. However, he found himself enjoying everyone's company. The commoners kept talking to him, and they had some amusing stories. He ate until he felt bloated and drank wine until he felt tipsy. Lola got up to clear the plates, but he waved her down. Instead, he got up and used his magic to send the plates whizzing out of the room, which dazzled his guests. Edward glanced at Belle and found her looking at him. He quickly looked away but couldn't help but look back again. When he did, she was looking away.

The flutters reappeared in his stomach, and he smiled tight-lipped. Belle reached across the table and wiped some sauce from James's face with a napkin. He batted the napkin away and sighed. Caleb laughed and so did Edward. He wished, secretly, that his mother would have been as affectionate as Belle was to James. But having a royal family meant that you had to lock things like feelings away. Belle half-smiled as she glanced at Edward, yet something in her eyes changed. She had never looked at him in that way.

He raised his hands in the air and made the instruments from the balcony play of their own accord. Happy, upbeat music filled the room and everyone lined up and danced. Bronze swung Lola around, and James danced with Belle. Edward walked over to them. His heart raced at a thousand beats per minute as she turned and noticed him. He took a deep breath and extended his hand. 'May I have this dance?'

She blushed and nodded. James nodded and walked over to the others, yet kept looking back at Belle and Edward with caution.

Edward placed his hand on Belle's hip and felt want surge through him. She pressed her body closer to his and looked up into his eyes. 'I know it's not possible, but I could swear you look different from yesterday.' It was true. The colour in his face was returning. His scars seemed less noticeable. His eyes were more brown than grey, and somehow, his nose seemed less pointed. Even his grey hair had turned to a sweet light brown. She spoke again. Her voice even seemed to dizzy him so much so that he almost lost his footing a couple of times. 'I can't believe you let all the guests out tonight for me. I was wrong about you ...'

Edward gulped. 'You were?' He hated to admit it, but after some thought on what she had said, she seemed to be perfectly right.

'Yes.' She smiled again, making her cheeks ball up and dimples appear. 'There's sweet, almost kind.' He felt himself drawing closer to her lips. Her scent took over him, and the thought of those soft, cupid bow lips on his almost sent him into a frenzy. The curse seemed to be the last thing on his mind. He shook his head and continued to dance. How could she possibly want him? No. He would just ignore it. But the glances ... the blushing. Surely, he couldn't be the only one to feel the electric pulse between them. He ran his hand around the small of her back and dipped her.

The haggard face of the enchantress entered his mind. This was the same ballroom, the same dance when he had sealed his fate. They gazed at each other as if they were the only ones in the room. His lips were inches from hers, and his heart was racing. Her lips curved into the sweet smile that could stop a man's heart, and he sighed. He lifted her up and ran his finger down her soft cheek. 'Go back to your family,' he ordered. 'I give you permission to leave.'

She looked at him blankly. 'I need to tell you something ...'

He shook his head. 'It doesn't matter what you have to say. I want you and your son to leave. Caleb will arrange for your things to be packed.' He walked away, leaving Belle standing alone and feeling stupid. Tears stung at her eyes. She hadn't realised she wanted him, but the realisation hit her with that dance. She stormed over to James and took his arm. 'We're leaving.' She looked at Caleb tight-lipped. 'He wants us to leave.'

Caleb breathed a sigh of relief. 'Good.'

'What?' She looked at him tight-lipped. 'You don't want us here either?'

'It's not like that!' Caleb called after them as Belle dragged James off toward the guest rooms. The prisoners walked back up to their rooms, all thanking Caleb for a wonderful dinner and asking him if it would happen again. He honestly didn't have an answer for them.

Stilt sneaked out through a door and sped up to the guestrooms. Edward finally having a conscience would ruins his plans. He scurried through the dark corridors, his light footsteps echoing maddeningly. He reached a brown arched door and pushed it open. Belle was undressing and gasped as he entered. She covered herself up. 'Get out!' she screamed.

He waved his hand dismissively and made himself comfortable on her futon. He glanced down at an open book. 'Oooh, reading a book, I see?' He looked inside. 'Feeling romantic?'

She scowled. 'I like romance books!'

He grinned. 'We always read what we crave ...' he trailed off, looking around the room. Finally, he raised a finger in the air and turned. 'Ah. I almost forgot. You need to kiss Edward.'

Belle flushed red as she pulled her dress back on. 'He doesn't want me to kiss him. He made that perfectly clear.'

He laughed quickly. 'Of course, he does, sweetheart. He won't because he is cursed.'

Her eyes widened. 'Of course! What Caleb said makes sense. If someone breaks the curse, then that person takes the curse ....' She dropped her head. She couldn't commit herself to imprisonment.

Stilt smile creepily, although he thought it was kind smile. 'Fear not, young Belle. True love's kiss will shatter the curse completely.' He wasn't lying. It would.

Her eyes sparked with wonder. 'You think he loves me?'

Stilt nodded and jumped up and down excitedly. 'Yes, yes, yes. Now, go and kiss him.'

She reached for the door and ran down the steps towards Edward's room. Stilt followed quickly. Belle's beautiful dress dragged along the ground and shimmered in the dim light. Her hair had come undone completely and looked a little wild, but it suited her small face. She banged on Edward's door and waited. Her breath caught in her throat and heart thumped loudly. Her hands trembled as she saw the door creak open. 'Edward,' she breathed.

'Belle ...' Edward's breath hitched. 'I told you to leave.'

'No.' She looked into his eyes with wonder, and her lips curved into a smirk. 'I don't think you want me to leave at all.'

He closed his eyes briefly. 'Oh, sweetheart, I do.'

She ran up to him and linked her fingers with his. He tried to push her away, but she held on to him. 'I know you're cursed, but if we kiss, it will break it.'

He shook his head. 'You will be cursed.'

She smiled. 'No, I won't.' Her heart thumped, and she etched her way up to his mouth. He placed his index finger on her lips to stop her but felt himself completely intoxicated by her. The feel of her lips was enough to drive him into a frenzy. He ran his finger across her bottom lip. Her heart thumped faster as she pushed herself closer to him. He wrapped his arm around her stomach, wanting to pull away from her. To protect her from all of this.

Her lips were just mere centimetres from his. Her eyes closed, and she pouted. As her lips grazed his, he felt his heart flutter, and it was as if fireworks had exploded in his stomach. He ran his hand up her back and through her silky hair. The strands slid through his fingers. Her lips moved with his in perfect synchrony. She had one hand on his arm and the other on his back. Light exploded around them, forcing them to separate. It invaded the space between them. Belle reached out for Edward. He held out his hand to grasp hers. Then, a splash of mist hit his face and he looked at Belle blankly.

Edward's featured twisted and changed. Belle looked wide-eyed at the handsome, tall man in front of her. He looked around and walked past her. 'Edward?' she called out, but he ignored her and kept walking. The door closed behind him, and Stilt was standing next to the door, waiting for him.

Stilt laughed. 'You're welcome, by the way.'

Edward scratched his head. 'What happened?'

'I broke the curse you had on you,' Stilt replied.

Edward looked at the short man, more confused than ever. 'Who is that woman in the room? I remember kissing the enchanting woman and then nothing.'

Stilt smiled. His memory wiping spell had worked. 'Then I helped you. That woman is a maid. We need to leave now. The curse keeping me here broke too. I can transport us there now.' He looked at the amulet on Edward's neck greedily. 'Ready?'

Edward nodded. 'I guess.' He looked back at the door. There was something about that woman. He shrugged it off and touched Stilt's arm. They transported to Dolorom.

Caleb ran up just in time to see Stilt and Edward vanish. He ran to the room and opened it. Belle was crying on the bed. 'What happened?'

'We kissed and then he left me.'

Caleb gasped. 'You're cursed!'

She shook her head. 'I don't think so. I don't feel any different. True love's kiss breaks the curse completely. Stilt told me.'

Caleb extended his hand. 'There's one way to find out.'

They walked down to the ballroom. The prisoner's doors opened and they ran out of the castle. Belle found James and looked for Bronze and the maids. Caleb sighed and looked at the bronze candlestick laying on the marble floor. Next to it was mouse. 'They're back to what they were,' Caleb stated.

They walked through the meadow. Caleb held one hand, and James held the other. She crossed the border and right into the snowy forest. There was no barrier. The snow was turning to slush and some green was apparent on the trees. 'I'm not cursed,' she said, confused. 'So it was true love?'

Caleb bit his lip. 'I guess.'

Belle cried. 'Then why did he leave?'

James shook his head. 'He doesn't deserve you. Let's go home.'

She looked back at the castle. 'Actually, I was happy here. Perhaps we can get your grandpa and aunts and have them move here. There are enough jewels here for them, and we can all be together. You can continue to sword fight.'

James grinned, and Caleb smiled. 'I admit this is like a family I never had. I'm happy to stay,' Caleb admitted. Belle looked out at the forest and sighed. Caleb and James were happy, and she could see her family again.

Yet the dull ache of Edward leaving stayed with her as a truth that could never be just a memory.

POWER ABOVE ALL

'Your Highness.' Stilt bowed his head. 'You're looking old.'

'It would seem that way,' she replied, tight-lipped. 'You're looking good, considering.'

He arched an eyebrow. 'I am?'

She laughed. 'For someone who ate his only child, yes, you are.'

A growl escaped his thin lips, and he ran at Lori, who simply vanished and reappeared a short distance away, leaning against a tree.

'Thanks to you!' he shouted.

'Yes, yes,' she said, sounding bored. 'Are you here to punish me, or have you called me for something worthwhile?'

He narrowed his eyes at her. 'I need your help,' he admitted. 'I have a prince with me, Edward, and I need to take his magic from him. He has an amulet that gives him unlimited power.'

'Edward?' she asked. 'Edward of Dolorom?'

'Yes,' Stilt said and evaluated her expression. 'Ah.' He smiled, wide-eyed. 'You know him, don't you ...?' He moved closer to her until they were almost nose to nose. She shifted uncomfortably as his amber eyes bore into her soul. He laughed manically, the stench of wine in his breath made her gag. 'Very well, it would seem. Tell me, why do you hate him?'

She ground her teeth and pushed past him. 'He ruined everything for me.'

'Ohh,' Stilt said excitedly. 'What did he do? Steal from you, kill someone you love, cheat on you?' His eyes lit up. 'That's it, isn't it? He lay with another while with you. Well, no wonder you're so bitter.'

'It was more than that,' she said. She looked up at the sky. Pain flashed across her green eyes, as if trapped in a painful memory. 'We were engaged. I trusted him. I gave him everything. I turned him into a frog as punishment, yet he has somehow gotten around that. Who did he find to kiss him?' She turned her gaze to Stilt. 'Who was the unlucky lady?'

Stilt shook his head. 'From what I hear, the curse was tampered with. He killed a princess to become a man again,' he tutted and smirked. 'I looked into his soul, and he holds more darkness than even you and I do. Yet ignorance masks it. Even if it did falter momentarily.'

'Falter?' She raised an eyebrow.

'Yes,' he replied. 'Edward fell in love. Belle is her name, but now, he doesn't remember who she is. She's alone at a castle, and he is here in Dolorom with me.'

Lori pursed her lips. 'He fell in love!' she stated. 'He's not capable of that.'

'Oh, I assure you he is. He really loved her too,' he said, loving how much it was getting to her. 'He would never have cheated on her, but then she really is something. You should see her—'

'Enough,' Lori barked. 'He doesn't remember her anyway. I don't care.'

'Lies,' Stilt hissed. 'Either way, you're welcome. He won't be getting his happy ending now. But,' he said, almost dancing, 'I will make him remember if you don't help me take the amulet from him.'

She gulped and ran her hand over her bracelet, which was silver with an oval blue gem on it. Unknowing to anyone else, it was the source of her unlimited power, and the lengths she had gone to acquire it had taken a lot of sacrifice. 'I will help you.'

Stilt laughed. 'Glad to hear it, Majesty. I knew you cared.' He winked, and she pouted at him. 'So how do we take that amulet?'

'A deal needs to be struck; that's how any sorcerer gets one of the few unlimited power sources. However, mermaids have certain powers. I know one who can help us,' Lori said, running her fingernail across the blue gem again. 'She's called Ursula.'

'Well'—Stilt grinned—'what are we waiting for then?' They both clicked their fingers and vanished, leaving behind a desolate forest and two dust-like figures in the air swept away by the cool breeze.

Lori and Stilt reappeared at the edge of a glimmering lake, looking out at the miles of water that was between them and what they need.

'How do we reach her?' asked Stilt. Lori grinned and held out her hand. A boat appeared. It was big and wooden. The sails were red, and the seats were coated in velvet.

'Ah,' Stilt said and got in. He considered for a moment to push her overboard when her back was turned, but she was far too powerful. She would just magic a way out and kill

The Enchanted Kingdoms

him. He decided to use her to get what he wanted then he would one day find a way to remove the source of her unlimited power and kill her. She had an immortal soul and had managed to keep her body going despite the original curse that took her youth and looks. Stealing beauty from others by using her cursed apples, she could stay young and beautiful. But her looks were fading. He could see the crow's feet by her eyes; her eyebrows still perfect and pointed were lighter than the usual dark brown. Her hair was a shade lighter too.

They sailed in silence until they reached a mound of rocks by a cliff. Stilt could just make out the top of a cave as the waves drew away. Lori reached into the water and let a swirl of gold liquid circle down into the cave. Minutes passed, and finally, a head broke the surface. A mermaid with a moss green tail and shells covering half of her face pulled herself up the side of the boat until she was face to face with Lori and Stilt. 'What do you want?' she hissed.

Lori's thin lips curved into an evil smile. 'Magic,' she said, wide-eyed.

'Magic?' Ursula repeated. 'You have magic!'

Lori continued to smile. 'A way for Stilt to take someone else's unlimited power.'

Ursula scoffed. 'Why would I help you?'

'A deal?' Lori's eyes glistened with wonder.

Ursula looked up at her with dark eyes. 'You'll owe me a favour. Whatever I need, when I need it.'

Lori raised an eyebrow. 'Deal.'

Stilt pushed in front of Lori. 'I need a way to get an amulet from a prince.' He sighed. 'I thought that by breaking the curse completely, the amulet would be free for the taking. I was wrong.' He ground his teeth. He hated to be wrong. 'No matter. Well, the amulet is his, and I cannot just take it from him. It's attached to a rose that is still at a castle.' He mentally kicked himself for not joining the dots before they left.

Ursula nodded and disappeared under the water. Several awkward silences later, Ursula reappeared with small vial of potion. 'Get him to take this and you will take his power for good. However, to own the power completely, you must get the root of the power. The rose you spoke of.'

Stilt nodded. 'Thank you.'

Ursula disappeared, and Stilt grinned. 'Now, we can leave.'

Lori shook her head. 'We need something else to bind the potion so you can hold the magic.'

Stilt huffed. 'You left that out.'

Lori shrugged. 'Oh, come on. Admit it, you secretly love spending time with me.'

'Loathe, you mean,' he muttered.

She cackled. 'Mermaid hair is important so one can carry unlimited power. As you well know, mermaids hold their own unlimited powers. Although different from a sorcerer's, they can hold it because of their hair.'

Stilt arched an eyebrow. 'Strange.'

'Yes.' Lori grinned. 'They are.' She sailed to the middle of the lake. Fog settled above the water, giving the circular lake a mystical appearance. She stopped in the centre and leant over the side of the boat.

'I wish ...' she hissed to the water's surface. Stilt rolled his eyes.

The boat rocked as hands grabbed the side. 'You wish for what?' the mermaid asked, her eyes greedy. She grabbed the side of the boat and pulled herself up until she was face to face with Lori.

'Your Majesty,' Lori said and smirked. 'You are the queen of this lake, aren't you?'

'How did you know?' the mermaid asked, her voice was floaty, innocent, but with an aggressive undertone.

'The seaweed crown on your head and the gold flecks in your eyes. It's obvious. I am a queen too. I can tell when I am in the presence of another great ruler.'

The mermaid smiled. 'I am Josephine.'

'I am Lori. This is Stilt, Prince of Darkness,' she stated.

'Prince of Darkness, eh?' Josephine asked.

Stilt bit his tongue. He never had such a title, but ever since the disastrous incident, he had been known as that. 'They used to call me the cunning snake. I always found a way to thwart my enemies, no matter how powerful they were!' he said, staring angrily at Lori. She laughed, dismissing him, and turned back to Josephine.

'I require mermaid hair,' she said, not wasting any time.

Josephine ran her hand through her wet yet untangled red hair. It was a dark red; that's how Lori could tell she was old. Younger mermaids from this lake had bright red hair. 'I cannot give you mine,' she stated.

'I require young hair. I need as much power as I can.'

'I have a daughter, Ariel. She will give you her hair. In exchange, I need something from you.'

'Of course,' Lori said, expecting nothing less.

'Find a sorcerer, someone to place a curse on my Ariel. She wants legs, to become a human. I can never allow this to happen.'

Lori grinned. 'I am a sorceress. However, I cannot grant such a thing. No one can. Although I can do something else. A curse that will only ever allow her, if she found a way to become human, to leave the lake for up to three days before she has to return or she will turn into sea foam.'

'What? No. I don't want her to die,' Josephine said quickly.

Lori shook her head. 'She would feel herself being lured back to the lake, and if she gets legs, they will turn back into a tail after three days. She would find a way to return to the lake and will never be able to become human again. It is all I can do,' Lori said. 'Now, do we have a deal?'

Josephine hesitated and looked down into her underwater kingdom. 'You have yourself a deal.'

Lori grinned and conjured up a vial of red and green liquid. 'Make her drink this. It will enact the curse.'

'Thank you,' Josephine said as she took the vial and swam to find Ariel.

Lori and Stilt waited. 'Never call me a prince of darkness again!' he said through clenched teeth.

She cackled and pulled her hair down from the tight bun which stretched her skin on her forehead. He noticed when her hair fell, it tumbled down past her waist and was slightly curly. She looked much younger, more innocent with it down. All except for the eyes; they gave her away. You can always tell someone's true nature by the darkness in their eyes, and hers were as dark as they come.

She sighed. 'You're never going to get over it, are you?'

He clenched his teeth. 'Obviously not.'

She huffed and plucked one of her black hairs and popped it into another vial. She waved her hand, and the hair turned into an oozing black liquid.

'What is that?' he asked.

She handed him the vial. 'This is an apology, the only one you shall ever get. Well, it's more of a pity gift. It will make your wife forget that you ever had a child, the one that you ate.'

He scoffed. 'I would say thanks, but this doesn't even come close to making up for it.'

'It's all I can offer you,' she stated. He snatched it from her and put it into his pocket. The boat rocked a little, and Josephine returned with Ariel. She had beautiful red hair that clung wetly to her face, neck, and chest.

'Hi, I'm Ariel' the chirpy redhead said excitedly. 'Mother says you need hair. Here,' she said. She was bobbing up and down excitedly. Lori had never seen anyone with so much energy. Ariel cut her hair with a sharp shell until her hair was shoulder length. As soon as the hair was on the boat, it became instantly dry and shone a little.

'Thank you, Ariel,' Lori said and smiled.

'That's okay. Hey, can I have that?' she asked and pointed at Lori's cloak.

'No!' Lori exclaimed.

'Sorry,' Ariel mumbled and swam back into the lake with a huff. Josephine rolled her eyes.

'Sorry, she's obsessed with collecting objects used by people.'

Lori forced a laugh. 'We will be on our way now, thank you.'

They sailed back to shore. Stilt had tried to transport himself using his powers, but the power of the lake prevented anyone from doing that. She looked properly at his jacket, which was sewn entirely with thread made from gold. It matched the colour of his straw-like hair; even his eyes, though amber, had a slight gold hue to them.

'I guess you spun the gold yourself?' she asked.

He grinned, showing his crooked, partially blackened teeth. 'Yes, lovey. As you know, I am the only man who can spin straw into gold.'

'Yes, yes.' She waved her hand impatiently. 'It looks beautiful. I have never seen anything look like that. When the light catches it, it's mesmerizing,' she admitted in a trance-like state.

'Want to strike another deal? I can make you the most beautiful golden dress,' he said, his beady eyes locked onto hers.

'No,' she said, turning away from the jacket. 'I know of your deals. I'd never be idiotic enough to make a deal with you, no matter how beautiful a dress you could make. After we get off this boat, we go our separate ways.'

Stilt nodded. 'Agreed.'

They jumped off the boat and waded through the shallow water until they reached the pebbly beach. Lori twisted the hair until it too turned into liquid. She magicked a little glass bottle and uncorked it. The liquid danced into the bottle.

The Enchanted Kingdoms

Lori poured the contents of the vial from Ursula into the bottle and pushed the cork back in it.

Stilt looked through jealous eyes. Lori was more skilled at sorcery than he was; despite the magical power, she had skill. He hated that and would never admit it to her. But he did appreciate it. Ursula was a sea witch, which meant her magic worked in a different way. Merlin prevent the use of sorcery to take other's powers from them. However, mermaids were not under his domain and realised that Lori must have made a deal with Ursula before to gain unlimited power. Stilt took the bottle.

'Don't forget,' Lori warned. 'Prince Edward does not get a happily ever after!'

PRINCE EDWARD

'Your Majesty,' Edward said. He knelt and bowed his head. He looked up at his parents. His stepfather, his hair now dark grey and hidden under a thick gold crown, sat on his white throne. His mother smiled, and her eyes filled with tears.

'Edward,' she said, and he stood. She jumped up off the throne and embraced him with a hug.

'Kathryn,' the King expressed in a dark, demanding tone. 'Pull yourself together.'

She bowed her head, still smiling, and sat back on her throne. She was only forty, and her husband was fifty- five. They had married when she was just seventeen. Edward was her child from a previous marriage. She and Edward's father married when they were sixteen. He died before their first anniversary. Fortunately, the king enjoyed her company at court so much that he wed her just a month after the accident that killed Edward's father.

'Edward,' King Charles started. 'We are happy for your return. We would like you to go back to your previous role as head of trade.'

'Of course,' Edward replied and walked out of the room.

'That was a frosty welcome,' said Johnathan, Edward's right-hand man from before he was cursed. Edward looked him up and down. He hadn't changed a bit, aside from looking a little older. His albino white hair still suited his pasty complexion. He still looked thin and scrawny, and his head still looked far too big for his body. 'I don't care. I have my old position back; my life back,' Edward stated.

Johnathan sighed. 'Majesty, you have been gone for five years. Things have changed. The king and queen have been trying for a child.'

'What's new?' Edward scoffed. 'He should give up. It hasn't worked so far.'

'They're trying magic now,' Johnathan replied.

Edward sat back and caressed the hilt of his gold-encrusted sword. 'I tried to help with my powers. Lot of good it did; I lost most of my magic that day.'

'The king is desperate,' he said.

'Hold on,' the prince said and sat forward. 'Did you say five years?'

'When?'

'A moment ago, you said I have been gone for five years.'

'You have,' Johnathan stated.

'I was not a frog for ten years,' the prince said, confused. 'You there,' he shouted to one of the guards. 'How long has it been?'

'Five long years, your Majesty,' the guard replied and returned to staring at the doors to the prince's chambers.

Maybe I was a frog for longer than I realised, thought Edward.

'Terribly boring job, being a guard, don't you think?' Edward asked.

Johnathan nodded in reply. 'If the king and queen have a child, won't you lose the throne?'

'If they have a boy,' the prince corrected him. 'And they will not have a boy!'

'How can you be sure?'

The prince laughed. 'Leave it to me, Johnathan.' Edward got up and exited his chambers. Now that he was back, his hair was slicked back, he was clean shaven, and he wore a white suit embellished with gold buttons and diamond cufflinks. He strode through the palace and out the back entrance.

'Stable boy,' he said, addressing a young man with scruffy hair. 'Bring me a horse; I'm going to see a friend.'

***

Stilt clicked his fingers. He arrived back at his home—a manor house covered in ivy. The garden was overgrown, the stone walls were cracked, and most of the windows were broken.

He looked around at the many surrounding fields with the same dead woods to the left and a rippling pond to the right. The house had not been looked after in his absence. Of course, he knew his wife, Sadie, was okay, after receiving reports from his spies who kept an eye on her while he was away. However, she may be physically well, but mentally, she was not. People now called her Crazy Sadie. He sighed as he approached the front door, knowing that if she saw him, it could tip her over the edge. He hesitated by the knocker when he heard a horse approaching. He turned and saw Edward on a magnificent white stallion.

'Stilt,' said the prince, breathless. 'I was hoping to find you. I knew you lived here.'

Stilt cackled. 'Edward, I was going to come and see you soon. How are you?' he asked, pretending to care.

Edward jumped off the stallion and walked up to Stilt. Stilt wrapped his arm around Edward's broad shoulders. Edward had grown fond of Stilt, seeing him not only as an ally but a friend. They understood each other's need for power. They didn't look down on the darkness in each other. They did not judge each other. Edward liked that, for so many looked down at him for his decisions, his selfishness, and his power lust. Stilt did not. When they had arrived back in Dolorom, Stilt had been extremely understanding of Edward's problems. He'd even given good advice on what to do next. Now, Edward hoped that Stilt could help him with another problem. 'My mother and the king wish to have a child,' Edward said.

'So I have heard,' Stilt admitted. 'What are you going to do about it?' he asked, devilishly.

Edward sighed. 'I have heard rumours that they may have found a magic strong enough to help them. However, if they have a boy, he will take the throne before me. I cannot allow this!'

Stilt smirked. 'Of course.' He looked at Edward with a mischievous grin. 'You are the prince. It does not matter that the king is not your father! You are the rightful heir to the throne. Your mother is a queen. How dare some little kid come into the world and take that from you? Perhaps, if they had a girl, then that would be okay?'

Edward smiled. 'My thoughts exactly.' Stilt hid a grin. Knowing Edward, of course, he had calculated all his options first. Edward continued, 'They won't give up until they have a child. However, like you said, if they have a girl, that would be okay. He is desperate for any child of his own, girl or boy. I don't think he would care.'

Stilt piped up. 'We must find a way. My wife, she is childless and is in the same position. I've tried to find a way for magic to help her, but nothing helps. She had her ovaries and other parts ripped out many years back,' Stilt admitted.

Edward turned slightly green. 'Oh gosh, how awful.'

'I know,' Stilt said. 'Anyway, with no ovaries, there is no way she can have a child, even with magic. But I can help your mother and stepfather, in exchange for their firstborn. I will, of course, make sure both children are girls.'

'Both children?' Edward asked.

Stilt nodded. 'I will make sure they can have more than one child, seeing as I am to take their first.'

'And you will make sure they are all girls if I help you?' Edward asked.

'Of course. I consider you a friend and an ally. I wouldn't trick you,' Stilt said with a menacing twinkle in his eye.

Edward lifted Stilt up onto the back of the horse then jumped up himself. 'I don't know if they'd agree.'

Stilt cackled. 'Of course. they will if they are as desperate as you say they are. For now, we need to find out who's helping them and kill them before they ruin both of our plans. Do you know who is helping them?' asked Stilt.

'Yes,' the prince said and whipped the horse, who was now galloping across the fields. Stilt looked back sadly at the house. He had hoped to see his wife. But once he returned with a child and gave the potion to make her forget what happened, then she'd be happy. They would be happy again.

'Who is it?' Stilt asked Edward.

'He calls himself Merlin,' Edward stated.

***

Spring was nearing. The shrubs of green shot through the mossy mattress. They rode through the forest, which showed little light, and toward centre of Cantata.

'Merlin, present yourself!' Edward shouted, once they were at the centre of Cantata.

'You'd think the magical hub of the world would be more than just a tiny cottage,' Edward said. Stilt rolled his eyes at Edward's arrogance. A man with a long dark beard tied into segments with little bands covered in purple beads appeared. The purple beads complemented his violet eyes. His wavy raven black hair, tied into a ponytail, reached down to his shoulder blades. He wore a long green velvet robe, patterned with gold thread. Stilt looked at it fondly. He was one of the few who had enough power to force Stilt into making it for him.

'Stiltskin,' Merlin said. His voice was low and gruff. 'It has been too long.'

'It's just Stilt now,' he replied and looked at the ground. 'You look well; you haven't aged a day.'

Merlin laughed throatily. 'I see you're still a coward.'

'Merlin, I am Edward, Prince of—'

'I know who you are, boy!' Merlin spat. 'A prince, soon-to-be king. A coward who abuses his power. A man who will stomp on anyone to get what you want. I've heard all about you.'

'At least, I am more handsome and wealthy than you are!' Edward snapped back.

Merlin raised an eyebrow and smirked. 'Arrogance, oh, how it must feel to be young and stupid. Ignorance is bliss as they say—'

'I am not ignorant or stupid! You think you can talk down to me because you are a powerful sorcerer? You used to be someone to admire; now, no one hears of you anymore. I used to go off your teachings when I found out that I possessed the magic. Now, you're a laughing stock, hiding in this tiny cottage, afraid to make new deals with anyone.'

Merlin gritted his teeth. 'I am helping your parents. Therefore, I will warn you not to get on my bad side.'

Edward smiled at Stilt. 'I do not care. If you help my stepfather, the king, he will go back on any deal he has promised you. That is what he is like. He is uncannily like me for someone who is not blood-related.'

Merlin laughed. 'I will rain havoc on Dolorom if he dares to cross me.'

'You could try, but I will rise against you, along with all the sorcerers I can find, with all the men I have. I will find a way to crush you and your stupid magical cottage.'

'Leave here now!' Merlin ordered, shouting.

'Refuse them help,' Edward said.

'Why should I? It is not you I made a deal with.'

'I need you too,' he protested. 'Tell them you refuse or I *will* make you pay.'

'Edward,' Stilt said nervously. 'This is Merlin you are talking to.'

'Yes, Edward. Listen to your cowardly friend. At least he isn't stupid enough to think he can take me on.'

'What did they offer you?' Edward asked. 'When I become king, I will give you that plus more. I will sign a contract, so I cannot break it.'

Merlin raised a tangled eyebrow. 'I want a ship, a unique ship.' Edward's expression twisted into one of frustration. 'You know what ship I am talking about, Edward. The same one you have been looking for. A pirate ship, with a particular pirate, owned and controlled by a very powerful boy.'

'I have been trying to get to Neverland for years; it's impossible,' Edward replied angrily.

'It is merely improbable, not impossible,' Merlin said and conjured up a contract and handed Edward a quill. 'Sign here. If not, I will help your parents. Oh, and I know what you want, it is evident. You don't want them to have a boy, for you will lose your right to be king first. If you do not get me what I desire, if you do not sign, I will make sure they have only boys.'

Edward begrudgingly signed the contract.

'You have three years from the moment you are crowned king to deliver the ship to me. Unless you die first,' Merlin stated. 'Now, leave.' He turned to Stilt. 'Oh, Stilt. I will need you to redo some of these threads at some point.'

'But they are made of gold; they cannot fray,' Stilt replied.

Merlin laughed. 'They haven't; they are just dulling in colour!'

'Every time I spin gold, it takes some of my power, I cannot—' Stilt protested.

'I do not care. You will do as I asked,' Merlin interrupted.

Stilt stared at him coldly. 'I will come here after I have finished my business in Dolorom.'

They walked away, and Merlin and the cottage vanished, leaving nothing but a sea of trees. 'You just do what he asks?' asked Edward.

'He has always pushed me around. I want to say no, but he is powerful. He could ruin me,' Stilt admitted.

'Ha.' Edward laughed. 'I would never let anyone speak to me like that, whether it was Merlin or the king himself. I would crush them,' Edward said and laughed. He stood proudly, pushing his shoulders back and chest out. His white jacket was untarnished and fitted well over his muscular stature. He put his feet into the silver stirrups of the horse and grasped the hilt of his sword before lifting it into the air. The beautiful gold lines cracked their way around the blade; the edge was terrifyingly sharp. The hilt was covered with rubies, and it was long and thick. 'How do you think I got this, Stilt? I took it from a king many years ago. I always get what I want. Remember that.' He didn't mention that his other sword had been broken by that enchantress. Well, he *almost* always got what he wanted.

STILT'S DEAL

'Majestys,' Stilt said and bowed. He brushed his hair from his face and smiled warmly at the beautiful queen.

The king looked at him coldly. 'What do you want, Prince of Darkness?'

Stilt bit his tongue. 'I see the name has caught on,' he said, making light of it. 'I was cursed; I could not help what happened. I hate myself for what happened. However, that is why I am here.'

The king arched an eyebrow and leant forward in his throne. 'What do you want?'

'I have heard rumours that Merlin has chosen not to help you. Edward can confirm.'

Edward nodded stiffly, which was followed by a sigh from the queen. 'We know; he sent us a message.'

'Well,' Stilt said, smiling broadly. 'I am here to offer you a deal. I will give you the chance to have children. You will not be able to find any other sorcerer who has the power to do it, aside from Merlin.'

The king stood up and ordered the guards to leave. They marched out leaving the king, queen, Edward, and Stilt alone. 'What do you want in return?'

'Your firstborn child. I will guarantee that you can have more than one,' he said, getting straight to the point. He could see that the king was not one to skirt around things.

'No,' the queen said.

'Enough, Kathryn!' the king barked and walked over to Stilt.

He extended his hand, and Stilt shook it. 'You have yourself a deal, Stilt. Make your preparations,' he said and turned to Edward. 'Give him your chambers so he can carry out his work. He must have space and comfort to carry out the preparations for such a spell.'

'No!' Edward protested.

'I was not asking,' the king replied sternly and left the throne room. Kathryn ran over to Edward and hugged him.

'I have missed you so much, son,' she admitted. 'It has been incredibly boring without you here.' She even had a regal air when she hugged. Her eyes were jade green, unlike her Edward's, whose were brown. She had broad shoulders, but the rest of her was petite. Her thin, colourless lips suited her square face perfectly. Her brown grey-streaked hair was tied into a knot. A gold crown sat above it.

'I'm home now, Mother; I will not be leaving again.'

'Please don't,' she whispered and let him go when the guards entered the room. The king had always been jealous of the mother-son relationship they shared, due to not having a child of his own. So they tried not to be affectionate to one another when he was around or even when the guards were around.

***

Over the next few days, Stilt worked in the prince's chambers. He slipped the potion into Edward's drink when he had the chance. The tasters tried the wine first, but as they had no magic, the potion did nothing to them. Edward drank the wine as he sat by the open fire with Stilt. 'The king is in brighter spirits since receiving the news,' Edward said, smiling. 'I am happy for them both. They will have a daughter, I will become king one day, and everyone will be happy. Everyone wins.'

'Yes, we all do,' Stilt said, and they clinked glasses. Unknowing to Edward, his powers were slowly seeping into Stilt as they drank and laughed. Edward still had a small amount of his original magic left; however, he didn't notice the power leaving him.

'I must go,' Stilt said and yawned. 'The potion is almost complete. I should have it ready by the morning.'

'Perfect,' Edward said and stood up. 'Then I can have my chambers back. I cannot believe he just gave them to you. No matter, I will have much more than this soon.'

Edward strutted out the doors, followed by two guards and Johnathan, who followed Edward around like a lost boy.

Edward strode into the palace gardens and asked the guards and Johnathan to leave him. He breathed in the warm air. It's unseasonably warm, but this was Dolorom. He broke a sweat at the thought of going to Agrabah in the summer. It would be unbearably humid. However, as head of trade, he would have to go. There was one place he was terrified to visit—Forosh.

The fishing capital of the world, it was yet home to one woman he never wanted to see again. Lori. A lump formed in his throat. He caressed his amulet for comfort, unknowing that it was now just an amulet with no real power. With unlimited power, he could fight her. She might be more talented than he was at sorcery, but at least now, they would be equal on the power front.

Haunting Fairytales Series

The clouds rolled in from the east as darkness pinched the sky. The green hills faded from view as blackness coated the kingdom. Edward smiled as he looked out at the horizon. He missed Dolorom with its rich hills and mountains, beautiful scenery, and modern, clean streets. The air smelt cleaner, too. Tears brimmed in his brown eyes as he let the relief of being home wash over him.

***

Stilt finalised the potion, which looked like liquid silver, and poured it into a glass bottle. He walked into the throne room proudly. The king jumped up excitedly. Kathryn sighed and followed him. She wasn't happy about giving up their first child, but the king's orders were final. The king took the potion and handed it to Kathryn. She bit her tongue and suppressed the raging need to smash the bottle on the marble floor. Instead, she forced a small smile and allowed the guards to walk her and her husband to her chambers. Once there, she drank the potion and lay with the king. The reality of becoming pregnant, carrying a child for nine months, and then handing it over brought tears to her eyes. Instead of letting her emotions show, she swallowed hard and pushed the thought to the back of her mind.

Stilt left the castle and jumped on the back of his horse. Nerves filled him as headed for the border toward Fainland, a scenic kingdom with luscious plants and exotic fruits. As he galloped across the border, which wasn't too far away, the nerves overwhelmed him. He was about to see his wife again for the first time since she took him to the castle and told them to lock him up. Not that he blamed her. He would have done the same if he was her.

***

Edward nodded at Johnathan. 'I must visit Stilt. Tell them I will be back in time for the trade meeting with the King of Northmanni,' Edward said and jumped onto his stallion. He rode over to the border into Fainland and through the long, pretty meadows. He reached the cobbled streets of the small town, Atford, and headed over to Stilt's house. 'Stilt,' he proclaimed on seeing him by the door.

'Hello, friend,' Stilt said and smiled. 'Nice of you to visit. Is there anything you need?'

'Just a social call,' Edward replied and jumped off his horse.

'Please, come in. I warn you, my wife, Sadie, is not well. She was throwing things at me all night. No, she only throws soft objects, so I am sure that she is calming down.'

Edward laughed. 'Female hysteria, eh?'

'It's not as simple as that,' Stilt said. 'She is within her rights to be angry with me.'

'I'm home, my love,' Stilt said as he creaked the door open. He had been in town getting groceries. He was planning to make Sadie a soup to slip the potion Lori gave him into, yet she deeply mistrusted him.

Edward ducked as a large book was thrown their way, just missing their heads by inches. Next came a candlestick, which narrowly missed him. The woman, who was in her late forties with crazy, blond hair stuck up in odd places, squinted, and hurried over to Edward. She stopped just inches from him and looked up at him. Her eyes were like big blue orbs. She glared into his soul.

'She's rather intrusive, isn't she,' Edward said to Stilt nervously. Sadie was still gazing up at him curiously.

'Who are you?' she shrieked, making Edward jump.

He gulped and forced a kind smile. 'Edward, Prince of Dolorom.'

'Prince,' she spat. 'Why are you here? Come to take Stilt away? Good. Take him!' she shouted and rapidly walked away.

Edward looked after her. Her corset bodied pale blue dress was stained, and it looked like she hadn't washed in months. However, Edward could see that underneath all the crazy, she could be a very attractive woman.

'She seems ... nice,' Edward lied and followed Stilt into the drawing room. Stilt poured them both a scotch.

'She won't take the potion that'll make her forget. Well, she won't accept any drinks or food from me, which I could spike the potion in them,' he grumbled. 'I told her of the child. She was not interested.' He downed his drink and poured himself another.

'Maybe I could offer her a drink?' Edward asked.

'Maybe ...' Stilt pondered then poured the contents of the vial into the glass of scotch. 'Make her drink this.'

'Of course,' he said and went to find Stilt's wife. He found her sat by an unlit fire, surrounded by ashtrays, pipes, and books. 'Sorry, I thought it rude not to offer you a drink,' Edward said and smiled warmly. 'I completely understand your anger. It is not fair what happened to you. He should feel lucky to have had you in the first place; you are incredibly beautiful, if you don't mind me saying.' He sat next to her cautiously and placed the drink in front of her. She looked at it and hesitated.

'I am rather beautiful, yes, ha,' she said and cackled. He could tell that she was totally bonkers, though. 'Drinkie-drink time, drink my time away, tick-tock, and forever I ...'

She passed out after drinking the contents. Edward finished the rhyme, 'forgot,' he said and left the room. He found Stilt, who was crouched by the stairwell, trying to listen.

'It is done,' Edward said. 'All it took was a little flattery.' He winked at Stilt, who rolled his eyes.

'I must go,' Edward said on checking the time.

'Of course. Visit again?' Stilt prompted.

'I shall soon, friend.'

'We are just pawns on a chess board, my boy!' the king said as he made his move on the chessboard. Ever since Stilt had given Kathryn the potion, the king had been in a great mood and had taken to spending more time with Edward. 'The king, queen, and knight are the most powerful. But, you see, the queen is the most powerful player. Don't tell your mother I said that, though.'

Edward laughed. 'So what am I?'

'That depends on how you play,' he replied. 'You see, the pawns, like this, can be taken out as if they are nothing. People are always willing to sacrifice themselves to protect the monarchy. It is the way it always has been.'

'As it should be,' Edward said.

'Yes,' the king agreed. 'However, the moment we try to protect the pawns, we are weakened.'

Edward looked down at the chessboard with disdain. He never lost a game, but seeing as he was playing against the king, he would have to let him win. 'I know what you're saying,' Edward said as his stepfather said 'checkmate' and won the game. King Thomas looked a lot happier. Growing up, Edward always thought that the king resembled a dragon with intrusive, intimidating forest green eyes. He was muscular; his arms looked as if they were going to break the seams on his jacket. He strutted wherever he went, and his tongue was long and sharp hidden behind straight, white teeth. The chalky appearance to his skin matched his hair, which was as white as paper.

'In my game, the king will always win,' he said and stood up, grinning. 'How is the trading coming along with Forosh and Milborn?'

'Milborn have reciprocated,' Edward said proudly. 'Forosh, on the other hand, well, their queen is a tough one. She wants double what we have offered in exchange for their fish and wool.'

'She is a tough old cookie,' Thomas admitted. 'Go there, charm her. They have the best fish in the world; we need them. We can sell them at high prices, but we must get a good deal. Offer her an extra two thousand gold pieces and not a piece more. Get us this deal, Edward,' he ordered.

Edward had been afraid he'd ask that. 'Of course, I will leave at first light,' Edward said and looked at his stepfather.

King Thomas noticed that Edward was looking more handsome with age. Especially without the horrendous patchy beard that he had taken a liking to growing when he was a teenager. His hair was now slick and determination was evident behind his deep brown eyes. He had an air about him, intimidating yet charming. 'You'll make a fine regent for my children should anything happen to myself and your mother,' the king said.

Edward nodded, knowing that he would never be a regent. He would be king; there were no two ways about it.

'I must go and see to Kathryn. She has missed her monthly bleed, which means she may be pregnant. We did try at the right time for her to become pregnant.'

'Let's hope so,' Edward said, feeling a little nauseous at the detailed information about his mother's cycle. The king left, and Edward ordered the guards to prepare his things for the trip tomorrow.

Johnathan ran into the room 'Edward, I mean, Majesty, I have news!' Johnathan said. 'That's why I requested an audience with you. The queen, they believe she is pregnant. A seer told her they were twins, two girls.'

'Wonderful news,' he replied. It was great news but expected.

Johnathan had expected a greater reaction but continued anyway. 'I heard that you're leaving tomorrow.'

'Yes,' Edward said. 'You are to stay here. I need you to keep an eye on things here. My stepfather is getting old. With only girls as children, it will not be long until I am king.'

Johnathan bowed and left the room. Edward decided to get an early night, not knowing what, or who, he would face in Forosh. The last time he was there did not go well. That was, after all, where Lori and her family reigned.

THE EVIL QUEEN

The waves scattered the moonlight. Long breaking waves of grey and white crashed onto the deck, accompanied by a fierce, howling wind. You couldn't tell where the dark sky ended and the sea began. Edward looked through his telescope but could see nothing but darkness.

The mercenaries staggered about the deck, some throwing up over the side of the ship. A couple of them were yelling that one of their own had gone overboard. Edward took it upon himself to go up and cut a sail. A lot of time at sea in his younger days when trading had taught him a thing or two about getting a ship through a storm. After some time, and after losing several men, the storm calmed, and they were soaring toward Forosh. The white cliffs became visible through the telescope as they approached the island. The red leaves from the many trees that littered the green land had fallen onto the ground. The small amount of sand there was tinged grey. He had never seen such a depressing beach. They sailed past the beach and toward the main harbour.

'They're not known for their beaches, are they,' one of the mercenaries said.

'No, we have golden beaches in Dolorom,' the prince replied, proud of his kingdom. It was a beautiful kingdom; clean, cobbled roads, rich green trees and grass. Golden beaches, and the sun shines throughout most of the year. The only thing it lacked was fish. Forosh was known mainly for its fishing and wool industry.

They sailed into the well-maintained harbour, and there waiting for them was a crowd of people. All of them waved, dressed in silks and satins, with over-the-top jewellery. The ship docked and men ran to tie it. Edward stepped off the ship and smiled charmingly at Forosh's wealthy subject.

***

Back in Fainland, Stilt sat in his house feeling depressed. Sadie had not said a word to him since taking the potion. She seemed to be in a constant dream-like state.

'Stilt,' a shrill voice said from behind him. He turned and wiped his forehead; covered in sweat, he had chased the horse around the field until finally catching it. His power was surging, and sometimes, it felt like too much. Sometimes, he couldn't control the pure amount of it, but he did like how invincible he felt. Although it shouldn't have worried him, he was concerned about Edward. He would soon find out once he tried to use his powers. The magic was all used up, and when it was gone, it was gone. Edward would surely take it out on Sadie and his unborn child. As much as it was hindrance, he believed he had done the right thing. He would do his best to protect the few he cared about from Edward's status. For now, he could only focus on the woman who stood behind him. The woman he hated.

'What do you want, Lori?' he asked. Her heavy-lidded brown eyes looked tired, and her hair was up in a high ponytail for a change. Her hair was darker again, her skin more youthful, her lips were a deep red again.

'Where is Edward?' she asked impatiently.

'I do not know,' he admitted and poured himself a scotch.

Lori ground her perfectly straight teeth. 'I want to make sure he is living out his unhappily ever after. We have a deal.'

He downed his drink and poured another. 'I'd offer you one, but you're not a guest here. Leave.'

She walked over and threw the bottle of scotch at the wall. It shattered and scotch spilled onto the floorboards, mixed with broken glass. Stilt did not jump. Instead, he drank his drink. 'Well, that was immature of you,' he stated and sat down.

'Get me Edward,' she ordered.

'Yeah, yeah, I will.' He waved his hands dismissively.

'No, it's not 'yeah, yeah, I will.' You will do it, now!' she said and knelt in front of him. She placed her hands on his head. Her long, painted red nails dug into his scalp. She locked her gaze with his and ran her hand down his neck. 'You will find Edward and bring him to me, or I will kill your wife,' she said sweetly and tapped his cheek. 'Now, off you pop. I'm fed up with not being listened to. Maybe I should start ripping out people's hearts! Maybe then people will listen.'

'Lay a finger on my wife,' Stilt warned, 'and I *will* destroy everyone you love.'

'Good thing I love no one,' she said and sat across from him. Her laced black ankle boots looked odd with her black and red ballgown style dress. 'Empty threats.'

'And no one loves you!' he said snidely. 'Anyway, so are yours. You won't kill anyone,' Stilt said and sat forward, staring at her stonily. 'You couldn't even kill Edward.

Instead, you cursed him to be a frog. You wouldn't even show your face when he called for you all those years back. You didn't confront him. When your mother died, you didn't even go to see her on her deathbed when she asked for you. You are more of a coward than I am. So you can wait. I will give you Edward when I am done with him. Then you two can argue for eternity for all I care.'

He saw weakness in her for the first time in a long time. She looked hurt, vulnerable. Stilt watched nervously as her eye twitched and lip trembled.

'You are right,' she said quietly. 'It looks like I need to stop helping anyone. I give people chances, and I am always made out to be the baddie. Someone who gives empty threats. That's fine. I'm known as the Evil Queen in these parts. I'd better start living up to the name.'

She walked out of the room, and Stilt followed. 'Get out of my house.'

'No,' she replied. 'Sadie?' she called sweetly.

'If you touch her, I will kill you.'

'Why are you worried?' she asked. 'I'm only full of empty threats. I am too cowardly to hurt her, right?' She spotted Sadie sat in front of the fire in the living room.

Sadie looked over at them. Confusion washed over her features. 'I've been thinking...' she trailed off and continued to look at the flames. Stilt sat down too and stared angrily at Lori. He would make her leave in a minute. Sadie, however, didn't care about the company. She wasn't even sure what was real and what wasn't anymore. She looked into her husband's amber eyes and smiled for the first time. 'I remember now. We were happy. I don't know why I was so angry with you. I love you,' she said softly. Stilt cried with joy and stood up with her. She flung herself into his arms. 'Always,' Sadie whispered.

'Alwa—' He stopped as his wife half screamed, half cried. He held her up as she went limp. The light left her eyes. He looked down, shaking. There was a hole in her chest where her heart used to be. As she dropped to the floor, the last thing he saw before Lori vanished was her holding Sadie's heart, still beating in her hand; the floor by her feet soaked in blood.

***

'Mirror, mirror, on the wall. Who is the evillest of them all?' Lori asked the mirror. The mirror warped into a face.

'You are, your Majesty,' it replied before moulding back into a silver framed mirror.

Lori fell to her knees, letting the heart roll out of her hands. Blood covered her dress and arms. Tears fell onto the dusty floor. 'I never wanted to be this person. I shouldn't have cursed him. I should have let him go,' she sobbed.

Henry watched as the queen showed remorse and regret. Both of which were a first. 'My Queen,' Henry started but was lost for words; they both were.

Lori wept and looked at Henry with an unbearable sadness. 'I need you now more than ever. I need you to help me kill Edward.'

Henry raised an eyebrow. He had met Lori after Mary died. Henry moved into the woods, and Lori had taken pity.

They both had one enemy in common—Edward. 'But you just said you never should have cursed him?'

'But I did,' she stated and stood up. She took her hair down and let it fall around her shoulders. 'He has shown no remorse, nothing. *He*, he is the evillest of them all, and I *will* destroy him for good. He killed your love; do you *not* want him dead?'

'I do. I did.' He hesitated, looking out of the smeared window. 'But I now have someone to look out for, someone to love,' he replied.

'Snow,' she said. She couldn't hide the envy lacing her words.

'She is sixteen. Now that her grandmother is dead, it won't be long until she takes the throne. Once the king dies, she will be alone. She will need me.'

Lori smirked. 'Ah, yes, the king. He is looking to wed again, is he not?' she asked.

'He wants only the fairest of them all,' Henry replied.

'They all do,' she groaned. 'Am I not fair, Henry?' she asked.

'You know you are enchanting. But in more of a seductive way, not in an innocent way. The late queen was innocent, beautiful, and kind.'

'I can be those things,' she said, smirking. 'Maybe I should become queen. A real queen.'

'Queen of Passion is still a queen,' he pointed out, as she had done so many times before. 'And you are a princess of Forosh.'

'Yes, but as queen of a land, I will have access to an army. I'll find a way to kill Edward and defend myself against Stilt.

He will come for me now that I have taken the heart of his wife.'

'I can see why he would,' Henry said bluntly.

Lori shrugged. 'Yeah, me too. At least, people will know not to go against me. Once word gets out, everyone will know what I am capable of. Except for here. This is a kingdom that knows little of magic. It is the only place where I am safe.'

'For now,' Henry said and looked out the window to the apple tree. He realised how evil he had been. To allow him to stay there, he had agreed to help Lori find victims to eat her cursed apples. But now, he was tired. Tired of magic. Tired of games.

'I want no part of this,' he stated.

'You made me a promise,' she said and walked over to him. Dried blood filled the gaps of her fingernails, and he had to hold back a gag. 'I will rip Snow's heart out if you don't obey me.'

'You love her too,' he shouted.

'No, dwarf,' she shouted. 'I envy her. Her beauty. Her charm. I'd have no problem killing her. Do you really want to call my bluff?' she asked.

He gulped. 'No.'

ISABEL

'Prince Edward,' the old queen greeted him. She placed her wrinkly hand out for him to kiss. He hesitated and kissed her ring instead. She seemed pleased enough with that and summoned him to the castle. Her eyes mirrored Lori's, which made sense considering she is her grandmother. Still, being back in Forosh brought back a flurry of memories that he would have rather kept buried. He followed the queen into the royal carriage. Coated in gold, with small windows and red curtains, was a reminder of how rich their country was. Although it was not as rich as Dolorom was. No country was.

Pear trees surrounded the entrance. A moat with floating lily pads and flowers circled the castle. On the drawbridge, yellow and purple streamers hung from the iron gate.

'We have just finished celebrating Forlod, the national holiday celebrating independence from ...'

'My country,' he stated. When he stayed in Forosh, they had reminded him almost daily that they had defeated Dolorom and gained independence. 'I know. Two hundred years. You must be proud.'

'That we are,' she said. Her voice was shrill and slightly nasal. 'We must feast.'

'Of course,' Edward replied. 'You have the most beautiful castle I have ever seen. Although I have seen it before, it still entrances me with its beauty.'

She looked at him tight-lipped. 'Trying to charm me won't work. Double or nothing, as I have said. I will accept nothing less.'

The subject of Lori hung in the air, and Edward worried that he would see her soon. 'We are willing to offer you an additional two thousand gold pieces. No more,' he stated in a monotone voice.

'Then I am afraid you have wasted a trip.' They stopped by the great hall. The princess and her ladies blocked their path.

'Princess Isabel,' Edward said as she curtsied. He bowed his head and looked up. Their gazes locked, and she grinned. 'It has been a long time,' she said, with an Eastern accent.

'I have missed you,' he admitted. She blushed and put down her white lace parasol. She looked amazing. Especially since the last time he last saw her. Well, she was only fifteen at the time. Lori's little sister. Now, she was twenty. Her amber hair fell in ringlets from her messy bun. Little roses dotted the bun carelessly. Her emerald green eyes were enticing, shown off by her thick black lashes, complemented by her olive skin.

She bit down on her lip. His heart raced as he watched the colour change from a pale pink to a rosy red. They were so plump, so kissable ... 'Edward,' she said, snapping him from his train of thought. 'Are you coming to feast?'

'Of course,' he replied. 'I'm glad you're here.'

'I had to come and greet you when Grandmother told me you were arriving,' she admitted. 'I didn't believe you had returned. You are more handsome than I remember,' she admitted.

He blushed, which was a rare occurrence. But they—Isabel, Lori, their mother, and their grandmother—were all daughters of passion; a type of deity. This meant that they were almost irresistible to men. However, Isabel had her own charm about her, a kind of kookiness that attracted him.

They walked behind the queen, just enough that they couldn't be heard. Edward leant in toward Isabel. 'Your grandmother is getting old. You will become a queen soon; are you nervous?' he asked.

'If Lori comes back, she will be queen. She is the eldest,' Isabel pointed out.

'Comes back? You mean she left?' Edward asked. The sound of her name twisted his stomach.

'No one knows why she left like she did. But she did ...' Isabel blinked back tears. 'She loved you. You must know. Please, tell me,' Isabel pleaded.

'I don't know,' he said. 'I haven't heard from her since we, er, broke up.' He adjusted his collar. Did it suddenly feel warmer?

'Neither have I,' a teary Isabel admitted. 'Maybe you were made to forget what happened? I mean you two were close. There is no way she would have just left and not told you.'

Isabel gasped and ran up to her chambers, leaving a confused Edward behind. He walked to the feast alone feeling slightly smitten with Isabel. He had never felt smitten before, and she was the most beautiful woman he had ever encountered. However, being back at the castle made him feel a little nauseous over.

Memories swamped the halls. He could hear Lori's laughter. Picture them as they ran around the orchard. How they sat side by side in the great hall. He knew, of course, that he had laid with another woman. That would be why Lori had disappeared, after cursing him to be a frog. But since then, he hadn't heard from her.

Isabel reappeared with a pink sparkling potion. 'It's a memory potion,' she said, answering his unspoken question. 'Take it.'

It wouldn't change anything. He honestly knew that the reason Lori left was probably down to him. He rolled his eyes and drank it, then fell to his knees, clutching his chest as the memories swarmed back.

He remembered Belle, at the castle. Someone had made him forget. Stilt had made him forget her! Now, it made sense to why he was missing time, why it had been five years since he had been gone. He had been made to forget his time as a beast.

'I must find Belle,' Edward said and stood up.

'Do you remember anything about my sister?' Isabel asked, hopeful.

'I'm sorry, no,' he admitted. He gave Isabel a quick hug. 'I must go. I'm sorry,' he said apologetically and ran out of the castle. Memories of his one true love filled him up. The heart-wrenching thought of her alone after their kiss pained him. She must have thought that he did not love her. He had to set things right. He got onto the ship immediately.

Fortunately, they hadn't taken his luggage to the castle yet. He ordered his men to sail home immediately.

'What's happening, your Highness?' asked one of the men.

'I must find my love,' he stated. 'I remember everything ...' He looked out at the horizon, his expression twisting into one of anger. 'It was all Stilt. He did this. He made me forget them. I'm going to kill him,' Edward swore.

***

Edward returned to Dolorom. The familiar white cliffs and greenery greeted him. He looked at the island with cold eyes. Fury still filled him. He stomped back into the castle he had called home for a long time and packed his things himself. He wouldn't answer anyone's questions. He got on his horse and rode to Stilt's house.

When he got there, he saw Stilt through the window, crying. He was covered in blood.

'What's happened?' Edward asked when he walked in, staring at the blood with horror.

'She ripped my wife's heart out,' Stilt said between sobs.

'Who?'

'Lori,' Stilt answered. Edward's head went fuzzy. He held onto the side cabinet for support.

'She's alive?' he asked.

'Yes, and she hates you. She is the Evil Queen. She's coming for you,' Stilt warned.

'And I am coming after you,' he spat. 'You spelled me to forget Belle, James, the castle. My time as a beast!' Edward shouted.

Stilt sat up on the arm chair. 'Then kill me. I have nothing left to live for anyway.'

Edward looked around at the blood. Sadie laid on the floor. Now just an empty shell left by the crackling fire. 'I see you have been punished enough. You'd just better pray that Belle and her son believe me. In fact, you're coming with me as proof!'

'I cannot,' Stilt said, exasperated. 'Please just leave me to grieve!'

'No,' Edward pulled the cabinet down. The glass doors smashed on the floor, ornaments cracked, and books fell into a heap. 'Help me!' he screamed, tears falling down his face. 'I will use the last of my powers to get us there.'

Stilt panicked. 'Wait. First, we should go to the castle to check everything is okay. I added a time spell to the potion so the pregnancy would be quicker. She should be almost full term. After we check, I promise to go with you. Deal?'

'Fine,' Edward said. He wanted to say goodbye to his mother anyway. They rode back to the castle. The blood on his waistcoat dried as the wind whipped around Stilt. The castle was in sight, and Stilt tried to come up with a plan.

Edward huffed as they rode. 'You do have something to live for. Your soon-to-be daughter.'

Stilt smiled yet felt incredibly selfish to do so. 'You're right.' He didn't want to face a future without Sadie. But the child was promised to him. She was to be his daughter, and he must take care of her. He was glad he wasn't cursed anymore! The love curse, to crave the flesh of those he loved, was a cruel one. Because of it, he had eaten his own child. A memory that would haunt his nightmares and waking moments, always.

When they arrived at the castle, the king welcomed them. 'We have excellent news. We were going to tell you before you ran off in a hurry,' he said.

'What is it?' asked Edward.

'It's definitely two girls. We have had many confirm it. Considering this, I have decided that my daughter will be crowned queen once I die. Providing I have no more sons after their birth.'

'What?' Edward felt the colour drain from his face. 'I mean that's great news.'

Edward and Stilt went to Edward's chambers to talk more. 'It is supposed to be sons only. Me!' Edward hissed once he had dismissed the guards.

'And what would you have me do?' Stilt asked.

'Anything. There must be something,' Edward said quickly.

Stilt pondered. 'Perhaps she could enter an eternal sleep, a death-like slumber? They will have no choice but to proclaim you a king then. My daughter will be taken away from this land so they cannot find her. Once they give her to me, of course.'

'Perfect. Do it,' Edward barked.

'What will I get?' Stilt asked.

'My forgiveness,' he said.

Stilt considered it for a few minutes. Edward was a powerful ally to have. Also, Stilt had grown fond of the arrogant prince. 'Fine.'

Haunting Fairytales Series

Stilt cast the curse. 'On her sixteenth birthday, she will prick her finger on a spinning wheel and will fall into an eternal slumber. As with every curse, it needs a get-out clause.'

'True love,' Edward said and grinned. 'At sixteen, she will not know what love is.'

'Of course,' Stilt said menacingly. 'And only true love's kiss can break the curse.' Green mist seeped from the room and into the queen's stomach, who was napping on an upstairs futon. Edward left the room, pleased with the curse.

Edward packed and was rearing to leave. 'Are you ready to go?'

'Yes,' Stilt said. 'The girls will be born within the month. We will make it back in time for the birth.'

'We will,' Edward said. 'Congratulations.' Although angry, he had promised forgiveness, and he was a man of his word.

'Thank you,' Stilt replied. 'I have decided to call her Cinderella.'

'That's a beautiful name,' Edward said and took Stilt's hand. 'Do you want me to do it or do you want to?'

'I will,' he answered quickly. They vanished and reappeared at the castle. Storm clouds covered the skies.

'Belle,' Edward shouted and ran into the castle. 'Belle, James.'

Belle stomped out, holding her son's hand. Edward looked at them. James was a year older than when he last saw him. Yet he looked so different. Taller, more handsome. He was at least sixteen years old yet looked older.

'You left!' Belle said, tears streaming down her cheeks. 'You shouldn't have come back.'

'I didn't choose to leave. I was made to forget you both and the castle. I took a potion, remembered everything, and now I am back.'

'You don't expect me to believe that, do you?' she asked.

'No, you shouldn't,' a familiar voice said from behind Edward. He turned and saw the Evil Queen.

'Lori,' he spluttered. He opened his mouth to say more but couldn't speak. He was lost for words. Sadness and guilt crept over him as he looked her up and down. She hadn't aged a day.

'Belle, Edward is a liar. I am his ex, and I am here to help you. He left you here to rot. Made up that story. I feel sorry for anyone who falls by the hands of *him*,' she spat.

'No,' Edward said, finding his voice. 'Belle, don't listen to her.'

Belle looked back at the castle. Caleb entered the ballroom, looking back and forth between Edward and Belle. Belle's father walked down the middle staircase and cleared his throat. 'What's going on?'

Belle look from Lori to Edward, puzzled. 'I'm not entirely sure.' After they all moved into the castle, Belle's sisters grabbed all the jewels in the castle and left for the city, leaving Belle, Thomas, Caleb, and James alone.

James grabbed his sword, which was propped up against the wall, and pointed it at Edward. 'I believe the witch.' Lori frowned but smiled as James pointed the sword closer to Edward's chest. 'You've come back to hurt my mother again! It won't work. Not this time.' James looked through daring eyes, and Edward backed off. His hand jolted towards the hilt of his own sword, but he thought better of it. This was Belle's son.

Edward held his hands up. 'I swear I'm telling the truth. I love your mother.' His gaze averted to Belle. 'I love you.'

Her gaze filled with sadness and her chest tightened, but she didn't say a word. Instead, she looked at Caleb for an indication of what she should do. Caleb simply shrugged and gave her a sympathetic look. Lori stepped forward and was pushed to the ground with a thud. Stilt grabbed Edward's sword from him and pointed it down at Lori's throat. Lori touched the tip and heat ran up the blade until Stilt dropped it. She dodged the hot sword and jumped to her feet, throwing a spell his way, which he narrowly missed.

James stood between them. 'Enough!' His voice, although young, was demanding and authoritative. 'I've had it with magic. You all need to leave.' He looked over at Edward. 'Especially you!'

Stilt growled. 'That woman,' he spat, pointing at Lori, 'killed my wife!'

Belle gasped. 'That's terrible.'

'You did?' Edward asked.

Lori groaned. 'Who cares? She was crazy!'

Stilt clenched his fists. 'She. Was. My. WIFE!'

Lori looked from Belle, who was looking at Edward doe-eyed, to James. She sensed something from James. Something she could use. However, Belle would never buy her story now. With a flick of her hand, a hurricane of black mist swept from the ground and circled around them. They all stumbled around blindly. Lori touched Belle's arm and

The Enchanted Kingdoms

felt her beauty drain. A curse like this would take everything from her. She swept Belle, James, Caleb, and Thomas into the mist along with herself, and with a click, they all disappeared.

'No,' Edward cried and closed his eyes. He held back tears, yet one managed to escape and crawled down his cheek.

'We can get her back,' Stilt said.

Edward shook his head and sighed. 'Not if Lori has her way. Still, I must try!'

Stilt nodded. 'First, we will need something.' He disappeared through the corridors and returned with the enchanted rose, which he had encased in a glass dome.

Edward frowned. 'What are you doing with my rose? It is safe here.'

Stilt gulped. 'I ... we need it.'

Edward stretched out his arm toward Stilt and waited for a surge of power to come. Instead, a small spurt knocked the rose from his hand. Stilt knelt and grabbed the rose. Thankfully, the glass did not smash.

Edward looked down at his amulet and took it off. 'It's ... powerless.' He narrowed his eyes at Stilt. 'Did you take my power? Is that why you need the rose? Why you have been spending time with me?'

Stilt pursed his lips. 'I need it more—'

Edward launched himself at Stilt. Stilt dodged him. 'Try to understand.'

'Are you being serious?' Edward scowled. 'What could a wifeless, childless man possibly need power more than I for?'

Stilt's apologetic expression turned to one of hatred. 'Well, there go the feelings of guilt!'

Edward lunged at him again, but Stilt dodged him with ease. 'You'll have to do better than that.'

Edward smirked. 'Oh, I will. I will take Cinderella from you. I will take everything until you're left with nothing,' Edward promised.

Stilt looked at Edward challengingly, clicked his fingers, and disappeared. Edward stood alone in the cold castle, only comforted by the sweet memories he once had there.

NORTHMANNI

Lori stared at the magic mirror with disdain. 'I look disgusting.'

'My queen, you look lovely, especially for your age ...'

'I am thirty!' she screamed.

Henry looked at her wide-eyed, his gaze tracing over every putrid wrinkle. 'Thirty? I thought you were, if you don't mind me saying, hundreds of years old. That's why you make others eat your apples so that you can take their beauty?'

'I do that,' she said with exasperation. 'Because when I cursed Edward, the curse was so strong, it took all of my beauty and youth. The apples are the only things sustaining me. The problem is no one will eat one. No one trusts me. You found one person to eat the apple I gave you. Even you haven't found anyone to eat anymore.'

Henry nodded slowly and bit his lip. It wasn't that he couldn't find anyone to eat them. It was that he didn't offer them to anyone. It was an unfair thing to do, to take other's beauty.

The more Lori used her magic, the more it drained her of her beauty. One person's beauty would sustain her for around ten to twenty-five years, depending on their age. However, using the magic to heal Belle's father had taken everything from Lori. 'If I could find someone young and incredibly beautiful, then I would not need anyone to eat another apple for a while. But few possess such beauty,' Lori pointed out.

'Maybe you should just accept how you look. It's all about personality—' Henry offered.

'Oh, don't be dim,' she interrupted. 'The king will never agree to marry me when he sees how I look. He may be old, but as a king, he can have anyone he chooses. You need to find people to eat the apples,' she ordered.

Her chocolate coloured hair was tied up so tightly that it pulled the skin tight on her forehead. She turned her head toward the window of the shack and put her finger up to shush Henry. 'Belle and James are back,' she said and forced a smile as she swung open the door. 'How was your walk?' she asked an annoyingly beautiful Belle. She had considered offering Belle an apple. It would kill two birds with one stone. Edward would have his true love turned into a hag, and she would have enough beauty to sustain herself for a long time. Even with using magic. However, Henry had opened his mouth before Lori could decide, and now they knew about the cursed apples.

Belle's cupid bow lips formed a perfect smile. 'It was wonderful, thank you. We met a girl; she calls herself Red. She walks through the same forest every day to take food to her grandma. She's sixteen, the same age as James. They get along well. I'm thinking of taking him back there tomorrow,' she said and grinned.

'Great news,' Lori replied, bored. 'I must talk to you about Edward,' Lori admitted and took Belle into the next room. James went to sit in the garden with a book in his hand.

Belle followed Lori into her bedroom. The room was lavished with red velvet and gold satin. Although she only lived in a shack, it was surprisingly big and luxurious on the inside. 'I will get straight to the point,' Lori said and sat on her four-post bed, which was draped with gold curtains. 'I imagine you would like to get even with Edward.'

Her smile dropped as his name was mentioned. She felt an unstoppable, wild rage explode within her. 'I want him dead.'

Lori grinned. The curse she had used on Belle turned all passion and love for Edward to bitter hatred. She must have loved him a lot, for the rage she had for him was overwhelming. 'Me too,' Lori replied.

Belle lowered her head, and her expression faltered. 'I don't want James to get tied up in all this. Maybe I should try to forget him and just hope karma gets him.'

No,' Lori said a little too angrily. Belle looked concerned, and Lori quickly forced a smile and laughed. 'I just mean that I need your help. He and Stilt must pay for what they have done to all of us. If we do not stop them, they will continue doing it to whoever they like. Do you want more innocent people to suffer?'

Belle looked at the floor, grinding her teeth. 'Of course not. I just don't want James getting involved with it. I want him to have a violence-free, normal life.'

Lori looked at Belle sadly. 'I am afraid that's not possible. James is coming of age, and I noticed something about him. He possesses powers.'

'That's not possible,' Belle said. 'My family has no magical history.'

'I bet you don't know much about your ancestors?' Lori pointed out.

Belle ran her fingers through her long brunette hair and sat down at Lori's dressing table. 'No, I don't.'

Lori looked Belle up and down with envy. Her hair was so soft, long, and when the light hit it, hundreds of shades of brown shone. Her eyes, a honey brown, were perfectly defined. Black outlined her irises, showing off the flecks of golden brown. Her thick black lashes made her eyes more striking than Lori thought possible. The most annoying thing about Belle was, as Lori had noticed, no matter what Belle wore—an old rag, a dress, trousers—she always looked amazing.

'Your ancestors were powerful sorcerers,' Lori explained. 'I realised when you told me your surname was Sparken. Your ancestors are known in the magical world. They had unlimited powers. It often skips generations. James will grow into his powers. He has no idea of the amount that he possesses.'

'The amount?' Belle questioned.

Lori elaborated. 'Every sorcerer has a limited amount of magic. If used properly, it is enough to last a lifetime. However, when abused, most lose their powers. Only three have unlimited power. Merlin, me, and James. Your lineage is famous amongst sorcerers.'

'I don't want him to have these powers,' Belle said quickly.

Lori huffed. 'You have no choice. Anyway, it is a wonderful gift. He can help so many people with them. He will be able to protect himself against any threats.'

At that, Belle sighed. 'You make a good point.'

'Yes,' Lori said and stood up. 'It will not take Edward or Stilt long to figure it out. They will come for him. They may not be as powerful as James is, but they are far more cunning, and a billion times more heartless. They'll kill him. Once it gets out about his powers, and believe me, no matter how much you try to conceal it, it will get out.'

Belle stood up and clenched her fists. 'I will not let them hurt him.' She wondered where the sudden anger had come from. She had always believed strongly in forgiveness and had more tolerance than most people. Yet she knew that if Edward were standing in front of her, she'd rip his head off.

'Then,' Lori said, patronisingly, 'we must get to them first.'

Belle frowned. 'How do we find them?'

Lori scoffed. 'They'll come to us. Don't worry.'

Belle's stomach twisted in a way she didn't like, and a voice in the back of her head niggled *Murder is wrong. You love him, remember?* But then why did she feel so much hatred for the man? 'I can't kill him!'

Lori ground her teeth. 'You have to!'

Belle shook her head. 'Taking someone's life from them leaves a mark on the soul.'

Lori shifted uncomfortably. 'I'll let you think about my offer. Help me and I'll help you. I'll keep James safe and help him control his powers. You don't want him losing control, do you?'

Belle arched an eyebrow. 'Are you sure he's a sorcerer?'

'Positive,' she replied without hesitation. 'I'll help bring them to the surface.' Lori waited for a response but got none. She absentmindedly twirled her hair around her finger. Belle said nothing about Lori's appearance, which had drastically changed in the last month. Over James's sixteenth birthday, he had become more and more grumpy. Belle was sure it was because he wasn't around people his own age. Lori was right. If he did have powers, then control was key. Also, she didn't want Edward and Stilt coming for them. 'Like I said, think about it,' Lori added.

Belle had told Lori each heart-wrenching detail when they arrived. Belle, although angry, did see some truth in Edward's words but would never tell Lori that.

'I thought he loved me,' Belle said sadly.

'Ha,' Lori said and walked over to the door. 'He makes a lot of people believe that! You're not the first, and you won't be the last. Edward lied. He left with Stilt to get his kingdom back. He only returned to get the rose, which held power. I'll give you some time to consider my offer.' She left the room, and Caleb and her father returned.

'Belle,' Caleb exclaimed. 'I met someone!'

Belle grinned. 'Fantastic! Details?'

'Of course.' He laughed and sat next to her.

Thomas leant against the wall. 'He seems nice.'

'Nice,' Caleb said, wide-eyed. 'Oh, he is more than nice. He's so handsome and charming. 'He's my age and so witty. But that's not all. He said a cottage is for sale in the city, and I was thinking ...'

'You're leaving?' Belle gulped.

Caleb pulled at his collar. 'It's just the friends I have made all live there, and he lives there. Plus, the fruit market is booming, and I was thinking of buying an orchard and setting up exportation to the other kingdoms. Everyone knows Northmanni has the best apples.' Caleb couldn't hold in his excitement. 'Edmund knows all about it. He's given me some tips, and I think I could get somewhere with it. The orchard is selling for only one hundred gold coins due to the flooding, but it's nothing that some hard work won't sort.'

Belle forced a smile. She was happy for him, but sad that she'd be saying goodbye. As if he read her thoughts, he smiled sweetly. 'I will still see you.'

'You'd better,' she warned and grinned. 'So he's called Edmund then?'

Caleb nodded. 'Yep. Well, Thomas is taking me to look around the orchard and cottage again. So I'll be off. Tell James I'll be back for our fighting lesson this evening.'

Belle waved goodbye to them as they rode off on the horse and cart and sighed. James might need those sword fighting lessons more than she thought.

DEAL?

Edward eventually pulled himself out of his slump. He looked around the empty castle and felt afraid for the first time in years. He was without a friend in the world, and everything he loved had been taken from him. Lori was back, which was a shock. He didn't know how he felt. He loved Belle, of course, but something stirred inside him when he thought of Lori and the many happy years they had spent together before he ruined everything. The ghost of Belle's laughter echoed as he walked through the ballroom. The room where he realised he had fallen for her. Everything, for him, changed at that moment. He had spent a month in the castle, moping.

'Rumpelstiltskin, Rumpelstiltskin, Rumpelstiltskin,' he said. It was an old wives' tale. If you say his full name three times, he would appear. He waited anxiously and sighed when nothing happened. Suddenly, a loud pop sounded behind him, and he turned. Stilt stood there sporting his sword. The one he took from him just before they went to the castle and threw to the ground.

'Damn spell,' Stilt muttered.

'You betrayed me,' Edward said. 'I thought we were friends.' The childish words escaped his lips before he had a chance to think. Stilt looked unfazed.

'You were an ally,' Stilt replied. 'You have nothing left to offer me. My wife is dead. Everything I loved has been ripped away from me. That tends to bring the darkness out, even in the nicest of people.'

'Give me back my powers or I swear I will find a way to take away the one thing you have left in the world!' Edward promised. He noticed that Stilt was sweating, his hair was stuck up in places, and he looked like he had just left a war. 'What the hell happened to you?'

'Your father,' Stilt said, his mouth twisting in disgust. 'We have a contract, but he won't let me see Cinderella.'

'Hurt's, doesn't it?' Edward smirked. 'When people break their promises.'

Stilt laughed in response.

'What so funny?' asked Edward.

Stilt laughed again. 'That you honestly think it hurts. I'm used to people breaking their word. A person's word means nothing these days. Power is everything. It's an annoyance. It did not hurt me. You're such a pansy. 'Hurts, doesn't it?' mocked Stilt.

Edward would have launched himself at Stilt and hit him, but he didn't have the strength. He felt emotionally and physically drained. 'You vile old man.'

Stilt nodded in acknowledgment. 'I must be going.'

'Wait,' Edward shouted. 'Lori will be coming back for you. Lori is using Belle and James for her own gains. I need to find out why. If you leave me here, you're on your own. I will find a way to get back and make sure that little Cinderella never gets to meet you. Or if I have to ... I'll kill her myself.'

'Or I could just kill you now?' Stilt pointed out, grinning.

Edward laughed now. 'You could try.' He glinted dangerously. 'Or you can help, and when I am king, I can offer you everything. We can find a way together. To keep your daughter safe. I have the ability as a sorcerer to regain my powers somehow. With your help, we can be a team. Deal?'

Stilt considered it for a minute and sighed. 'You're right.'

'You're making the right choice,' Edward said.

'I know,' Stilt said. 'I won't kill you, and I will help you get your powers back.' Stilt extended his hand. Edward touched his wrist, and they both vanished and reappeared in a familiar place.

***

Belle watched James and Caleb as night fell. They were in the woods. The sounds of swords hitting each other and the occasional gust of wind was all that could be heard.

Caleb had bought the orchard and was leaving in the morning for the city. She had already made him a basket of bread and cheese to take with him. James had taken the news better than she thought. He shook Caleb's hand and wished him the best of luck. Then insisted that the student had surpassed the teacher and he no longer needed lessons. Caleb reacted by offering not to hold back and for them to battle it out tonight.

Belle couldn't help but giggle as she watched sweat drip down into Caleb's groomed beard. He looked aggravated more than anything. He was *really* trying to beat James. Yet with every move, James dodged and came back at him with force. So far, James was winning, by a lot. As the night grew colder, Caleb held his hands up in surrender. 'You're not too bad,' he said breathlessly.

James smirked. 'Like I said ... Student surpassed the teacher.'

Caleb smiled, genuinely, and extended his hand. 'You were a great student. I'm going to miss you.'

'You too,' James admitted. He wasn't great at showing emotion. He shook Caleb's hand firmly and put his sword away.

They walked quietly back to the cabin and heard a howl. 'Probably Red's wolf,' James said as they walked. He'd grown fond of Red. She was funny and strong. But she didn't want to hang out much. Instead, she sat alone in her cabin a lot, save for the occasional visit.

They reached the shack. Lori was examining her face in the mirror. 'I look gross.'

James shrugged. 'Can't argue that.'

Belle turned and shot him a firm look. 'That's rude. Apologise.'

'Sorry,' James said insincerely and walked off to his room. Caleb wiped his forehead and headed for the bathroom.

Lori turned. 'Your father asked me to give you this.' She handed Belle a note.

Belle,

Gone to Colomorgh to see your sisters. I don't know when I'll be back, but I will be staying at the Dead Man's Inn if you need me.

Griselda was caught stealing from Charles. I know as an old friend, he will let her go, but it's better if I go and see them in person. Griselda has been acting up, and I'm

worried about her. She needs me at the moment, so I'm going to stay there for as long as it takes.
Love you.
Father

Belle swallowed hard. The lump in her throat stayed regardless of what she did. Thomas had left, Caleb was leaving, and soon, she felt as if she'd have no one to talk to. She felt completely alone and, for the first time, vulnerable. She turned to Lori and sighed. 'I agree to your offer,' Belle said after weighing her other options. 'You've given me no reason not to trust you, and I must protect James. You'd make a better friend than enemy.'

Lori smiled broadly. 'You're a smart girl, Belle. First things first, I must marry the king.'

Belle's eyed widened. 'King of where? And why?'

Lori smiled seductively. 'The King of Northmanni. He is looking for a wife. He is a very powerful man for a mortal. Northmanni is one of the biggest in all the lands. He will help us achieve our goals, but I need to find a way to get more beauty for myself,' Lori informed Belle.

'Beauty is only skin deep,' Belle pointed out. 'You don't need to obtain more beauty.' She pulled her dark pink velvet cloak tighter. Her hair was tied up into a loose ponytail. Her dress was a dusty pink; it cinched in at her waist and flared out at the bottom. All of it was courtesy of Lori, who insisted that Belle needed new clothes. Now, Lori insisted they needed new looks, including James. He was up for the challenge, no questions asked, which shocked Belle.

'Again ... I need beauty,' Lori said, interrupting Belle's train of thought. 'There is only one in this kingdom who is beautiful enough that I would not need to take anyone's beauty for years.'

'You can't steal someone's beauty?' Belle asked sternly.

'You want to protect your son? Then you must trust in me,' Lori said before disappearing into her room. 'We start tomorrow,' she shouted before shutting the door.

Henry yawned and stretched out his legs by the fire. James walked down from his room and sat next to Henry.

Belle bit her cheek. She knew the apples were cursed, but to take someone's beauty and youth? It was ... different. Belle looked at her son and sighed. 'James.' He turned and looked at her blankly. She took a deep breath and continued. 'You know how I told you earlier that Lori thinks you have powers?' He nodded. 'Well,' she continued. 'I have agreed to help Lori hunt Edward. She's going to help you control your powers.'

Henry grumbled but didn't say anything. James turned. His light brown hair had turned a couple of shades darker. His voice had broken, and he was at least a foot taller. He was growing up so fast. 'I'm up for the challenge. Henry's been trying to help me bring my powers to the surface.'

'Nothing yet,' Henry said.

Belle smiled warmly at Henry. 'You have a good heart, Henry. How is Snow?'

'I went to see her today. She's growing up so fast. Sixteen now,' he said. 'She's opinionated, kind, funny, just like her mother was.'

'Someone else James's age?' Belle asked.

'Yes,' Henry replied. 'Her birthday was last week. I attended the party thrown by the king. He adores her.'

Belle smiled in response and made them all cocoa.

'You can come and meet her if you want?' Henry suggested.

Belle grinned. 'How sweet. We would love to. When are you thinking?'

Henry smiled. 'I'm seeing her tomorrow.'

Belle grinned and looked over at James. 'Tomorrow it is.' She hoped that being around more friends would cheer him up. 'I'm sure they will get along,' Belle added.

SNOW WHITE

Lori watched Snow from a distance. She heard the horse and cart pull off in the distance and smiled. Finally, Caleb had gone. She only wanted Belle and James there, and now, they trusted her. That was why she had taken Caleb and Thomas back. She could see that Belle would never willingly leave them. Slipping a love potion into Caleb's drink had been all too easy. He had fallen in love with the first person he lusted. It was even easier to use her mirror to spell Griselda into stealing and drinking liquor. Then made sure that a letter made its way to Thomas.

Lori had been cheated on by Edward a long time ago and had never forgiven him. Making sure he would never get his happy ending, she had made sure to take his one true love from him; Belle, and her son, James—a handsome sixteen-year-old with a talent for sword fighting and even more, he was a sorcerer. He couldn't control his powers yet, so Lori was helping him. With Belle and James on her side, she could finally get her happy ending by becoming Queen of Northmanni and killing Edward.

The queen died the previous month, leaving the king free to remarry if he wished, and if Lori had anything to do with it, then he would wish it. However, to be queen, she would need to steal someone's beauty using her siphoning apples, which she so often did, turning them into dwarves. And who more beautiful in the land than Snow White?

Lori gazed at her beautiful prey. Snow hid behind a tree, camouflaged by her white cloak. She was throwing snowballs at the guards then ducking before they could see who threw them. It snowed for most of the year in Northmanni. Lori shivered and grasped at the apple in her pocket and took a deep breath. Snow's midnight black hair ran straight down her back. Her skin was as white as the snow she threw, which made her blood red plump lips even more striking. Her dark eyes shone brightly behind thick black lashes. She wore a black dress underneath her cloak.

Snow sat on a rock, and Lori seized the moment. Lori pulled down her hood and approached her. 'Snow,' she called.

'Lori,' Snow addressed and scrunched her nose. 'What do you want?'

Lori faked shock at Snow's disgusted tone. 'What have I done to offend you, child?'

Snow looked at her with heavy eyes. 'I know that you grow apples to take people's beauty for your own. You're a wicked woman with bad fashion sense.' The last part hurt Lori more than she wanted to admit.

Lori placed her hand on her chest and felt her heart hammer underneath. 'My apples do not take people's beauty. They are magical. People say those stories because they want the apples for their own and don't want anyone else to have them. In fact, as a gift, I was going to offer you one.'

'Oh.' Snow looked down, disappointed. 'I'm sorry.'

Lori waved her hand dismissively. 'We all make mistakes.'

Snow's eyes sparkled with wonder as she gazed at the apple. 'Wait, so if I eat that apple … I will have magical powers?'

'Yes,' Lori answered and secretly congratulated herself on her acting.

'Oh, my gosh!' Snow said, delighted. 'What a truly wonderful gift. Thank you. Can I have it?' Snow begged, practically jumping with joy.

'Here you are,' Lori said and handed her the red apple. Snow took it and brought it up to her lips. Lori's heart thudded with anticipation.

Snow's smile turned to a smirk. 'You'll have to try harder than that next time, witch.' Snow threw the apple underarm, so it landed in the middle of the frost covered grass.

'I am not a witch. I am a queen,' Lori called after her and stormed furiously back to the shack. 'I bet Henry told her,' she muttered under her breath.

***

'Sweet pea,' Henry said, addressing Snow. She was sat with her feet propped up on the banqueting table, showing off her black laced boots.

'Henry,' she squealed as she saw him. She jumped up and hugged him. 'You've brought Belle with you, and, um ...?'

'I'm James,' he said and kissed her hand. She blushed slightly. He had a wide jaw, athletic build, brown eyes, and tousled medium-brown hair, which fell to his ears.

'I'm Snow, Snow White.' Their gazes locked, and Belle and Henry smiled at each other.

'Happy birthday for last week,' Belle said kindly. Belle and Snow had met through Henry the previous week, and Snow had instantly taken a liking to her, but she didn't know that Belle had a son—a handsome son, at that.

Snow continued watching James. He half-smiled at her. 'Thank you,' she said dismissively.

Belle laughed and went to meet the king with Henry. 'Be back soon.' She eyed James. 'Behave.'

They both nodded, and James looked down at Snow's bracelets. 'Not the usual attire for a princess,' he said, grinning.

She fiddled with the black strings covered with coloured beads. 'I don't care about others' expectations anymore,' she admitted.

'I like that,' he replied. 'Would you like to go for a walk? I've never seen the palace.'

Snow smiled widely. 'Of course. I like to throw snowballs at the guards when they're not looking.' She laughed. 'It's so fun to see them hold up their spears, looking around. Some dance around when I manage to hit their necks. The snow goes down their back.'

James laughed. 'God, it's good to be around someone my age. I'm stuck in with Mum and Lori most of the time.'

'Lori? That evil cow!' Snow gritted her teeth as they walked into the garden.

'She's helping us. My mother fell for a man who was a liar and broke her heart! I'd love to get my hands on him and make him feel the same pain that she felt!'

Snow scoffed. 'Lori steals people's beauty and kills for fun, apparently. It's not nice to hear about what happened to your mother, but Lori is worse.'

He shrugged. 'I don't know what she's like, to be honest.'
'What happened to the man who hurt Belle?'

James put his hands casually in his pockets and shrugged. 'No idea. Hopefully, he's dead. I think we may actually hunt him down.'

Snow hid a grin. 'Dark.'

James pulled an apple out of his pocket and a small knife. He cut a bit and offered a piece to Snow.

She pressed her lips together as she looked down at the piece of apple. *Trust Lori to send someone else.* She pulled a silver dagger from her boot and pointed it at him. 'You're working with Lori, aren't you? Trust her to send some handsome guy to come and woo me, thinking it would work.'

He smirked. 'You think I'm handsome?'

She growled and pushed the dagger closer to his stomach. 'Answer me!'

He looked at the dagger cautiously and took a couple of steps back until he hit a tree. 'Whoa, calm down. I'm not working with her in the way you think. It has nothing to do with you.'

She glanced at the apple. 'That will take my beauty! Did she send you?' Snow shoved the dagger forward until it was pressing into his stomach, almost breaking the skin through his shirt. Snow leaned in until their noses were touching. 'Answer me honestly, or I promise I will gut you!'

'You're a psycho!' he exclaimed. 'I bet Henry doesn't know you carry a dagger around with you. What else do you have on you?'

'That's none of your business,' she spat. 'Now, answer me!'

He placed his hand on her arm. 'It's a normal apple. I'm not stupid.'

Snow raised her eyebrows. 'Debatable.'

He frowned. 'Ouch. You don't even know me ... yet.'

'Erghh,' she groaned. 'If it's a normal apple, then take a bite.'

He took a deep breath and brought the apple to his lips then took a bite. Snow waited, but he stayed as handsome as ever. 'See, Princess? I was just hungry.'

'Oh,' she said yet didn't move the dagger.

'Well ... I've never met a woman so ... terrifying,' he admitted. Grinning, he showed off his pearly white teeth. He was taller than her, by half a foot. Yet she had a presence that scared even him.

She gulped and steadied herself. 'I don't care. I know she sent you!'

'She did not,' he said with exasperation.

She raised a perfectly arched eyebrow. 'Fine.'

James smiled. 'I know we've just met, but I think I'm going to like you.'

'What? You don't know me!'

'I'm attracted to psychopaths?'

'Urghh,' she complained. She pushed the dagger down the side of her boot and let him go. 'You're not as charming as I first thought.'

'I don't usually disappoint,' he moaned. 'Anyway, I was joking. I like that you're different, even a little psychotic.' He half smiled. 'And you look cute when you're angry,' he added.

'I am not cute when I am angry,' she said, grabbing the front of his shirt until she was face to face with him. 'I could easily cut your heart from your chest without a second thought,' she spat.

He looked at her doe-eyed. 'Adorable.'

Her face flushed red. 'I wish I never met you.'

He grinned. 'Don't lie.'

'I'll hurt you,' she warned you.

He laughed. 'You couldn't hurt a fly, Princess.'

'Want to bet?' She pulled her dagger out and listened for a buzz against the quietness of the snowfall. A fly buzzed past her and landed on the wall that stood near to them. She edged her way over and with lightning speed brought the dagger down. James looked at her wide-eyed. On the end of her dagger was a twitching fly.

'Fair enough,' he said and shrugged.

She turned and let out a patient breath. *That was intense.*

Belle and Henry waved as they walked out of the palace doors. 'How are you both getting along?'

She smiled sweetly. 'We're getting along great. He's such wonderful company,' she lied.

James side-glanced at her. 'You really are a psycho,' he whispered.

She gave him a sideways glance. 'You have *no* idea.'

SHELLS

They arrived at the lakeside. Stilt smiled reassuringly at Edward. Edward had been here before when he used to visit Prince Eric when they were children. He looked down at the misty water. 'How will a lake get me powers?'

Stilt cackled and dance in the water until it reached up to his knees. 'It's what's in the lake.' Without warning, Stilt submerged into the depths. He used his newfound power to cast a spell that rippled through the water. Then he swam back up and looked over at Edward. Stilt was almost glowing.

Edward looked behind Stilt in astonishment. Stilt looked backward and saw Ursula smiling unnervvingly at them both. 'What do you want?' Shells crept around her stomach to her belly button in the same paatern that they did on her face. Her tail splashed the water, spraying them all. She pointed a long, sharp nail toward Edward. 'That one's handsome. Perhaps we can make a deal?'

Edward bowed his head, begrusdingly. 'I am Edward, Prince of Dolorom.'

'Oh, a prince.' She giggled and swam closer to the water's edge. 'Perhaps we can make a deal then. I'll grant you what you need if you make a mermaid fall in love with you.'

'You?' Edward asked.

'No.' She laughed. 'That wouldn't be hard. No, a certain redhead I have plans for.'

Edward sighed. 'I wish I could agree—for what I need, I need badly. However, my heart is taken by another.'

Ursula rolled her eyes. 'You loyal types,' she said slimily. 'Fine, as a prince, you have access to other royals?' He nodded. 'Good,' she said. 'Then bring me a prince for my mermaid to fall for, but don't make it obvious.'

He nodded. 'Prince Eric of Milborn.'

'Great,' she said. 'Now, what do you need?'

'Powers.'

Urusula looked back at Stilt. 'Ah, so this is the one you stole the powers from?'

Edward growled. 'You helped him?'

She pouted. 'Aww, if I knew how handsome you were, I wouldn't have,' she lied. 'Well, I can give you powers. However, I would be giving you some of my own power. Make sure you use it well.' She ripped one the shells from her face and screeched. It left a red patch where her skin used to be.

She handed it to Edward who examined it suspiciously. 'What do I do with it?'

'Harness its energy,' she stated. 'Keep it on you at all times. I recommend attaching it to you. Or just keep it in your pocket.'

Stilt, who was back on dry land, coughed. 'Great, ready?' he asked Edward.

Edward looked back at Ursula. 'When do you need Prince Eric?'

'You'll know.' And with that, she swam off.

TIME FOR THE TRUTH

Snow looked down at the picture of her mother holding her as a baby with a huge smile plastered on her face. Next to her stood her father who Snow barely remembered. 'You know,' Snow said to the picture, 'I barely remember either of your voices,' she admitted.

Tears splashed onto the glass. 'I'm sorry.'

Henry knocked on the door. Snow wiped her eyes and placed the picture down on the dresser. 'Hey, Snow.'

Snow looked at the floor. 'Hi.'

'Just wanted to see how you were holding up. It's a year today since your mother went missing…'

'I know!' Snow exclaimed. 'I'm not going to forget it, am I?'

Henry pulled himself onto the bed, his little legs dangling over the side. 'I want to talk to you about that night.'

Her stomach twisted. 'What?' she asked cautiously. She didn't want to talk about it simply because she couldn't handle the truth. That night, after stepping on her mother, she had to wash the remains of her shoe then go around pretending she didn't know what had happened to her mother. Pretending that she hadn't known she was turned into a frog. Pretending that her boot hadn't ended the life of her last parent.

'About your mother, how she went missing …'

Snow's breath hitched. Did he know all this time? Her stomach flipped, and she held back the bile that threatened to spurt out of her mind. The only way to deal with the pain was to pretend to be heartless, which was what she had done.

Snow had dressed in nothing but red and black since her mother died and had done nothing but try to fight 'evil magic' in the form of Lori. Snow had noticed dwarves popping up all over the place and found out about Lori's apples. Snow hated magic; despised it even. It was what had turned her mother into a frog, therefore causing Snow to accidentally kill her.

She had spent years trying to track down the culprit but no one knew, and Henry denied knowing anything about it. Henry sighed. 'I have been dishonest.'

Snow arched an eyebrow. 'How so?'

'I was there the night she went missing.'

Snow felt sick. She could see it now—her name branded as a murderer. Was she not a murderer? She scratched at her wrist to take her mind off the pain of the conversation, in fact, digging and scratching her wrists were her best distraction. Henry continued, taking Snow's pause as wanting more information. 'She was turned into a frog.' Snow went pale, which was surprising considering how white she already was. She sat down. Henry took this for shock and went on. 'A man I was a servant to, the same man who made that snowflake necklace for you, was a sorcerer. To free himself from the curse to be a frog, he had to turn someone else into a frog.'

Snow felt dizzy.

'He killed her.'

'What?' she spluttered.

Henry hung his head in shame. 'I'm sorry I didn't tell you. This must be quite a shock.'

Snow nodded her head slowly. 'I ... I don't know what to say.'

Henry sobbed. 'I should have told you sooner.'

'How? How did he kill her?'

'Stepped on her,' Henry admitted, feeling sick.

Snow stood up, shocked. She had blamed herself all this time, and Henry had known the truth all along.

'Sorry,' Henry said.

'Forget it,' Snow said and left the room. She walked down the corridor and met James and Belle on the way. Henry ran behind Snow.

Snow huffed; she just wanted to be alone so she could throw daggers at her wall. 'What are you doing here?' she asked bluntly.

The tone did not go unnoticed. Belle looked from Henry to Snow. 'Sorry, we just came to speak to the king on behalf of Lori.'

'Lori is an evil witch,' Snow said, angrily.

'She is helping us. I trust her,' Belle admitted.

Snow turned to Henry. 'And you ... Do you trust her?'

Henry bit his lip and looked at Snow sadly. 'She can be reckless, sometimes bad. But I do trust her. Sometimes, the villains in our stories are just hurt. She's just had a bad life. She wouldn't hurt those around her.'

Snow frowned. 'Yet it was you who told me to be wary of her!'

Henry sighed. 'Well, yes. I may trust her with me, but probably not with you.'

'Well,' Snow said, 'it appears I can trust no one.'

Henry sighed at the dig. 'Right, Belle and I have some dealings with your grandfather on behalf of Lori. I admit. Remember, she isn't a bad person, Snow. Just misunderstood. What have I said about judging people?'

Snow looked at James quickly then looked back at Henry. 'That we should give everyone a chance until they prove us wrong. However, I only take my own advice now.'

Henry let out a patient breath. 'See you both in an hour for dinner. We will be feasting with the king in the ballroom,' Henry said and walked off with Belle. Henry glanced back at Snow before rounding a corner. She used to be so sweet. So royal. So good. Since Mary died, she had turned darker. More revengeful. He hoped, strangely, that perhaps James could help her.

Once they were alone, James turned to Snow. 'Yes, prejudging people is a terrible thing to do.' He grinned and arched an eyebrow.

'I follow my intuition,' she said moodily.

'What does your intuition say about me?' he asked and took her hand.

She pulled her hand away from his and took a deep breath. 'It says I should probably not get involved with you.'

'I'm one of the good guys, sweetheart,' he said.

She frowned. 'I am not your sweetheart!'

James's expression darkened. 'What's the matter?'

'Nothing.'

The playful smirk turned into a hard line. 'Seriously ... are you okay?' He placed his hand on the side of her arm.

She pushed it off. 'Please, leave it.'

She walked off toward the gardens.

***

The guard looked down dreamily. 'That's the most delicious looking apple I have ever seen,' he said as he picked it up off the blanket of snow. The other guard tried to snatch it.

'Apples are my favourite fruit!' the other guard said.

The guard held the apple close to his chest. 'Tough, it's mine,' he said and took a bite. The other man walked off grumpily. Lori appeared not far from him, smiling.

'Guess you'll do,' she said, waiting for the apple to take effect. She was glad now that she had taken a walk around the palace grounds. Rarely did she get to actually see someone eat an apple. He shot down to below half his size, and his face warped and wrinkled. 'What have you done to me, witch?' he asked.

She laughed and vanished, leaving the guard alone. His wife would surely leave him now; he was almost unrecognisable. Angrily, he stormed to the castle and ran into Snow. 'Sorry, Princess.'

'What happened to you?' she asked. He was wearing the royal guard's jacket which dragged across the grass.

'I'm Michael,' he squeaked. 'A witch stole my looks. I shrunk to a dwarf's size and lost all my looks.'

'Lori,' she said angrily. He was not the first to appear in their kingdom spewing the same story.

'I ate an apple—'

'Yes,' Snow interrupted. 'Heard it before. Probably my fault. I threw it after she tried getting me to eat it.'

'Where does she live?' Michael asked, grinding his teeth.

'Dead Forest,' Snow informed. 'I have been secretly gathering a group of people to fight her. You will get revenge and potentially get your beauty back. We can take her out, and in doing so, I will hopefully find the person who murdered my mother. She just disappeared,' Snow said and looked back. James was approaching. 'Meet me in the dungeons later; we will be having a meeting there,' she whispered.

The man nodded and walked away. 'What was that about?' asked James, who had caught up with her.

'I thought I told you to leave me alone.'

James smiled. 'Thought I told you that I'm not working with Lori to destroy you? I'm just looking out for my mother.'

That hit her where it mattered. She understood. If it were her, she would have done anything to protect her mother, had she known she was in danger or upset.

James swallowed hard. 'Why do you still dislike me? You seemed quite smitten with me to begin with?'

Snow opened her mouth to speak but closed it. She was speechless for once. She had an excuse to dislike him when she thought he was working with Lori. But now, she didn't. Maybe it's because she was scared of getting hurt, and handsome, confident men like him always end up hurting girls. 'I just know your type,' she said.

'You don't know me. Give me a chance. I wasn't lying when I said I liked you!' James stated.

Snow took a deep breath. 'I'm not looking for a relationship if I'm honest.'

He grinned. 'Well, can we at least be friends?'

'Yes,' she replied and walked with James to the top of the garden. 'If we are to be friends, then I must know if I can trust you. Tell me something personal about you.'

His expression darkened. 'I like daisies.' She laughed, but he groaned. 'I can't help it,' he admitted. 'They're so pretty.'

Snow bit her lip then smiled. 'Enough with jokes. Tell me about your life. How did you end up here?'

James brushed the snow off a log and gestured for Snow to sit down then sat down next to her. 'My grandfather was cursed by a beastly man. My mother and I went to the castle to see if we could make some sort of trade. He was cursed to die. Anyway, when we got there, the man who cursed my father lifted the curse and kept us there as prisoners. Except he treated us nicely, I guess. My mother fell for him.'

'Oh,' Snow said.

He sighed and fiddled with the hilt of his new sword. It was a present given to him by Lori for joining her plans. 'He thought of himself as a beast. I know now that he was cursed to be as ugly on the outside as he was on the inside.'

Snow grinned. 'Wow, was there a beast?'

'Well, he wasn't actually a beast. It was more of a metaphor, I think ... Anyway, I was being taught to sword fight so didn't mind staying. I wanted a way to protect my family so used the castle as a way to do that.'

Snow nodded. 'I would've done the same thing.'

He raised an eyebrow and smiled. 'Well, it was a mistake. Long story short. Mum fell in love with him. I should have been there to talk some sense into her. Maybe then she wouldn't have sought comfort with him.'

Snow looked at his expression. She could see he was hurting over it. He was remorseful after all. 'Anyway,' he continued. 'He kissed her and the curse broke completely, and then ... he left.' Snow showed nothing but compassion. He noticed she had an almost innocent aura about her. Well, he would have believed it if he hadn't got to know her. 'I found out more when they left. I read through diaries. Stilt ate his own child!' James's eyes widened. 'Like his own real-life child. Lori cursed him, which I don't agree with.' Snow didn't look surprised. Instead, she gave him a told you she was evil look. He continued. 'And Edward was a frog for years. Apparently, the first kiss didn't work, so he found another. She became a frog, and he killed her. Then he came to the castle to get more power, and the enchantress used his own ego to trick him into a kiss ... Snow?' He realised she was no longer listening. Her face had warped into one of pure anger.

Snow opened her mouth, tears brimming in her eyes. Tears of anger. 'That man, Edward. I think the woman he killed was my mother. She died as a frog. I thought for so long that I had killed her. I stepped on her and only found out this morning that she was already dead. I hated myself for so long, and now, I barely have any family left, only my grandfather, the king. The fate of the kingdom, the continuation of the dynasty falls to me. This man, Edward, ruined everything!' She stood up and pulled out her dagger. 'Where is he? I will remove his head from his shoulders!'

Tears fell like a veil down her face, and for the first time in a long time, she felt vulnerable.

James grabbed her hand and lowered the dagger. 'We'll have to be careful. I want him dead too. Join me with Lori and my mum. We are going after them.'

'I can't,' Snow admitted. 'I have promised the people whose beauty she stole that we would destroy her. A group of dwarves out for revenge. I've been hiding them in the dungeons. We were planning an attack.'

'Ask for their help,' James offered. 'Tell them to wait. If they help us kill Edward and his sneaky friend Stilt, then we will take Lori out. I promise.' James took her hand in his and looked into her eyes. 'We will get our revenge. Let's help each other. It'll be our little secret.'

She looked back into his and grinned. 'So what do we do first?'

HOME

Edward finally arrived at the iron gates of Dolorom. A guard peeked into the carriage. 'Your Majesty,' he said and bowed.

Stilt walked alongside Edward. 'It has been a long journey. I must get back to the castle.'

The guard bowed again. 'Of course, Your Highness. Would you like us to escort you?' he asked.

'Please,' Edward said. They followed alongside the carriage on horses until they arrived at the gates of the palace.

They could have just reappeared at the castle, but the constant use of magic was wearing them out. They didn't mind the scenic journey.

'You're home,' Edward's mother said and hugged him tightly as he walked into the room. 'Where did you go?'

'Long story,' Edward said tiredly. He looked down at his mother's stomach, which was now flat instead of rounded. His mother beamed. Her hair looked softer, and she looked radiant. He had never seen her look so motherly. 'Congratulations,' Edward said.

'Would you like to meet them?'

Edward grumbled. 'Yes, of course.'

Stilt smiled broadly. 'I would love to meet my daughter.' The queen frowned but said nothing.

She led him up to one of the top rooms, which had been converted into a nursery. As he entered the room, he saw two cribs, side by side. He walked over to them slowly and looked inside. The left child looked up at him and smiled. 'Aw, she likes you,' his mother said. He smiled back the little girl then looked at the other. She was asleep. 'I'm going to find it hard to part with one,' she admitted.

Both girls had blond hair and blue eyes. 'We've called ours Aurora,' she said. 'Stilt, I believed you named yours—'

'Cinderella,' Edward finished, knowing already.

'Yes,' Stilt said and picked up the beautiful child. She cooed lightly in his arms. His eyes bulged with tears. He wished that, more than anything, Sadie could have been here to see this.

'Aurora and Cinderella, my sisters.' He couldn't help but smile. Little Aurora kept smiling every time she looked at Edward. It was adorable. 'I need to go. Stilt and I have unfinished business.'

'Don't leave again,' Kathryn said, tears brimming in her eyes. 'Every time you leave the gates, I never know when, or if, you are coming back.'

Edward placed his hand on her shoulder. 'I will do my best, Mother.'

'I know you will,' she replied, her lips spreading into a warm smile. 'I love you, son.'

Edward nodded in reply and walked out of the room, leaving Kathryn alone with her daughters. One of which, she would have to give to Stilt. It killed her inside because she wanted, needed, to keep them both together. But King Thomas would not agree. A deal was a deal, and he was happy to keep to it. One daughter, and maybe more children after, was enough. He wouldn't even look at baby Cinderella for fear of growing attached.

Stilt cried as they walked down the corridor. 'She's beautiful, and once we have completed our quest, she can come home with me. The king and queen will have her here until then.'

Edward and Stilt walked into his chambers where Johnathan was lying on his bed. 'What the bloody hell do you think you're doing?' Edward barked, noticing that Johnathan had his feet up, reading one of Edward's books. Johnathan jumped off the bed and dropped the book on the floor then scrambled to pick it up and put it back on the shelf.

'So sorry, Your Highness. I was just—'

'I need your help,' Edward said, firmly. 'Even if you are a blithering idiot, you are loyal. I don't know who I can trust anymore. There is a woman, Belle. I love her. I need to find her and bring her here. My ex, Lori, has her.' Edward paced around the room. Johnathan had never seen the prince looking so distressed. 'So much to do,' Edward mumbled. 'I have to keep to so many deals.'

Johnathan scratched his floppy white hair and pressed his lips together. 'It will be okay, Majesty.'

'Will it?' Edward asked. For once, he spoke to Johnathan, not with anger or authority, but with fear.

'What do you need me to do?' Johnathan asked.

He took a deep breath. 'I have heard whispers that Lori lives in the Dead Forest near Northmanni. I didn't believe the whispers until now. Send spies to the town. They will be looking out for a sixteen-year-old boy, James. Brown hair, brown eyes. Belle, brown hair, brown eyes, beautiful. Lori, black hair, green eyes. And a dwarf, Henry. I can't help but feel that he is a part of this all. He has a personal vendetta against me. Send them, the boy and Belle must not be harmed. Lori is dangerous, so they cannot make themselves known.' Johnathan bowed and left the room to find spies to bribe with gold.

'Majesty, the king would like to know about the trade deal with Forosh,' a guard said who entered the room.

'I could not do it,' he admitted. 'I will go over there again in one month. In the meantime, I have much bigger things to do. Johnathan will be head of trade in my absence.'

'And where shall I tell the king you're going, Majesty?' the guard replied.

Edward smirked. 'Tell him I will be going to Milborn with Stilt.'

***

'Prince Eric of Milborn,' a guard announced. A handsome man around twenty-five walked out, sporting a devilish smile. 'Good to see you, old friend,' Eric said. His voice was light and fun. Edward remembered back to when he was young. Eric was fifteen the last time he saw him.

'You're all grown up,' Edward said, grinning.

'And you're looking older too. What are you now? Forty?' Eric joked.

'Thirty-nine,' Stilt replied, grumpily. 'Lovely reunion, but we have things to get on with.'

'Who's the old guy?' Eric asked. Stilt huffed.

Edward laughed. 'A friend; we have business to attend to. I just wanted to stop by and say hello while I was in the kingdom,'

Eric raised an eyebrow. 'What do you want from me?' he asked, knowing Edward all too well.

'Have you married yet?' asked Edward.

'I haven't found anyone who I love yet,' admitted Eric. He leant in closer to Edward and whispered, 'They're all so prudish and boring around here.'

'Know what you mean,' Edward admitted. 'Well, I have someone I'd like you to meet.'

'Who?' asked Eric.

'A little mermaid,' Edward replied, grinning.

Eric scoffed. 'A mermaid? You're kidding, right?'

'Nope,' Edward replied.

Eric walked them into the castle. 'They are half fish,' Eric said as he walked next to Edward.

'Just meet her, once. As a favour to an old friend?' Edward persisted, looking around at the white walls. Everything in the kingdom had a seaside feel to it. The shell ornaments, the pillars, statues of Neptune.

'I'll meet her, but I will not marry her!' Eric said and brushed down his white blazer in which gold buttons ran down the centre.

'Thank you,' Edward said.

'What about you?' Eric asked. 'A lucky girl managed to snatch you up yet?'

'One,' Edward admitted then looked at the ground solemnly. 'Unfortunately, she has been taken from me.'

'Sorry to hear it,' Eric said and slapped Edward on the back. 'So when will I be meeting this mermaid?'

'Now,' Stilt said, who was walking behind them. 'We leave now.'

THE DWARFS

Snow pointed at a yawning dwarf. 'This is Fred, but I call him Sleepy. He is always drifting off during our meetings. It's from the side effects of the spells that take their beauty from them,' Snow informed James. 'And this one is Sneezy; he keeps having allergic reactions to almost everything,' she said sympathetically. He looked around the dungeon. In the middle of the dimly lit room was a wooden table. It looked out of place with the rest of the room, which consisted of stone seats, a barred window, and chains attached to the wall. He looked at the dwarf who was rubbing his nose. They all looked ugly. James felt pity for them. They were all once men, who simply ate an apple and had their lives ruined. 'That one's Doc. He was a doctor before, so it fits.' She shrugged. 'And that one is Bashful. Always blushing away.'

'No, I'm not,' Bashful said as his face filled with colour.

One dwarf extended his hand to Edward. 'I'm Gregory; Snow calls me Happy,' he said a little too enthusiastically.

'Nice to meet you.' James shook his hand and looked at Snow. 'How are we going to do this? We are nine people.'

Snow smiled. 'Ten if you include Henry.'

'Will he help?' James asked.

'I'm sure he will,' she said and shrugged. 'I can get guards, too. I can pay men to help us. Experienced sword fighters, assassins, and thieves.'

'Let's fight bad with bad. Make sense?' Gregory said.

Snow rolled her eyes. 'Oh, now you have a moral compass. You're planning on helping to kill a woman, and you're judging me on who I get to assist us?'

'Well, if we have to commit murder, then we must do it in the right way,' Gregory replied.

'Oh, shut up, you blithering idiot. We will use who we have to!' Grumpy said. 'I trust you, Snow. You're the only one helping us. So what do we do?'

James stepped forward and knelt by the table. 'There are two men worse than Lori. Edward and Stilt. Edward killed Snow's mother then left my mother. Stilt ate his own child and is helping Edward. They are our first target. Lori hates them, and they hate her. They are our key to destroying her.'

Snow smirked. 'We have all been pawns in their games for far too long. It is time that we start playing them at their own game. We are going to be the ones who give them the push they need. I have spies right now finding out information about Edward, Stilt, and anyone else they have been in contact with. We are going to bring them down.'

'To do that,' James said, 'we are going to join Lori. To pretend that we are on her side to bring Edward and Stilt down.'

***

'Your Highness,' Lori said to King Charles. She had gotten her beauty back after taking the last man's beauty, and she looked incredible. Her dress was silk, reaching to the floor, and dark red, matching her lips. Her hair fell like satin around her heart-shaped face, and her eyes were glossy and dark.

'Can I help you? How did you get in here?' he asked. She lifted her hand, and a pink mist hit his face. 'You're so pretty,' he said after, in a hazed state.

'Thank you, you are so charming,' she replied and sat next to him. They were sat looking over the pond, which was frozen over.

'I cannot believe I am saying this, but will you marry me, um?'

'Lori,' she said. 'Yes.'

'Lori,' he repeated dreamily. 'Your beauty is outstanding. We will wed at the end of this month.'

'Wonderful,' she replied as he leant forward. She gulped and begrudgingly kissed him. As she walked away, ready to spread the good news, she smiled down at her hand which was holding the head of a pink rose; spelled with a powerful love potion. It would have only worked with her beauty at its peak. *Well, that was easy.*

RED

James wolfed down his chicken and potatoes as he mulled over their plan. His part was probably the easiest. He looked at the door as Snow walked in. He noticed little things about her that he didn't before. Like how cute her dimples were when she smiled. How she kept pushing her fringe out of her face, and when she got nervous, she would pick at her fingernails. That she would always have a hole in her tights within half an hour of wearing a new pair. That her boots were always tied sloppily. 'Hey,' he said, feeling a little breathless. She grinned and sneakily poured a little whiskey into his goblet. 'What are you doing?'

'Having a little fun,' she stated. 'Come on, never had whiskey before?' she asked, giggling.

'No, actually,' he admitted and drank it. 'That tastes vile.'

She laughed. 'I know, I hate it. Was fun to see you try it, though.'

'I really hate you sometimes,' he said and huffed.

'Aww, damn! I'm going to cry,' she said sarcastically and ate some chicken. 'Anyway,' she whispered. 'Update. I know where Stilt and Edward are. Apparently, they are in Dolorom.' James leant in closer to her and noticed that she smelled subtly of strawberries with a hint of vanilla. He felt himself go lightheaded for a second then shook it off. 'A woman, Red, she lives nearby. Apparently, Stilt had something to do with her mother's death, and she wants revenge.'

'I know her, Red. We're friends,' James said.

'Oh,' Snow replied. 'Good.'

James looked puzzled. 'So she's in?'

She shook her head. 'Not yet. I will go and see her. I've not actually met her.'

'We will go to see her. I know her,' he pointed out.

'Okay,' she breathed. 'We'll leave this evening. Now, pass me the water,' she demanded.

He handed her the water. 'Are you okay?'

Her eyes widened. 'I'm fine.'

He brushed his fingers along her hand. 'If you want to talk to me, I'm here whenever you need me, Snow.'

She looked down. 'I'll be fine.'

He tousled his hair. 'Still, I'm with you.'

She gazed into his eyes; her own sparked with madness. One minute, she was crying, and the next, laughing. Still, she maintained an air of grace—she had to, she was a princess, after all.

***

'Red,' James said and hugged her. Her hair was a dark brown but still lighter than Snow's. She wore studded black boots and black trousers with a bright red top. The most unique thing about her was her eyes. Surrounded with black lashes, slightly tinted red, were bright violet eyes that shone in the moonlight. Beside her was a wolf, staring at Snow and James hungrily.

'I'm Snow,' Snow said and looked down at the wolf nervously.

'Red,' Red replied and shook Snow's hand firmly. Snow noticed that Red looked, well, cool. She had the whole "I'm a badass, and I don't care what people think" look about her, and Snow kind of envied the fact that Red seemed to pull it off better than she did.

'To what do I owe the pleasure of this late-night visit, James,' she asked, cooing his name. Snow held her breath for a second and gritted her teeth.

James placed his hand on her arm and smiled the most charming smile. 'Do I need an excuse to see one of my favourite girls?'

Snow coughed loudly. 'Can we get down to business? We have important things to discuss.'

'Of course,' James said and held back a grin. 'You know how we were talking about Stilt and Edward? Well, Snow would like for you to join us with our plan. She's going to explain it all to you now.'

Red invited James and Snow into her tiny shack, and Snow revealed every detail of their plan with Red until Red was on their side. They would all approach Lori, explaining their 'motives' after James had spoken to her first. They were all now making their moves in the game, not knowing who would end up winning.

'Today is the day,' Snow said, grimly. 'Today, Lori becomes my stepmother.'

'She'll be dead soon,' James stated and shrugged.

'She'd better be.'

James sat down and sighed. 'I went to see Red. She's gone, Snow. Only a wolf is there. Do you think she just up and left because of the danger?'

Snow shrugged. 'I don't know. I can send out spies to try and find out where she is, though.'

The Enchanted Kingdoms

'Please do,' James replied. 'She doesn't seem like the type to just run.'

'No,' Snow admitted. 'Guess not.'

'She was courageous; she didn't mind a bit of danger. I'm going to miss her. She made me laugh,' James said.

Snow smiled in response then looked down at the floor. 'I could make you laugh if I wanted too!' Snow said under her breath.

'What?' asked James.

'Nothing.' She hated to admit it, but in a way, she was glad Red had left. James had a soft spot for her. Not that she should care, even though she did.

James leaned in closer to Snow. 'Have you briefed the dwarves? We will be meeting at Lori's tomorrow. Once she is wed, Lori will send the army to invade Dolorom. We have weeks, if that, to prepare ourselves.'

'I have and I know,' Snow said and smiled sweetly. 'I'm so sick of every conversation I have of late being about killing or secret meetings. I need to have some fun.' She picked up some snow, wearing her leather gloves, and made a snowball, throwing it at James' head. 'That's a ten out of ten, there. Right on the nose.'

James shook his head. 'Nice effort, Princess. But I'd give that a six out of ten. Maybe a seven for effort.'

'Oh, really?' Snow said, rolling another snowball. 'We shall see.'

***

'You're what?' Belle asked, astounded.

'Getting married,' Lori replied simply.

Belle looked at Lori through wide eyes. 'Married? How did you get him to want to marry you so fast?'

Lori shrugged. 'I have my ways. Now, we will use what is soon to be my army to attack Stilt and Edward. Where is James?'

'Spending time with Snow. They're really hitting it off,' Belle replied, smiling.

'Of course, they are. She's gorgeous; why wouldn't he want to be with her?' Lori said. Belle noticed that envy attached itself to Snow's name on Lori's lips.

Belle smiled and turned to the fireplace. 'I got the outfit, thank you.' Lori had gotten Belle an outfit made. Black trousers, heeled pink boots with laces, and a fitted fuchsia pink halter-neck jumper. Belle tied her hair into a high ponytail and let bits fall around her face. 'The outfit is perfect for fighting in. Easier than a dress.'

'This is for you, too,' Lori said and handed Belle a box. Inside was a dagger around half a metre long. The handle was gold and blade silver. She handed her a scabbard to strap around her leg to hold it in.

'Thank you,' was all Belle could manage. It was all seeming too real now.

'James's powers will show themselves soon, I believe,' Lori said.

'I'm sure,' Belle said and left the room.

Lori walked over to the mirror. 'Mirror, mirror, on the wall. Who is the fairest of them all?'

The mirror warped into a face. 'Snow White is the fairest in all the land, Your Majesty.'

Lori screamed in frustration and walked into her room, where she pulled on her black top, red trousers, and riding boots, and stormed out of the house. She wore her hair in a braid and it bounced on her back as she jumped on a horse and rode it back to the castle. Lori knew that James' powers would only come in if he was in danger, or someone he loved was. She realised after he kept trying and nothing happened that he just needed the right motivation.

CURSES

Stilt looked down at the hole in the garden he had recently dug and sighed. Tears rolled down his cheeks as he used his powers to lift the coffin into the air and lowered it into the hole. He threw a rose on top of it and filled the hole with dirt. He put the gravestone he had made into the ground and knelt in front of it. 'I promise you, darling, I will avenge you. I will bring up our daughter, and I will make things right.' His voice broke at the end, and he stood up. Rage pulsated through him as the memory of Lori holding his wife's heart floated unwantedly through his mind. 'I'll kill her.'

He felt a hand thump down on his shoulder and squeeze. 'Beautiful send-off,' Edward said.

Stilt didn't look up. 'I will not rest until Lori suffers as much as I have!'

Edward nodded, looking down at the headstone. 'I know.'

Stilt sniffed and looked away from the grave. 'We should leave for Northmanni.'

Edward felt the shell pulsate in his pocket. 'Great ...'

'What?' asked Stilt.

Edward huffed. 'A message from Ursula.'

He showed Stilt the shell. On it, in ink, read I need that prince. Now. Throw him into the lake. He will be saved. That's all you need to know.

Stilt raised an eyebrow. 'Will he trust you?'

'I've done trade deals with him in the past.'

The Enchanted Kingdoms

Stilt grinned. 'Well, what are we waiting for?'

***

Lori placed the apple into the cauldron. Green smoke hovered above the cauldron. She placed the apple sneakily into the kitchen. It sat on the apples in a basket that would be used to make a crumble pudding for the wedding. Since becoming engaged, Lori had gained access to every part of the castle, to Snow's annoyance.

She had taken two more people's beauty since then. Snow, however, was no longer the object of Lori's beauty desires. No, she needed Snow to stay looking beautiful. She needed James to fall helplessly in love with her. So when Snow takes a bite of the apple and falls into a death-like slumber, James will be forced to use his powers to awaken her. His powers will be active, and then she can use him as a weapon.

She watched Red with great annoyance. James seemed comfortable around her; they laughed, they joked. He approached her about Snow, Red, and some other men, joining the plan as they wanted rid of Stilt and Edward too. But she couldn't have Red on her side. She would cause a disruption between James and Snow. Snow could always be used as a weapon against James, and Lori needed that. She needed Snow to be her leverage.

***

It was midnight. Belle was in her room, reading. The light from the little oil lamp shone out from under her door. Lori vanished from inside her room and reappeared by Red's shack. She peered through the window and noticed that no one was inside.

'What do you want?' Red said from behind Lori. She turned, and Red was holding a knife. Her pet wolf by her side.

'Hello, dear.'

Red snarled. 'Why are you here?'

'Here,' Lori said, handing Red a little vial of white potion. 'I have given the others theirs too. It's a protection potion. It will keep you from physical harm. I need to make sure you all stay safe throughout our plan.'

'Why didn't James and Snow come with you?' she asked, hesitant to take the potion.

Lori pursed her lips. 'They are, if you don't mind me saying, at the castle, cuddled up by the fire.'

Red smiled. 'I hoped they would finally get together. I could feel the sparks between them.'

'Yes. So take this,' Lori said, holding the vial out for Red to take. Hesitantly, she took the vial, popped out the cork, and drank it.

'What no—' Before she could finish her sentence, Red disappeared into a pile of dust then transformed into a wolf. Lori, with a wave of her hand, took Red's voice.

'Good luck telling anyone about this,' Lori said to the wolf who was looking around sheepishly. Lori turned and cast the death curse on the other wolf that lunged at her. Before it reached Lori's throat, it whimpered and fell to the ground. Red lunged at Lori, who whacked her against a tree. While Red was unconscious, Lori cast an entrapment spell, keeping Red in the shack or the surrounding area by a mile. 'Time to put my plan into action.'

Tomorrow, she was to go to the castle to wed. Tomorrow, Snow would eat the apple. Tomorrow, everything would change.

***

'What?' Snow screeched.

'I will be marrying Lori,' the king said with a sparkle in his blue eyes.

Snow looked at him tight-lipped and curtseyed. 'As you wish,' she said bitterly. 'When will the wedding happen?'

'Tomorrow.'

'So soon?'

He smiled dreamily. 'Yes.'

'Fine.'

'You will marry this year,' the king said simply, 'to the duke.'

Snow opened her mouth but closed it again. What could she say? She fiddled with her bracelet. 'What if my heart is with another?'

'Then,' the king said angrily, 'I suggest you keep your virtue and remember your duties.'

Snow nodded stiffly and walked out. He had been spelled, she was sure; still, she couldn't argue against the king's wishes.

James headed down the corridor. 'I came to say goodbye …'

Snow grabbed his hand. 'Wait.'

His lips curved into a smile. 'Always.'

Her heart skipped a beat. 'I have to marry the duke.' Tears brimmed in her eyes and one escaped, trickling down her cheek to her chin. James wiped it away with his thumb and brought his lips to her ear.

'Then I will just have to enjoy you from afar.'

Her breath hitched, and he turned and brushed her lips against his.

Her sweet smell flooded his senses. He ran his hand through her hair and held his breath, pressing his lips against hers urgently. Warmth spread through him as her lips moved with his, not sweetly, but demanding. He wrapped his arm around her back and pulled her closer to him. Her body pressed against his, making him flush. He ran his hand down her side and let the dizziness go to his head, drunk from her kiss.

The sounds of guards marching up the hall distracted them both, and with great resistance, James pulled away regretfully, to keep from spoiling Snow's name. She was panting, her chest heaving. 'We must never mention this again.'

He gulped and took in a deep breath. 'Of course.'

A LONG SLUMBER

Lori walked down the aisle wearing a beautiful, long, white lace dress. It dragged along behind her, and so did Snow, who looked grave as she begrudgingly made her way to the arch decorated with red and white roses. Everyone in the kingdom was there, waving flags, cheering for their new queen.

Snow caught James's eye, and he gave her a sympathetic look. The vows seemed insincere, and Snow swore she saw Lori gag a little as her grandfather kissed her. Finally, when the ceremony was over, Snow walked over to the food table.

'Tasted already for you,' said one of the servants who had been spelled. 'Apple pie.'

'Thank you,' Snow said, taking the bowl. James walked over and hugged her tightly.

'What was that for?' Snow asked.

'You needed it,' he said. 'Plus, I like hugging you,' he admitted. Snow realised he no longer looked confident. If anything, he looked a little shy.

'I like hugging you too,' she admitted and took a bite of the apple pie.

He wrapped his arm around her stomach. He went rigid, not knowing how to react. He pulled her closer to him. She pressed against him and dropped the bowl of apple pie. She felt dizzy yet excited. She could smell his scent. *This was a hug, nothing more*, she tried to think. But the way he looked at her said a thousand words. Things were no longer sarcastic or cute, it was physical. He brought his lips close to hers. She felt tingly. His beautiful scent consumed her as his lips almost brushed against hers.

This morning, he had acted as if their kiss had never happened, so she presumed it was just a silly moment easily forgotten, but his urgency told her that it was something more; much more.

Her head flopped back. At first, she thought she was going to faint, but then the garden and everyone in it started spinning around her until she was limp

'Someone help!' James shouted, holding her up.

Lori came running over. 'Oh my, what happened?' Lori asked, scooping up the rest of the pie. 'I will get this checked.'

James felt devastated as he watched Snow being taken away. Later that day, he was informed that she was not dead. Yet she would not wake.

He crept into her chambers and felt his powers surge inside him.

Clicked footsteps followed him. 'You need to use your powers to wake her. Only you can. I have tried,' Lori stated from behind him.

'Did you do this to her?' he shouted.

'No, of course not! Why would I?' Lori asked. He bit his tongue and walked over to Snow.

'How can I wake her?' he asked.

Lori smiled sweetly. 'You must use your powers to draw out whatever evil, spell, curse, or poison that is inside her.'

'You sure seem to know a lot about this,' James said suspiciously. Lori didn't answer, just nodded. James concentrated until his powers showed. Lori clapped with delight as she saw it. Yet no matter how hard he tried, he could not wake Snow.

In Snow's slumber, she was in a world of perpetual darkness and called out for James, but no one came. The more she feared she was in purgatory, the more the sky changed. It was a dark night, yet stars shone against the canvas.

'You will be here one day,' a voice said from behind her.

She turned and saw an odd looking man. 'Am I in Hell?'

The man laughed and shook his head. 'No.' He looked around. 'I am the future.'

'Future?' Snow arched an eyebrow.

'Yes.' He ran his hand through his slick back hair and looked at her with orb black eyes. 'Everything that is to come is for a reason. I am here to warn you.'

'About what?' she asked. 'How am I here?'

'You are in a deep sleep.' He sat on a rock and gestured for her to sit on a rock opposite him. 'Your path is already laid out for you, no matter what you do. However, your destination can be changed depending on the decisions you make.'

Snow nodded. 'What do I need to do?'

'When the time comes, you will have to betray the people you love the most and side with those you hate. There will come a time when you have no heart, when you will own something more valuable than you can imagine, and one where you will be the key to everyone's happy endings, including yours.'

'And James's?'

The man smiled creepily. 'Yes ...' he breathed. 'I cannot tell you everything, but I will say that no one will understand why you will do the things you will do—they will all hate you—but in the end, they will realise you were their saviour.'

Snow took in a deep breath. 'If I don't?'

'Their happily ever afters will be lost forever ...'

***

James felt his powers grow stronger every day that Snow was in her slumber. He often sat by her side, feeling totally helpless. Even if he was the key to waking her up, he didn't know how. His powers had just surfaced, and if he used them wrong, he was worried he could do damage to her.

'You can wake her up with a kiss,' a man said, who appeared in the dimly lit room. 'True love's kiss.'

James pulled out his sword and stood up slowly. 'Who are you?'

The man stroked his beard, which James noticed was tied in segments and sported a lot of purple beads. 'I'm Merlin.'

'The Merlin?'

'So you've heard of me,' Merlin stated.

James looked at him questioningly. 'Of course. Who hasn't?'

Merlin sat down next to the bed. He crossed his legs under his long purple robe. 'Thank you.'

James put his sword back into the scabbard and sat down by the lit fire. 'Lori told me about you. You're a legend.'

Merlin laughed throatily. 'Was. I had that pointed out to me recently. Anyway, I am here on business.'

'What do you want?'

The Enchanted Kingdoms

Merlin sighed. 'Some are making waves in the world of magic! Waves that have and will continue to destroy lives. I would like to put an end to powers outside of my domain.' He looked down at his gold pocket watch. 'I cannot control what I do not have access to.'

'Stilt, Edward, and Lori?' James asked, knowingly.

Merlin nodded. 'I need you to learn to control your powers.'

James scoffed. 'I can't use my powers to wake Snow up, let alone to help anyone else.'

Merlin shook his head. 'I want you to come with me. Let me help you with your powers then take Stilt down with me. Along with Edward, and eventually, Lori. Although, she will be the hardest to break.'

'What will I get in return?' James asked, arching an eyebrow. 'Aside from you helping me to control my powers, I have much to do here and battles to fight alongside Lori. I promised Snow.'

'Well, I have told you how to wake Snow up. True love's kiss,' he pointed out.

'I don't—' James started but stopped on seeing Merlin's knowing look. He bent over and brushed his lips against Snow's. They were plumper than he thought they'd be. He stepped back, and her eyes flung open.

'What happened?' a breathless Snow asked, clutching her chest. James rushed to her aid and helped her sit up.

'You went into a slumber,' James informed her. 'Like a coma. We don't know how, but we will find out!' he promised.

Snow looked around, puzzled. 'So I just randomly woke up?'

'Uh, yes,' James lied. She jumped off the bed and looked around, noticing Merlin for the first time.

'Who are you?'

'Merlin,' he replied.

'Why are you here, and what do you want?' she asked, cutting straight to the point.

'James,' he admitted. 'I need his help to take down two men.'

'Stilt, Edward, and Lori,' James told Snow.

Snow grinned. 'We already have a plan for that. And one to take down Lori!'

Merlin smiled. 'Care to tell me this plan of yours, Snow?'

Snow looked at James. He nodded. 'Fine, sit down.'

SLAIN

Grumpy pushed his food around his plate. 'Where the bloody hell is she?'

'Calm down, I'm sure she's on her way,' Happy said. 'Cheer up. You're always so grumpy.'

'Well, yeah, look at me!'

'Everyone calm down,' Sleepy said and yawned.

'Yes, everyone please calm down,' Lori said, who appeared by the door. 'Snow's taking a nap. She won't be coming.'

'How do you know—' Grumpy started, but Lori raised her hand and all the dwarfs rose off the ground.

'I know everything. Snow confided in Henry, and he told me everything in exchange for Snow's protection. He knew your plan would fail, and he was right. Did you really think you could all take me down?' she cackled.

'You ruined our lives,' Sneezy shouted.

Lori rolled her eyes. 'No, you ruined your lives. If you didn't plot against me, then this wouldn't have happened. You only have yourselves to blame.'

'Wh-what are you going t-to do?' Happy stammered.

'This,' Lori said and flicked her wrists. Their necks twisted. The sound of cracking filled the dungeon. They clutched at their throats, gasping for air. Lori swiftly moved her hand, and broke their necks. The dungeon was filled with floating dead dwarfs. She took a deep breath. Slowly, each of them simultaneously dropped into piles of dust.

She wiped her hands together then exited the dungeon. 'Now, for the real work to begin.' She saw the wand on the table and picked it up. 'Oh. Thank you.'

***

James jumped on his horse—a beautiful stallion gifted to him by Snow—and rode to the gates. Snow was in the garden, as per usual, picking apples off a tree. She was wearing a white cloak, embroidered with black patterns down the side. And, as always, she wore a corset-style top with a skirt, black tights, and boots.

'Hey there,' James called out. A stable boy took the horse to the stables.

'James,' she said, smiling. She ran over to him, basket swinging from her arm, and hugged him. He hugged her back. She rested her head on his chest for a little longer than she should.

'I missed you,' he admitted.

'It's been twenty-four hours.' She laughed but couldn't help but smile.

'Still ...' He started.

'I missed you too,' she admitted. He stood back and grinned. That was one of the few times when she showed him any affection at all.

'Good,' he said and grinned. He reached out and brushed off the snow that had landed on her jet-black hair. She looked longingly into his eyes; those honey brown eyes melted her. She breathed in his scent and felt a little lightheaded.

'So my mother has left to meet Merlin,' he said, 'which means we have Lori alone. I'm worried she may try to hurt your grandfather.'

'She wouldn't dare,' Snow said, pulling out her dagger.

James groaned. 'Calm down! Stop grabbing your dagger every time her bloody name is mentioned. We are meant to be lying low. Where are the dwarfs?'

'They left,' Snow said angrily.

'What?'

'I don't know,' she admitted. 'They just disappeared. I have sent out people to find them,' she admitted and sat on a bench. They looked out at the winter wonderland in front of them.

'Looks like it's just us then,' James said.

'And Merlin,' Snow pointed out. 'Your mother has gone to meet him. Why didn't you just tell her ...'

'She's too close to Lori!' He ground his front teeth. 'She would tell her; she trusts her. Then Lori would know that Merlin wants my help.'

'Good point,' Snow said and brushed her hair out of her face. The wind had crept over Northmanni and the snow fell lightly. Soon enough, a blizzard started, forcing Snow and James inside the castle. They ran up to her chambers, and James sat in front of the fire.

'Lovely room,' he lied. Snow was just as bad as Lori was with the gothic interior.

'I know it's a bit dark, but I like it that way,' Snow said. She took her cloak off and threw it onto her four-post bed.

'A bit?' He looked around. 'Everything is either black or red.'

She laughed. 'They're the colours of my soul,' she joked. He rolled his eyes, and she joined him on the sofa in front of the crackling fire.

'That kiss ...' James started.

Snow placed her finger over his lips. 'Thought we were never to talk about it again. Plus, it didn't mean anything, right?'

He pulled away. 'It didn't?'

'I meant for you,' Snow said, blushing.

His eyes narrowed. 'Did it to you?'

Snow lowered her gaze. 'I ...'

James leaned in and gazed into her eyes, sliding his hand down her hair then her neck, his gaze tracing over her as if he would never see her again and needed to take in every detail. 'I will never let anything bad happen to you.'

Snow blushed. 'I ...'

'Snow speechless?' He laughed. 'Well, there's a first for everything,' he said with a playful smile. He slid his fingers down to her wrists and noticed the scratches. 'You hurt yourself?'

Snow pulled her sleeve down. 'It's not what you think.'

James sighed. 'Snow, if you ever feel in pain, come to me. Promise?'

She leaned in. 'If I do, do you promise to always make it better?'

He nodded. 'Always.' He lifted her wrist to his lips and kissed it softly. 'Always, my Snow.'

Her heart skipped a beat. 'Will you stay with me tonight?'

His eyes widened. 'I – Yes. I would love that.'

She smiled coyly. 'I've never felt so vulnerable,' she admitted.

'It's not a bad thing.'

'I could get hurt.'

He shook his head. 'I could never hurt you.'

She took his hand and led him to her bed. 'If I must marry someone I do not love, then I'd rather spend just one night with a man who ...'

'Yes?'

'Nothing,' she breathed. Slowly, she slipped off her dress. His face reddened as she bared herself, laying on the silk sheets, illuminated only by the candlelight. She looked down at his breeches and smiled.

He climbed on top of her and kissed her, his lips demanding. 'Always my Snow,' he whispered.

KING'S DOWNFALL

Belle looked at Lori with disgust. 'You're not wearing that, are you?'

Lori looked down at her dress and shrugged. 'What's wrong with it?'

'You look like you're attending a funeral. Let's add some colour,' Belle said brightly and walked over to Lori with one of her own yellow dresses. Lori backed away.

'No, no, no …' Lori repeated as Belle got closer. 'I'm not wearing that. Look, black is my colour.'

'At least try it!' Belle begged.

Lori's face twisted into one of disgust. 'No, it's just so … colourful.'

Belle laughed. 'That is the point.'

James popped his head around the door. 'What's going on?'

Lori turned and sat at her dressing table, brushing her long dark locks. 'Your mother is trying to make me hideous!'

James looked at his mother questioningly.

'I'm trying to make her look less morbid,' Belle said.

James laughed. 'Yeah, right.'

'Enough,' Lori huffed. 'Have you managed to use your powers properly yet?'

James sighed and sat on the footstool. 'Only managed to turn an apple into a worm. Considering that is all I have to practice with here!'

'You managed to transfigure an item into a living creature? James, that is incredible!' Belle praised.

'Yes, yes. Incredible,' Lori said dismissively. 'With more practice, you will be able to do things you couldn't have imagined in your wildest dreams.' Her eyes were greedy, locked onto James. He was the key to ending Edward's miserable existence for good.

'I just want to wake Snow up,' James admitted. 'I've failed her.'

Belle patted his shoulder. 'You'll find a way, sweetheart. I have complete faith in you.'

'We must discuss, first, our plan,' Lori said. She placed her black birdcage veil on, which covered one of her eyes. 'The king's army will not invade Dolorom unless Dolorom is an immediate threat. The king will not allow it, which means I need to bribe more of the guards. I need to infiltrate the king's guards and lords of the land. Once I have them on my side, we can overturn the king's decision. Unless, he dies first, of course!'

'Lori,' Belle gasped. 'You wouldn't? He's your husband.'

'I wouldn't allow it,' James said, brandishing his sword.

Lori rolled her eyes. 'Put your weapon down, for goodness' sake. I'm not going to kill him,' she lied. 'I need you to leave,' she said to Belle.

'Leave?' Belle and James chorused.

'Yes,' Lori answered. 'I need you to go to Merlin. A powerful sorcerer. I need him on our side. We don't have what you would call a good history. But he will listen to someone like you. Kind, beautiful, innocent.'

'Where does he live?' asked Belle.

'The centre of Cantata.'

'The centre of our world?' Belle repeated.

Lori rolled her eyes. Living with Belle meant that she would probably end up with her eyes stuck in her forehead. 'It's in the Enchanted Forest next to Dolorom.'

'I will go. What do you want me to say?' asked Belle.

Lori handed her a rolled-up piece of parchment. 'Give him this. It's a letter detailing our plan. Also, entertain him. Make him like you. We need him on our side, Belle. Do not let us down.'

***

'Majesty,' Lori said as she approached her husband. His grey hair was slicked back, and his red cloak covered his protruding belly.

'My love,' he replied and put his arms around her.

She forced a smile and escaped his grip. 'Why won't you let me use the army? Am I not queen?'

'You are,' he said and sat on his throne. 'But Dolorom is the biggest land. We would not win, and the attack is unprovoked.'

'But please,' she said and fluttered her lashes at him. Since taking more people's beauty, she was looking better by the week. Her hair was shiny, softer, and darker than it had looked in years. Her green eyes shone like emeralds, her petite frame paired with her soft features made her look so innocent.

'No,' he said. 'Sorry, my love. Anything else I would do, but I cannot send my troops out to be slaughtered.'

'Of course, I obey my king's orders,' she said and went over to the little globe. She opened it and pulled out a bottle of mead. When he wasn't looking, she activated the death curse, one which drained her, then and there, of all her beauty. She quickly left the room. Making sure not to show her face to him. Her footsteps clicked down the stone steps. She stopped by the kitchen. She snuck an apple into the kitchen's supply and waited for someone to eat it.

A little less than an hour later, everyone in the castle was running around frantically. A guard burst into Snow's room where she was resting her head on James's shoulder.

'Princess,' the guard said.

'What is it?' she asked, standing up.

'I'm terribly sorry to be the one to tell you, but the king is dead.'

REVENGE

The sudden death of the king shocked the kingdom, more so Snow. She had been awoken in the early hours in the morning and had to hide James in her closet. James stepped out of the closet and quickly pulled his shirt and breeches on then tousled his hair. 'Snow.'

'Don't.'

He held her hand. 'I'm so sorry for your loss.'

She walked away from him and grabbed a pipe from her draw. She stomped around the room, her breath rattling as she puffed on a pipe. 'What the hell are you doing?' asked James as he snatched the pipe from her mouth.

'It relaxes me!' she shouted.

'It's unhealthy,' he replied and walked over to her bed. 'She killed him, James. She killed him! I know it. I'm going to kill her.'

'No.' He walked over and placed his arms on her shoulders, knowing that she was talking about Lori. 'We will get revenge, but if you go up there now and attempt to kill her, you will be charged with treason. Princess or not. Lori is in charge now. We must play it safe.'

Snow knew what he was saying made sense, but she was livid. She couldn't see anything but the image of Lori being stabbed to death. Snow screamed and threw her dagger at the wall, which stabbed into a painting. 'I will prove she killed him then.'

James bit down on his bottom lip. 'If she did it with magic, which I imagine she did, then you couldn't prove it. Lori mentioned killing him, but my mother and I said no, and she said she was joking.'

'And you kept that to yourself?' Snow screamed. 'Whose side are you on?'

He pulled her into a hug and stroked her hair. 'Yours, Snow. Always yours.'

He pulled her down onto the sofa. She nuzzled into his chest. He hugged her in front of the fire while she wept into his jacket. Hours passed like minutes. The crackling of the fire and howling from the wind outside the window was all that could be heard above Snow's sobs. She eventually cried herself to sleep. James didn't want to move, in case he woke her, so he'd just laid there. He smiled as he looked down at her tear-stained face. She was pouting slightly as she slept, and the crease on her forehead from anger disappeared. Her fingers linked with his and a realisation swept over him; this was all he would ever need.

***

James took Snow's hand and looked into her eyes. 'I will be back soon, okay?'

She sighed. 'I don't want you to go.' He smiled at that. They were growing closer every day, yet he still didn't have guts to admit how he felt to her. She was just as stubborn.

He looked at her darkly. ''It's only one day. Keep yourself safe. Don't do anything reckless!'

'I can't make any promises,' she said and winked. 'I'm kidding,' she added on seeing his concern. 'I'm just going to try and find out what happened to the dwarfs and Red. I know something is up.'

'Don't get caught,' he replied. Henry entered the room.

'Snow,' Henry said. 'It is time.'

'Wish you could stay for the funeral,' a teary Snow said.

'We made a deal with Merlin. I have no choice. Look, I've been meaning to tell you something.'

'Yes?' she said.

'I ...' He stopped himself. 'I'll tell you when I get back,' and with that, he disappeared.

Henry cleared his throat. 'Ready?'

Snow gathered herself and brushed down her black top and trousers. 'Coming.'

'How are you? We haven't spent much time together,' Henry said.

Snow kept her head held high. She felt as if she was losing her mind recently. Since waking from that slumber, she hadn't felt okay at all. 'I'm fine. My dwarfs disappeared, and so did mine and James's friend, Red. I want to find out what happened to them.'

'Oh, well, to be honest ...' Henry started.

'Do you know something?' she asked him, stopping in the hallway.

'I will do anything to keep you safe; you know that,' he said. 'Lori found out about your plan to take her down.'

Snow gasped and put her hands over her mouth.

'You're kidding? She'll kill me.'

'She won't,' he said. 'I made a deal with her.'

'You did what?'

'In exchange for telling her who was a part of the plan, she promised never to harm you,' he admitted.

'Where are they?' Snow asked through clenched teeth.

He hung his head. 'I'm sorry.'

She shook her head with disbelief. 'No,' she cried. 'I promised to protect them.' She ran away from Henry and into the gardens. The church bells sounded as she sat on the bench. The snow was melting, now leaving a horrible slush on the ground.

Her head was spinning. James told her not to do anything reckless, and he was right. Lori was in charge, and anything could happen now. But she needed justice.

'Red,' Snow exclaimed and ran to the stable, grabbing James's stallion.

In a panic, she galloped down the winding road to the town then over to the Dead Forest until she reached a familiar shack. It was Red's. A wolf shot out of the door on hearing the commotion. Snow put her hands in the air and tried to turn the horse. The wolf, however, did not attack. Instead, it rested its head on a log and whimpered.

'Red!' Snow shouted. 'Red, where are you?' The wolf howled loudly. 'You know something? You're Red's pet, aren't you?' The wolf howled. 'What happened to her?'

After an hour of listening to the wolf howl, the wolf and Red gave up trying to communicate in any way. 'I'll be back,' Snow promised and rode over to Lori's shack. She knew Lori wouldn't be home as she was at the king's funeral. The king who she had murdered.

Snow jumped off the horse and tied him to the apple tree. In a manic state, she plucked all the apples from the tree and threw them at the shack before finally falling to the ground. I promised to keep them safe, and now, they're dead. Lori is in power, and Edward is still alive. James is gone. I am alone, and Henry betrayed me. She repeated those words in her head until they were deafening. She put her hands over her ears and screamed. The church bells sounded to pronounce the end of the funeral.

Grandfather, I'm so sorry. I will avenge you. All of you, Grumpy, Sneezy, Doc, Sleepy, Happy. Her thoughts were distracted as she saw the wolf again. It was near the shack but appeared like it couldn't go any further.

'Oh, James. I need you right now,' Snow said aloud and jumped back onto her horse.

URSULA

The undercurrent carried her to the shore. She found the rock she sat on every day and looked out onto the beach.

The beach she could never stand on.

In front of the pebbly stretch were glorious fields, rich with corn. Some of them had crops so high that Ariel wondered what it would feel like to get lost in them.

Oh, what an adventure that would be.

'Ariel,' her sister's voice hissed from behind her.

'Hey, Coral,' Ariel said dreamily as she watched a man and woman holding hands as they walked merrily down the bay, smiling, laughing.

Oh, how would it feel to hold hands with another and walk in the sun? How would it feel to walk? she wondered.

'Mother told me not to utter a word to you!'

'A word,' an eel hissed that slithered its way around her small stomach.

'But they are watching you,' her sister said.

'Watching you,' the eel repeated. Ariel batted the eel away with her tail and turned. Now taking more notice of her sister.

'You are not my sister,' Ariel said. 'You look just like her. But you have more of a loneliness behind your eyes. The smell of corruption, deceit, and desperation follows you.'

'I'll get you one day!' The sea witch cackled and turned back into her plump, ugly self. Her tail, unlike the others, was a mossy green. It felt the same as moss too. Her hair was like black seaweed clinging to a rock. Her eyes, which were barely visible due to the black bags hanging beneath them, were a putrid shade of green. The colour of jealousy. Her fingernails were more like talons, and shells were embedded into one side of her face and her stomach. If you had to ask for Ariel's opinion, which you would get whether you wanted it or not, Ursula was a disgusting slime ball with a bad temper and jealous streak.

No matter how desperate Ariel was, and she was pretty desperate. Never, ever would she make a deal with the sea witch. Nope. Never.

'Leave me alone,' Ariel demanded.

'You know,' Ursula said, who was now side by side with her, stroking Ariel's hair longingly. 'I have always wondered what it would be like to have magical hair. Beautiful red hair, like your mothers. Like yours. Like the others.'

'My father said not to listen to a word you say,' Ariel said, poking her finger onto Ursula's large chest.

'Your father is a liar! My family line *is* the *legitimate* heir to the throne. Your father took it from us,' she spat.

Ariel laughed. 'I don't know that much about it. But if I had to guess, I'd say that the *legitimate* heir to the throne would *never* have allowed someone to take their power from them. That shows weakness and our kind does not need weak leaders. Now go and wallow in your underwater cave, witch, and stop bothering me.'

Ursula snarled. She looked at Ariel, who was more vibrant than the others, with envy. She secretly liked the bubbly streak she pretended to despise and felt sad if anything. Sad that she, the different one, the one with a green tail and black hair, was not befriended by the only other mermaid in the lake who felt like an outsider.

Everyone knew Ariel wanted to be a human, and they'd say things like *It is such a shame that she is so odd.* Being a princess was nothing but an annoyance to Ariel. Even though anyone else in the lake would do anything to be in her position.

Being a princess meant she found it more difficult to sneak off and look at the people as they went about their daily lives. It meant that she was expected to do princess things, like sing, like, all the time.

Ursula swam away with her pet eel and left her alone.

Ariel's hair had grown back since she cut it to give to a woman, at her mother's request. It now reached down to the top of her tail. 'Ariel,' a small little fish whispered. 'Your father is waiting for you.'

'Cullum. How are you?' she asked with delight. She hadn't seen her little friend all day. 'I've been watching the people walk past. One woman was dancing as she walked. What a fun thing that must be to do.'

'S-sounds great, Ariel. But, w-we really should go,' Cullum stuttered. He was the smallest fish in the lake, by far. The size of one those little crockhoppers. Which were shoes. But Ariel had believed that crockhoppers were to wear on your hands. A dear friend of hers had informed her of that. Her friend was well travelled, so he must be right.

She had only seen humans who lived near the lake wear them on their feet. She giggled to herself, thinking about how odd those people must be, to wear crockhoppers on their feet. She decided that if she were ever to become human, then she would have to set them straight.

She swam back under the lake and made her way past the tall seaweeds without getting herself tangled, again, then over to the rocky wall to the kingdom. The sound of music carried through the water.

'The show,' Ariel said and gasped as she realised why there was music. That song was to play just before the main event, and *she* was the main event.

EXPLORING

Ariel hid behind the large pillar that held up the front of the palace. The seashell opened, and she wasn't in there. She had to improvise. If not, then her father would be so mad.

She swam out to where everyone was watching the show. She was behind them. Her father looked furious as everyone looked blankly at the empty shell.

'As I entwine myself in the seaweed of power,' she sang. Everyone turned and smiled. She swam through them. Most thought it was part of the act. Her father, the king, knew it was due to lateness.

'I look out at the blue abyss,' she continued. Her voice was beautiful. Light, powerful, and it had the slight sound of bells ringing to it.

Ariel's sisters joined her and harmonised with each other. Ariel had the best voice in the kingdom. The subjects clapped as the event finished and the shell closed.

'Ariel,' her father's voice boomed once they were alone in the palace hall. She hid behind a pillar. 'You were late, again!'

'Sorry, Father,' she said and swam out. 'I was exploring.'

'Always exploring. Start acting like the princess you are!' And with that, he swam off. His massive blue tail disappeared around a corner.

Cullum swam out from behind some seaweed. 'You okay, Ariel?'

She huffed and sat on the white marble seat. 'No,' she admitted. 'Maybe he's right.'

'No, he's not,' Cullum protested. 'You're fun; you're different. Nothing is wrong with that.'

'Hmph.'

'Want to watch the people?' Cullum asked, hoping it would cheer her up.

'Don't feel like it,' she admitted and swam off, humming the tune from the show. She moved effortlessly through the water. Ursula watched Ariel through her magic orb.

'Soon, when he fulfils his promise, Ariel will have no choice but to accept my offer. I will bring them all down,' she said to the eel.

'How do you know it will work?' hissed the eel.

Ursula laughed evilly. 'He will bring me a prince. I will make it so he falls in near Ariel. Being Ariel, she will save him. I will make it so they fall in love then I will offer her the deal. She has always said no to me, through distrust, but this will tip her over the edge.'

'Then you will kill her?' the eel asked. It swirled around the cave; it's black body slithering slimily.

'No,' Ursula said, smirking. 'Queen Josephine made a deal with the Evil Queen, so if Ariel ever takes a potion to become human, then she would turn to sea foam if she didn't return to the lake for good after three days. I will make a deal with the king and queen. I will make it so she cannot return to the lake unless they give me their crown.'

'I love it,' the eel hissed.

***

'Here we are,' Edward said as they appeared on the pebbly bay.

Eric looked out over the waters. 'Where is this mermaid?'

Stilt walked over to the water and turned to Eric. 'Stay here. Edward and I will be back momentarily.'

Edward walked over to the edge of water. Stilt waded through until he was submerged and set off a spell. He reemerged with wet hair covering his face. He moved it out the way and joined Edward at the water's edge.

Shortly after, Ursula appeared. 'Did you bring a prince like I asked?'

'Yes,' Edward replied. 'He is waiting in the bay. He's happy to meet this mermaid you mentioned.'

'Idiot,' she spat. 'You weren't supposed to tell him. I needed him to fall into the lake near her so she would save him from drowning. I cannot have her know this was planned.'

Stilt growled. 'You're the idiot. You should have said.'

She frowned. 'It was implied.'

Edward sighed. 'I will take the prince, wipe his memory of our conversations, and throw him into the lake.'

Edward stepped forward. 'Make sure he doesn't drown. He's one of the few people I actually like,' he admitted.

'Aww, you have a caring side. Who knew!' Stilt said sarcastically. 'Let's get Eric, wipe his memories of us, and throw him to the fishes. Then we can go!'

Stilt took Edward's hand before he could protest and they reappeared by Eric's side. Stilt, with a wave of his hand, took Eric's memories and pushed him into the lake. Ursula swam over and nodded at Stilt then dragged Eric down into the murky depths. She took him back to the surface for air before dragging him underneath again near to where Ariel was. She left him in the water and swam off, smiling.

***

'Oh my,' Ariel said when she saw the man who was trying to swim back to the surface. Eric managed to get to the top, but a wave pushed him back under. Ariel swam over to him with a frantic Cullum by her side. She placed her arms around his waist and swam to the surface. She made sure to keep his head above water as he spluttered until they reached the rock that she would watch the people from. Eric coughed as he laid on the rock before looking up. His eyes, she noticed, were a rich green. He had laugh lines, and his hair, though wet, was the most adorable shade of brown. His outfit told her that he must be royal.

'Can you hear me?' asked Ariel. He fell back unconscious after seeing her red hair. She took him to the bay and laid next to him, half in the water, so her tail wasn't on show.

Cullum bobbed a few feet away. 'I-is he alive?' She placed her ear against his foot. 'I can't hear a heartbeat,' Ariel said, panicked.

A seagull flew down from the sky and landed next to her. 'Hey, Ariel,' it said. Most couldn't hear animals, but being one herself, she could.

'This man,' Ariel rushed out in a panic. 'He fell in the lake. I think he may be dead?'

The seagull stroked its beak. 'Did you check his pulse on his foot, like I always told you to?' he asked.

'Yes, no pulse.' Suddenly, the prince woke up, coughing again, and turned on his side. The seagull, Jack, flew over to another rock and remained out of sight.

'What happened?' Eric asked. He looked up at the girl with wet red hair and smiled. She was beautiful. Her eyes were the colour of the lake and twice as enchanting. Her pink lips shimmered in the sun. Her sun kissed skin paired well with her bright red hair. Although an odd combination, she pulled it off incredibly well.

'I couldn't hear your pulse. I thought you were dead,' she admitted. *Her voice*, he thought, *was the most beautiful voice he had ever heard.*

'I was dead?' asked Eric, shocked.

'Yes, I took your foot and listened for your heart beat and heard no—'

Eric laughed. 'My foot? Why would you ever think to listen through my foot?' he asked, looking at his bare foot. 'You listen through someone's chest.'

She blushed and looked over at Jack, annoyed. He shrugged and flew off. 'Sorry,' she mumbled. 'A friend told me that was how to listen for one. Oh, sorry. You lost one of your crockhoppers in the lake.'

'My what?' the prince asked, still laughing.

'You know; you wear them on your hands to keep them warm.'

'You mean gloves?' Eric asked.

'No, well, you were wearing them on your feet,' she pointed out. 'They're supposed to be worn on your hands.'

'My boot, you mean.' He raised an eyebrow. 'You're not from around here, are you?'

'Not on this land, no,' she admitted.

He smiled. 'Did you save me?'

'Yes,' she said and flushed pink.

'I don't even know why I was around here,' he admitted and felt his head. 'I must have banged by head at some point.'

'Oh,' Ariel said, keeping her tail still hidden.

'I won't forget meeting you, um—'

'Ariel,' she said and took a deep breath. He was the most handsome man she had ever seen.

'Ariel,' he repeated, dreamily. 'Well, Ariel, may I invite you to come to my castle? I will throw a feast in your honour as a thank you for saving me.'

'Oh,' Ariel said and looked at Cullum sadly. 'I'm afraid I cannot. I must go. I, uh ...' She looked over at one of the boats on the bay. 'I must swim back to my boat; it's not far. Goodbye.'

'What, but ...' She disappeared under the water. He panicked, waiting to see her resurface. Finally, she did. He shouted after her until she was out of sight. He wrung out his jacket and thought about how odd all of that was. Still, he couldn't get her out of his mind.

The Enchanted Kingdoms

CHANGES

'Ariel ...' Coral started. She swam gracefully over to where her sister was sulking. 'Father shouted at you again, huh?' Ariel turned and wrapped her arms around her sister. Unlike the rest of her sisters, Coral cared about her. The rest were only interested in powers, killing, and eating. Coral did those things too, of course, but she understood why Ariel wouldn't partake in those activities.

'I was out exploring,' Ariel cried.

Coral put her sister at arm's length, keeping her hands on her shoulder, and looked into her eyes. 'You were looking at the humans again, weren't you?'

Ariel saw that Coral wasn't mad but worried. Coral looked nothing but sympathetic. She was just a year older than Ariel was, who was the youngest. Ariel nodded, her bottom lip trembling. 'I want to be like them. They are not cruel, like us! They do not kill ...'

Coral groaned. 'They kill, Ariel. They kill fish; they kill our friends. They've killed mermaids, and they kill each other. They are worse than us. We would never kill our own unless necessary.'

'No,' Ariel shouted, pushing Coral away. 'Father tells these stories to scare us. I watch them; they don't do those things. They love, they laugh, they have fun.'

Coral was almost a mirror image of Ariel, except for the eyes. Coral's were darker than Ariel's bright blue ones. 'Ariel, please, try to join in with us,' she begged. 'It has been so boring without you. You keep disappearing. Remember when we had fun? You and I, causing mischief. You used to want to be like me when we were younger. What happened?' asked a tearful Coral.

Ariel straightened up. 'I grew up and realised that I have my own destiny to fulfil. I love you Coral. You're different from the rest of them. But you belong here, and I do not. I thought about trying to be the princess you all want. I tried, but it is not who I am. I must try to become human, if only for a day. I want to just see what it is like.'

Coral's expression darkened. 'Cullum admitted that you met a man who almost drowned. Cullum is worried about you, Ariel. He wouldn't go to anyone else, only me. He knew I was the only one who wouldn't punish you. I want to help you, to talk some sense into you before you make the biggest mistake of your li—'

Ariel twirled upwards until she was above Coral. 'No! Just because your life is boring, just because you must marry someone you don't love, doesn't mean I have to.'

'That's not fair,' Coral replied, shocked.

'How isn't it?' Ariel asked. 'You're trying to stop me from being who I am! Don't you understand? I hate being a mermaid. I always have. And you, you don't even have the guts to tell Father you don't want to marry Shell. He is a horrible merman, and you don't love him. He doesn't treat you right!'

Coral pressed her lips together, holding back tears. 'Please don't ...'

'No,' Ariel replied. 'I'm leaving, please, feel free to go and tell Father and everyone else that I am going to become

The Enchanted Kingdoms

human. They will lock me away forever in the underwater dungeons.' Ariel swam off toward the sea witch's cave.

Coral just bobbed in the same spot for a while, staring at the rocky wall covered in shells and little sea creatures. She looked back up to the shipwreck, which was around fifteen metres from the dip she was in. Hardly anyone knew about this place; that's why she knew she'd find Ariel there. Their old hiding spot from when they were children.

***

Ariel peeked around the entrance to the cave. Darkness coated the cave, which just made the hissing that echoed throughout the cave even creepier. Ariel's heart pounded so fast she wondered if she was going to have a heart attack. She pushed forward and swam through the cave until she reached the back. It was bigger than she had imagined it would be. There were two tunnels going off in opposite directions. She could hear cackling coming from the right one. 'There you are,' she said aloud and swam through the grotty tunnel. She popped out the other side into a ginormous stone room with no windows. Ursula was staring into a mirror. 'I was wondering when you would pop by. How are you, my love?' she asked, turning and spinning in the centre of the room. A cauldron appeared and so did her eel.

Green liquid oozed and bubbled in the cauldron. Ursula used magic to keep it in there. Ursula danced and twirled as she added ingredients to the cauldron.

'So I guess you are here because you want legs?'

'Yes,' Ariel admitted. 'Will you help me?'

'Of course,' Ursula said sweetly. 'You seem to think I am some evil witch, but I am not. I am an outsider, like you. I want to help you.'

'I don't know if I can believe that,' Ariel said, crossing her arms. 'How do I know that this won't kill me?'

'Simple. If I kill you, I will be killed by your father and everyone in the lake will come for me. I am not an idiot. If you're done insulting my intelligence, then please, take this. You'll just have to trust me.'

'What do you want in return?' Ariel asked, taking the potion.

'Simple. For you to stay away from the lake, no matter what. For you to go and see your prince and get your happily ever after.'

'What about my family? I won't see them again?' she said, tearfully.

Ursula shrugged. 'Small price to pay. They will be fine. Probably glad to be rid of you,' Ursula said. 'I mean that in a compassionate way. Also, you have three days on land. If you wish to stay human, you must kiss your prince or return to being a mermaid.'

Ariel nodded, eyeing Ursula suspiciously, but took the potion anyway.

'Ariel,' Coral said who swam into the cave, but she was too late. 'What have you done?' she shouted at Ursula, who shrugged and smiled. Ariel's beautiful tail separated and turned into legs. Ariel gasped for air. Coral grabbed her sister and swam her to the surface. She took her to the bay and dropped her there. 'What have you done?!'

Ariel coughed until she got her breath back. 'I have legs!' She gasped and started wriggling her toes. 'I have legs!'

'Ariel,' Coral warned. 'Mother and Father will be furious. I may be able to strike a deal with Ursula to reverse the potion.'

'No,' Ariel shouted. 'Please, Coral.' She took her sister's hands. 'You're the only one I trust. Please, take care of Cullum and don't tell Father or Mother until I decide what to do. I have three days, apparently. If I kiss him, I stay human, and if not, then I return to being a mermaid.'

'Please make the right choice,' Coral begged. 'But if you decide to stay human, Ariel, I love you regardless and just want you to be happy,' Coral said and swam backward. 'If you need me, come to the water's edge and say my name. I will come for you.'

Ariel stood up, fell over, and then stood up again. Once she got her balance, she danced around ecstatically. Jack, the seagull, flew down and landed on a nearby rock.

'You have legs,' he said excitedly.

'Yes, aren't they wonderful?' she asked. She couldn't stop looking at them.

'We must get you some coverers,' he said, meaning clothes.

'Oh yes,' she said and covered herself up with a rag that had been left on one of the canoes. She tied it at the back. 'How do I look?'

He looked her up and down and nodded approvingly. 'Beautiful. So where is the prince?'

'The palace,' she said excitedly.

BELLE

Stilt and Edward walked down the winding road. 'Fresh air,' Stilt said, breathing in. 'The air is so clean out here!'

'It is,' Edward agreed. Any comment on Dolorom was a comment to him in his eyes. 'We need to leave tonight really,' Edward said, itching to go to Northmanni. Seeing Belle again, holding her, telling her how she changed his views on everything was the most important thing.

Stilt nodded. 'Yes.' They both heard it, a carriage coming up the winding road. On both sides of the road were woods that went on for miles. They were in the middle of nowhere.

'We will magic ourselves to Northmanni,' Edward stated. 'It has been nice to just walked and relax, though.' Stilt had suggested the walk, suggesting that it would clear their heads for the inevitable battle, and he was right. Edward felt better already. They both moved to the side of the road to let the carriage go past. 'Then,' Edward continued, 'Belle.'

'Yes, we get Belle ... oh,' Stilt said on seeing an angry Belle jump out of the carriage. Edward looked her up and down. She was wearing trousers, a fitted top, a dagger was in a scabbard strapped to her leg, and a bow and a quiver of arrows were on her back.

'You!' Belle said, pointing at Edward. 'I was hoping more than anything that I'd bump into you!'

'Me too. Look, I need to explain things to you properly.'

'Save it,' she shouted. 'The both of you singlehandedly destroyed mine, and by the sounds of it, many other people's too.'

'We never intentionally meant to hurt either of you,' Stilt said. 'Hear Edward out,' he insisted.

Edward sighed. 'Lori is using you. I told you about her before!'

Belle pulled her dagger out of the holder and pointed it at Edward's neck. 'You have ten seconds to tell me something substantial, or I will remove your head from your shoulders.'

'Okay, everyone needs to calm down,' Stilt said. Belle pushed the dagger forward more until it pressed into Edward's windpipe. He pushed Belle's hand back a little.

'I love you,' he started. 'I do. Even if you kill me now, I love you. I was spelled to forget you,' he said and looked at Stilt angrily then looked back at Belle. 'For the curse to break, I must have loved you. If I didn't, the kiss wouldn't have done anything.'

On that, she lowered her dagger and stepped back. 'Of course, but ...' She hesitated. Why wouldn't the hate disappear? 'But I really hate you. Like, I really do.'

Edward furrowed his brows. 'Over that? I didn't peg you as they type who could hate so much!'

'I'm not!' she snapped. 'What's wrong with me?' She tried to force herself from stabbing the dagger into him, but the urge was too strong. She pushed it toward him.

Stilt watched as a seemingly conflicted Belle pushed the dagger towards a hurt Edward's stomach and flicked his hand. Belle lost consciousness, and Edward caught her.

'What happened?' Edward asked, astonished. 'Surely, she can't hate me that much over something that didn't even happen?'

Stilt shook his head. 'I think she's cursed.'

Edward's mouth tightened. 'Lori,' he growled.

Edward and Stilt magicked themselves and Belle back to Dolorom castle and laid her down on Edward's bed. Edward ran his finger down her cheek and kissed her lips.

Seconds felt like hours until she woke. Belle looked at Edward hazily. He half leaned in, waiting for her to come around and kiss him. The other part of him hesitated, ready to jump back in case she attacked him.

Neither happened.

Belle sat up and looked around with wide eyes. Several realisations fell into her head. It felt as if the past month had been one long daydream. Her hand shot to her mouth as she gasped. Stilt and Edward looked at each other then back at Belle. She looked up at them with tears in her glassy brown eyes. 'Lori ... she's going to kill you. She's using my son. I think she even sent my father and Caleb away. She's hurting people and stealing people's beauty. She's Queen of Northmanni and ...'

Edward placed his hand on hers. 'Calm down. We can sort this.'

She pulled her hands back and wept. 'This is all my fault.'

Stilt shook his head. 'It's not. It's partly mine, but mainly Lori's ...' Edward snarled at him. Stilt bit his lip. 'Mainly Lori's,' he pointed out.

Edward huffed. 'He's right. We can get her back. I promise.'

She reached out and touched his lips. 'I was so used to seeing you with scars and well ... everything else that I only got to admire how you actually look for a moment before ...' She looked up at Stilt and frowned. He fiddled uncomfortably with his sleeve. She looked back at Edward. 'I never actually got to tell you ...' She stopped. Her heart throbbed in her throat. 'I love you.'

Warmth spread through him. 'I love you too,' he admitted. Never did he think he would say those words and actually *mean* them. 'I love you,' he said again and lifted her off the bed. He spun her around as Stilt looked on, sickened.

Love had shattered the curse.

'Oh, I, God, I hate magic!' Belle admitted.

Edward, still holding Belle's hands, kissed her, and suddenly, all the worries, fears that he had, seemed to melt away with her touch. Everything that he had been through was worth it. She was in his arms, and this time, he would never let her go again.

'Where are you going?' Stilt asked, looking at the carriage.

'To visit Merlin.'

Stilt shook his head. 'Don't bother. Whatever you need, he won't help. Not when you're allied with Lori or us. He hates us all.'

Belle pressed her lips together. 'I see. Well, shall we go back to Northmanni? I want to see James.'

Edward nodded and escorted her to the carriage.

HUMAN

Eric walked his usual route back to the lake as he had done every night since meeting Ariel. His hope of ever seeing the fiery redhead that called shoes crockhoppers and made him laugh more than he had ever laughed in his life was fading. He rubbed his eyes twice and looked at the blurry figure ahead of him. His vision corrected. It was her, his dream girl, talking to a seagull, dressed in an old rag.

'Ariel?' Eric shouted over at her. She turned and grinned, showing off her beautiful pearly white teeth. She went to run over to him, but tripped on the bottom of the rag, and fell onto the pebbles. Eric ran over and helped her up. 'I can't believe it's you.'

'Hi. I'm human,' she exclaimed then put her hands over her mouth. 'I mean, of course, I am.'

'Right,' he said slowly and raised an eyebrow. 'Where are you from?'

'Uhh, a different place to here.'

'Well, I know that.' He laughed. 'Why are you wearing a rag?'

She twirled. 'Coverer.'

He laughed boyishly. 'It's a rag. Shall we get you into a dress at the castle?' he offered.

She giggled. 'A dress? Um, sure,' she said.

They strolled toward the castle. Eric couldn't stop laughing at the things Ariel was coming out with. 'You're rather unusual.'

'Oh,' she replied and pouted.

'It's a good thing,' he admitted. 'I haven't met anyone like you before. You're like a breath of fresh air.'

She couldn't stop looking at his face. His chiseled features, his hair, now dry, was curly. She thought it was adorable.

'You're really nice, too,' she said, smiling.

'Ah, you've only just met me,' he joked, smiling mischievously.

***

Belle and Edward cosied up for the ride. Belle felt peaceful, happy even. 'I feel like I've been missing out,' she said.

'On what?'

'Love,' she admitted.

He stroked her hair and grinned. 'I never knew it could feel this good.'

Stilt, who was sitting across from them, looked as if he may vomit. 'Oh, thank God!' he said as the carriage came to a stop. 'We're here.'

'Oh, it's not that bad,' Edward said and laughed. He followed Stilt out and helped Belle out of the carriage.

'It's nauseating, watching you two. I liked you better when you were a swine,' Stilt admitted.

Belle grinned at Edward. 'What happens now?'

Edward smiled back. He couldn't help it. 'We defeat Lori, get James, and return to Dolorom.'

'James has powers now.'

Stilt raised an eyebrow. 'Does he?'

Belle pursed her lips. 'You will not try to take them from him!'

Stilt laughed. 'You're kidding, right? We have unlimited power now. What would we need with his?'

'Lori said ...' She stopped herself. Of course, Lori had said that. She turned to Edward. 'Never mind. I just can't wait for us to be a family.'

Edward raised an eyebrow. 'You mean it? We can be a family?'

'Of course,' Belle said and smiled.

'Oh, Belle,' he said and lifted her up, twirling her around. 'I love you so much.'

'I love you too,' she said, blushing. She was sure she could never get tired of saying that. 'Can't we return to the castle in Milborn?'

Edward shook his head. 'Sorry love. It has to be Dolorom. I have a kingdom to run.'

'Of course,' Belle said, shaking her head. 'I just want out of all this. I don't want a part in any of this anymore. I just want a peaceful life.'

Edward took her hand. 'I promise you we will have that. I will make sure of it. For now, I must help Stilt with his quest. I must help kill Lori. While she is alive, I will never be happy. She will always find a way to ruin my life. I must keep you safe.'

Belle bit her lip. 'I can go back and pretend that everything is fine. Work from the inside.'

'Excellent idea,' Stilt said.

'Out of the question,' Edward said and gave Stilt a discerning look. 'Belle will not be returning there. She will be smack in the middle of all the chaos. I will not let that happen!'

'Oh, you won't *let* me, huh? Since when did you dictate what I do or don't do?' Belle said, putting her hands on her hips.

'Let her do it,' Stilt said, interrupting their bickering.

Edward froze. A letter flew in their direction with a familiar wax seal. It was from Dolorom. The raven sat on his shoulder. He took the letter off, and it flew off into the sky.

Belle and Stilt watched with anticipation. He read it several times before looking up. 'Northmanni are planning an attack on Dolorom.'

Stilt shrugged. 'So? They'll beat them.'

He shook his head. 'No, they won't. Lori has built a huge army, apparently.'

Belle walked over and stroked his hand. 'We will do everything we can.'

Stilt looked at Edward. 'What do we need to do? My little girl is there.'

Edward looked at them both darkly. 'We need to go to Milborn. They are our biggest allies.'

He grabbed Belle's arm, and they all vanished and reappeared in Milborn. Belle scowled. 'I wanted to check on my son!'

Edward looked at her apologetic. 'Sorry. I promise this won't take long.'

They looked up at the palace. Moss clung to its walls, and the drawbridge was down. It cast a shadow on the courtyard where townsfolk were in their carriages trading things like fish and corn. The kingdom was bustling with people. The little road winding down to the pebble bay, had walls either side a couple of feet tall, covered in ivy and plants. Statues of Neptune and fountains littered the castle's entrance, and the iron gates were even in the shape of a clam.

'Best mussels in all the lands. Forosh have the best fish. Milborn has the best crabs and mussels,' Edward told Belle.

They walked into the castle and were confronted by guards. 'What is your business here?'

'We are here to see Prince Eric,' Edward replied coolly.

'Names?'

'Stilt, Belle, and I am Prince Edward of Dolorom.'

'Of course, Prince Edward,' he said quickly. 'We will tell the prince.'

Moments later, Eric appeared with a human Ariel sporting a baby pink dress. 'You're the little mermaid from the boat,' Stilt said and smiled. 'I see you have legs now.'

Eric looked at her questioningly. 'What?' asked Eric.

Ariel's cheeks flushed pink. 'I was a mermaid. I was given a potion to become human so that I could see you.'

Eric smiled. 'You became human so you could see me again?'

She nodded enthusiastically.

'Ariel, you're in danger. Ursula is here, in human form, to make sure you don't return to the lake,' Stilt said.

They all looked at him. He looked around and shrugged. 'Really? It's not hard to connect the dots. She's a jealous person. She desperately wanted the prince to fall into the lake. We gave Ariel's mother a potion so Ariel would turn to sea foam if she ever became human for over three days ...' He looked around again. 'What?'

Ariel asked. 'That makes no sense. I won't be going back to the lake.'

'You must,' Stilt said. 'If not, you'll die.'

'No! How do we stop it?' Eric asked, panicked.

Stilt smiled. 'I have a plan.'

They all huddled together and nodded as Stilt relayed the plan to them. 'Ready?'

'Yes,' Ariel said.

Edward turned to Eric. 'Dolorom is under attack.'

Eric grimaced. 'Who from?'

'Northmanni,' Edward said bitterly. 'We need more troops. Our kingdoms are allied, and we have sent you troops in the past.'

Eric nodded. 'Of course. I will talk to Father. In the meantime, please make yourselves at home,' he said and hurried off to find the king.

MORAL COMPASS

James furrowed his eyebrows and looked down at the compass. 'So how exactly does this work?'

Merlin placed his hand on top of his compass and smiled warmly. 'It's a moral compass. It works when you're using your magic for good. When you use your magic for bad, it will temporarily paralyze you.'

James looked up at Merlin and put the compass into his pocket. 'Why do I need to use it?'

Merlin sat across from him and stroked his long beard. 'It will give you complete control of your powers, and make sure you only use them for good. You do only want to use them for good, don't you?'

'Of course,' James mumbled. 'Thank you.'

'No need to thank me. As of now, you're my apprentice. I have a task for you,' Merlin said in his deep, gruff voice.

'Yes?'

'Well, Snow's plan has not worked.'

'You don't know that,' James replied.

'I know Lori slaughtered the dwarfs, and I know Red was turned into a wolf. Unfortunately, even you cannot tamper with a curse. Not with your moral compass. Only sorcerers who are not attached to moral compasses can tamper, break, and cast curses. Lori, Stilt, Edward, and Gertrude are the only ones who can.'

'Lori won't,' James said, feeling disheartened. 'Poor Red.'

Merlin lowered his eyes to James's compass. 'If you can find a way to bind Lori, Stilt, and Edward, and bring them to me, then I will help your friends.'

James nodded. 'I can do try.'

'Remember,' Merlin said. 'You must use your powers for the right reasons. Do not harm them, just restrain. The spells we have been practicing, the method, is the same for the binding spell. Here is the incantation,' Merlin said, handing him a piece of paper. 'Say it in your head.'

James nodded and memorized the incantation. 'I will be back,' he said and disappeared on the spot. Learning how to finally do that was an achievement for him. He felt in control, but not as powerful as he apparently was.

***

Loving her was an honour. Her hair was as vibrant as her personality. Her ideas were so mind boggling that they were bordering on genius. She breathed life into every room she entered. Eric was falling helplessly in love with her.

'I never thought you could fall in love so quickly,' he admitted to Ariel.

She was sprawled across his bed, with no shoes on, or crockhoppers as she called them, and was wriggling her toes. 'I don't care if people think it's odd or not. I love you. You just know it's right when you meet the one. Do you care about what people think?'

'Not anymore,' he said and sat on the bed. He stroked her cheek and leant in toward her. Her heart hammered loudly the closer he got. His scent filled her senses. Being around him was a sensory overload. He kissed her like he had never kissed before.

'You're a good kisser for a fish,' he joked.

'So are you, for a human.' She twirled his curly hair around her finger. 'I can't believe we stayed up all night talking.'

He laughed. 'I haven't stayed up all night since I was a child. Edward came over and me, him, and a few others went camping and told ghost stories all night.'

'What is a ghost?' she asked.

'The spirit of a deceased person,' he said darkly.

'Oh,' she said glumly.

'I do believe we have a ball to attend,' he said.

Ariel grinned. 'I have always wanted to dance. A dinner and a show—it will be amazing.'

'It'll be the best one we will ever have had.'

***

'They are in Milborn?' Lori asked the spy.

'Yes, they are in Milborn,' he repeated. 'They are attending Prince Eric's ball to announce his engagement.'

'Engagement to who?' she asked.

'Some commoner apparently. Ariel,' he said flatly. 'Sorry I couldn't bring more news. However, I did find out that Milborn are sending troops to Dolorom in anticipation of your attack.'

Lori drank her wine and put it on the table. 'We will see,' she said and polished her nails. 'I have always been one for balls. Arrange for my carriage and luggage to be prepared. We are going to Milborn. Also, fetch me Snow, will you?'

He bowed his head and left the room, leaving Lori alone at the long table. Before long, Snow stormed through the door.

'What do you want?' she asked. Lori noticed that Snow was looking a little crazed. Her eye was twitching, she looked tired, her hair was a mess, and she was breathing fast.

'Snow, take a seat.'

Begrudgingly, Snow sat down and looked at Lori stonily. 'What do you want?' Snow repeated, impatiently.

'Belle is involved with Edward again,' Lori said simply. 'One of my spies saw them together.'

'No,' Snow said, feeling betrayed. 'And James, have you heard from him?'

'Yes. Apparently, he has been making deals with Merlin,' Lori said and gave Snow a knowing look. 'I know about everything. I can no longer trust anyone, so I want to offer you to be my ally. I know you hate me, but I can bring justice to your mother. Edward, I promise, will die. Along with Stilt. And I promise to keep James safe. I need to you to accompany me to a ball being held in a kingdom far away. We will find Edward and Belle there. We will arrest him and Stilt for their crimes and bring them here.'

Snow sat in silence and considered her options. 'And you promise me that no harm will come to James or Belle? She may be with Edward, but she is a good person. I can see that.'

She smiled. 'I promise no physical harm will come to either of them,' Lori promised.

Snow lifted her hand in the air. 'Or curse ... you will do nothing to them!' Lori nodded in response. Snow nodded. 'Then, I am on your side. I will go with you.'

Lori smirked. 'More than that, you will trick them into coming here. Belle trusts you; so does James.'

Snow bit her lip so hard she could taste blood. She was going to betray the people she cared about. She was turning out to be just as bad as the people she hated. 'Fine.'

'Once they are out of Milborn, they are out of their jurisdiction,' Lori pointed out. 'I cannot arrest them there, but I can arrest them the second they leave Milborn.'

'What will happen once they are arrested?' asked Snow. Lori raised her hand, and with one of the pointed nails, she motioned a slit across her throat. Snow nodded and stood up. 'When do we leave?'

'Dawn,' she stated. 'I will have the servants prepare your things. Do not mess this up!' Lori warned.

'I won't.'

Snow walked back to her room. *I've made a deal with the devil.* She opened the door to her room and saw James sat by the fire, his feet up on the table.

'James,' she said. 'You're back early.'

'Yes, I am,' he said, smiling. 'I have so much to tell you. Red was cursed to be a wolf.'

'Oh. That would make a lot of sense. I went there and saw a wolf. I think she was trying to communicate.'

James noticed that Snow didn't look compassionate at all! If anything, she looked blank. James continued. 'Also, I am so sorry, but the dwarfs are dead. Lori killed them ...'

'I know,' she replied. 'I'm leaving in the morning.'

'Why?' he asked.

'Lori wants me to go to some stupid ball with her in Milborn.'

'I'll go with you,' James said.

'No,' Snow said a little too quickly. James looked at her suspiciously. 'It'll be boring.'

'As long as I am with you, I don't care.' She felt butterflies in her stomach then sighed. How could she ever tell him how she felt once she betrayed his mother?

'James, I want you to know that no matter what happens, I–'

A guard interrupted them. 'Your luggage has been prepared. You leave at dawn at the front entrance. You have your own carriage.'

'Make it for two, please. I will be coming along,' James said. The guard nodded and left. 'What were you going to say?' James asked.

'I was going to say that I care about you.'

'Oh,' he said, feeling a little disappointed that it wasn't more. 'Well, I care about you too. Even more than that.'

Snow didn't reply and got onto her bed. James gulped. 'Guess I'll see you in the morning. Look, are you okay? You seem a little ... down.'

'I'm fine,' she snapped.

'Okay, well, know that no matter what happens, you will always have me. I promise,' James said and left the room, leaving Snow feeling ten times worse.

MASQUERADE

Blue and purple drapes covered the walls of the ballroom. Three magnificent chandeliers hung from the high ceiling, and the glimmers from the crystals reflected off the marble floor. Tables surrounded the sides of the room, and the large space in the middle had been cleared for dancing. A band stood preparing their instruments on the small stage and a long table stretched across the top of the hall. It was filled with delicious foods, imported from other kingdoms, and mussels and crab from their kingdom were the special dishes.

Ursula, who had turned into a human to make sure that Ariel did not return to the lake, entered the hall. She had pretended to be a cook and took pleasure in the job. After all, she got to rip lobsters apart and chop the heads off shrimp.

Ariel could tell who it was, due to the eyes, but pretended not to notice.

'Everything to your liking, Majesty?' Ursula asked and bowed her head.

'Yes, thank you,' Ariel said quickly. 'Bring the engagement cake in at eight on the dot.' Ursula bowed and left the room. Belle, Stilt, and Edward stayed hidden from Ursula's sight, and they told the guards different names from their own.

Ursula walked away, smiling. Ariel would turn to sea foam at midnight, and as long as she kept Ariel at the palace until eleven, then she could return to the lake and strike a deal with the king and queen for their crown in return for the safe return of their daughter.

***

Lori rode into the palace grounds and stepped out of the carriage, wearing a disguise. She could not risk being noticed. She had the guard introduce her as the Queen of Forosh. She had made sure that the real Queen of Forosh did not come by sending a spell in a letter that caused a nasty stomach bug.

'Majesty,' the king said. 'Welcome to Milborn. We're delighted that you could make it to our son's engagement ball.'

'Pleasure to be here,' she said.

Snow and James pulled up. 'Is Lori here too?' James asked. 'You said my mother is here with Edward. Lori will kill them.'

'I sent them on a detour, and Lori is not here,' Snow lied. 'It's just us. I paid another woman to pretend to be Lori.'

'I see, good thinking,' James praised. Of course, Lori and Snow had devised a plan. Lori would be in disguise, and she would tell James it wasn't Lori. Then Lori would go in the carriage and leave early. Snow would get Belle, Edward, and Stilt into a carriage by telling them Lori was approaching and they had to leave.

However, on the road, Lori would reveal her true face, and she and Snow would arrest them. All Snow needed to do first was to persuade Stilt, Edward, and James to put on the bracelets that would stop their powers for five days.

Snow felt incredibly guilty but played her part well. She dressed up nicely. Her lace purple dress dragged behind her as she walked. Her raven black hair was half up, half down, and curled, with silver sparkles on the tips. She had on a red cloak with white fur up the front. She took it off and handed it to a guard. The palace and its grounds were bustling with people turning up for the ball, all wearing the most beautiful dresses and masquerade masks. James wore white trousers and an emerald green waistcoat over his black and white top. His cufflinks were purple to match Snow's outfit. They both had masquerade masks on colourful sticks to cover their eyes. They were gorgeous; both purple with gold and black beads, gold lace outlining it.

Lori stepped out wearing a silver ball gown. Her hair was down and wavy; her mask was a full one with silver feathers coming out of one corner.

Music boomed out from the hall. Ariel greeted them. She was wearing a sea blue ball gown that shimmered a little in the light. Her red hair was up with a few curls dangling from the bun, and she wore pearl earrings that matched her pearl necklace. 'Thank you so much for coming.'

'Thank you for having us,' Snow said and hugged the soon-to-be princess. James kissed Ariel's hand.

'You're Belle's son,' she remarked.

'How did you ...?'

'Same eyes, same expressions, same hair colour, same smile,' Ariel said and grinned.

'Oh,' James said and laughed. 'Where is my mother?'

'Inside,' Ariel said and let them past.

Eric walked over to them and Lori, who was in disguise. 'Majesty,' Eric said and bowed to Lori.

'Majesty,' Lori said and bowed back.

He turned to James and Snow. He shook James's hand and kissed Snow's. 'Thank you for coming,' Eric said. He was wearing a full white suit embroidered with gold stitching and buttons. His sword was in its scabbard. James spotted his mother at the back of the room. She was wearing a magnificent yellow ball gown which flowed out and was covered in little gold beads. Her hair was tied up into an elegant bun, and pearls fell from her ears. Her mask was an eye mask, like theirs, but it was plain gold and had three yellow feathers on the side.

Next to her was Edward. He wore a similar outfit to Eric's, except the stitching was silver and he had no sword. Stilt, who was next to them, was looking smart too. His hair was cut short and was swept to one side. He wore a black tuxedo. His cummerbund was green with silver spirals. Belle saw Snow and James and waved them over. Snow looked behind her and saw that Lori had gone off to mingle. James picked up two glasses of champagne from a passing waiter and passed one to Snow.

Snow raised her eyebrows. 'Alcohol?'

'It's a special occasion,' he said and shrugged. 'You look beautiful, by the way. I feel lucky to have you as my girl tonight.'

She felt her stomach knot on hearing 'my girl.' She wanted to be his girl always. But she never would be, especially not after tonight.

'Mother,' James said and hugged her. She held him tightly and asked him for a word. They entered the dimly lit corridor where waiters were frantically running back and forth with trays of drink and canapés.

'Stilt and Edward aren't bad, James,' Belle whispered. 'You have to trust me, okay. We have been lied to, by Lori. Stilt was forced to do what he did. Edward was forced to forget us. Look, I believe them. I love Edward,' she admitted.

He could see the anticipation in her eyes. 'I trust you. But are you sure you can trust them? Are you sure this is what you want?'

'I am certain,' she replied.

James smiled. 'I just want you to be happy,' he said.

He was taller than she was now, only by a few inches, but Belle looked up at her grown-up son teary eyed. 'You look so handsome. Snow looks beautiful tonight. You make a lovely couple. She seems to make you happy.'

'She does,' he admitted. 'I'm going to tell her I love her tonight.'

Belle grinned. 'She will say it back, I'm certain.'

***

The music started, and James put his hand on Snow's waist, looking longingly into her eyes. 'I know you hate Edward. However, my mother loves him. Apparently, he didn't do everything he has been accused of doing. I don't know if that includes the death of your mother. I hate to ask you because I know it causes you so much pain, but can you give him the benefit of doubt? They have been good to my mother. They seem like good people,' he admitted.

The Enchanted Kingdoms

She gulped. 'Of course.'

'I expected more of a fight. I'm surprised,' he said.

She forced a smile. 'You know me. Full of surprises.'

'Yes, you are,' he started. The music changed its tune. It was upbeat and had a jazzy tune to it. He twirled Snow around and felt his hands go clammy. Never had he felt so nervous. 'I'm in love with you, Snow.'

'You're what?'

'I'm in love with you.' He looked longingly into her eyes, waiting for her to say something, anything.

'The cake,' Eric announced over the room as Ursula entered the hall. She placed it on the table and smiled. Snow turned to see and out of nowhere Ursula was bombarded by twenty guards. Stilt used his powers and pushed her to her knees. Belle appeared and wrapped the rope around her, and Edward grabbed a sword from a guard and put it up to her throat. While she was distracted, Stilt grabbed a small bag she was carrying and ripped it from her. She screamed at him to give it back to her. He peeked inside and saw three shining shells. The source of her powers. They took Ursula to the dungeons, and Ariel and Eric followed Stilt, Belle, and Edward out of the room.

'What are we missing?' Snow asked and grabbed James's arm. She looked over at Lori who mouthed, 'Tell me everything.' Snow nodded and left as the king explained to the crowd that an arrest had taken place, and it was nothing to worry about, for everyone to continue dancing. He then announced the opening of the buffet, to distract them, I imagine.

Stilt, in the chamber, held the shells. He spelled Ariel to break the curse. Ariel was flung into the air, dangling like a rag doll. A light surrounded her until she landed back onto the floor.

'You're a human for good,' Belle exclaimed.

'Ursula will be executed soon,' Eric informed her. Ariel nodded but felt bad for the sea witch even though she knew she had no other choice.

Snow saw her opportunity. She left James, went into the ballroom and gave Lori the signal to leave then ran back into the corridor. She pulled out five bracelets; only three were spelled to suppress powers. 'Lori is waiting for us. I have just heard from a woman I paid to pose as Lori. I sent Lori on a detour. She has a curse planned. Please, put these on. They will protect you all.'

She handed Belle, Stilt, Edward, and James a bracelet each. 'I'm telling you, it's the only thing that will stop Lori's curse.' She put one on herself.

Edward turned to Belle. 'Can she be trusted?'

'Yes,' Belle said and smiled at Snow. Snow's stomach knotted.

'I'd trust her with my life,' James said and put on the bracelet. They all put them on.

'Is there anything we can do?' Eric and Ariel chorused.

'We need to leave before she gets here,' Snow said.

Eric stepped forward. 'I will get your carriages ready.'

They all exchanged their goodbyes. Ariel hugged Belle. 'Anything you need, just ask.' Belle nodded.

'What will you do now?' Belle asked Ariel.

'I'm going to explain everything to my family then I will wed Eric,' Ariel said and smiled. 'Eric has sent the troops to Dolorom, which should prevent the attack or at least delay it.'

They hugged once more, and they all got into the carriage. Belle and Eric waved as they rode away. As soon as they were out of the gates, Snow held James's hand.

'I love you too,' she whispered and closed her eyes. James squeezed her hand. She knew this would be the last time she'd have this.

When they were on the road, another carriage bashed into them. 'What the ...?' Stilt said. They poked their heads out and saw Lori approaching them. Stilt tried to use his powers to protect them, but he couldn't. James did the same. They tried to remove the bracelets and couldn't.

'Snow?' James asked.

'Sorry,' Snow managed.

James let the betrayal rush through him.

Snow grabbed the bag with the shells and jumped out of the carriage.

Lori walked up to the carriage, and she, Snow, and her guards put them all in handcuffs.

'It is only Stilt and Edward who are being arrested,' Lori said and dragged them out of the carriage. 'However, to make sure none of you try to help, Belle and James, you will be held in custody until the execution.

'Execution?' Belle asked. 'No,' she screamed. James shouted at them to let them go, but Snow walked off.

She could hear James calling after her, begging her to help, but she didn't look back. She went into Lori's carriage and sat with a guard.

'Ready, Majesty?'

Snow nodded at the guard. Lori stayed in the other carriage to make sure none of them escaped. There were too many of them to magic back to the kingdom. So they travelled back by carriage.

Halfway through the trip, Snow swapped carriages and found herself alone with James and a guard. 'How could you?'

She looked down at the floor. 'I have a plan.'

'You do?'

She nodded. 'You're not going to like it, and in fact, you're going to hate me for everything that is about to unfold, but you'll have to trust that no matter what happens and where we end up, I love you and I promise to secure a future at the end of it all for us.'

His eyes widened. 'Let me go, let me help you.'

She shook her head, tears brimming in her eyes. 'This is the only way I can make things work. It's going to suck, but everything I am doing is for us. You must believe that.'

He lowered his gaze. 'I do, Snow. I do.'

GOODBYES

He could hear Belle's pleas and screams from the holding cell. Every tick on the large clock tower ticked down the seconds left of his life. Childishly, he hoped that Stilt would use his powers to save him. Or his mother and stepfather would come in at the last minute and demand his release. Or the more unlikely option, that Lori would have a heart and let him go.

His cell was cold, drips fell from the pipes in the corner, and rats ran around freely. Sometimes, one would come up to him and eat the crumbs of bread left on his plate. The slice of bread he'd get only once a day. He'd hoped that as a last request they'd at least allow him to dress up nicely and eat a good meal before he lost his head. He stood up and peeked out through the bars of his window. Crowds were gathering in the court below. Hundreds of people had made their way to the castle to watch him take his last breath. To watch as their queen beheaded him for a murder committed years ago. This was all because he had cheated on her, he knew that, and somewhere deep down, she knew that. Lori had convinced herself, however, that he was responsible for her entire life going to shambles, and she was using Mary's death to get her revenge.

He saw Belle amongst the crowd being held by guards. Stilt, unfortunately, sat in the cell next to him. This was how he knew he could not be saved. His only hope was locked away, too. He could hear Stilt's incoherent mumbling as he watched the clock tick to ten to twelve. His heart hammered quickly as if it knew it was beating its last beats. Beads of sweat dripped down his forehead, and Edward ran his hand, probably for the last time, through his greasy, scruffy hair.

'Stilt,' Edward called out but wasn't answered. Edward gulped as he imagined the sharp edge of an axe hitting his neck. 'Stilt, please. There must be some way. We were friends. I always regarded you as a friend. Don't let them do this to me. How are you giving up so easily? You have a daughter!'

Stilt coughed, his voice was cracked and barely audible. 'I can't help either of us.'

'You have to try,' Edward pleased. 'They will be coming to get me any minute now, please. Belle is watching. I cannot have her watch me. I don't even know why she is here,' Edward pleaded. He wanted to walk to his death with dignity, with his head held high, but he was breaking. Tears forced themselves out of his eyes. 'I don't want to die. I'm scared.' The childish words escaped his lips as the guards threw open the door. They looked at him and waited for him to do something. 'Has there been any changes?' he asked but already knew the answer.

'I'm afraid not. You must come with us,' they said and placed handcuffs on him. There were ten guards. Even if he could take down one, he'd never be able to get away from all ten.

'See you on the other side,' Stilt said as Edward was dragged past his cell. Stilt looked through the bars sorrowfully. 'Looks like we have both been taken for fools.'

'Goodbye, old friend,' Edward managed as he was taken down the winding steps. The cuffs cut into his wrists. The closer he got to the courtyard, the more his heart pounded, the more beads of sweat trickled down his nose. He tried to steady his breathing, but as the door opened, sunlight blinded him. He looked around for anyone he knew, anyone who could help him, but unfamiliar faces took up his view, all cheering for his death. He looked up at the block and panicked. Lori was sat up on a balcony, looking down at the scene. She was not smiling, which was unexpected. She looked indifferent if anything.

'Edward,' Belle screamed through the crowd. Edward desperately looked around the crowd for her but couldn't see her face. He just wanted to kiss her lips and look into her beautiful brown eyes one last time. But that wouldn't happen, and he didn't want her to watch what was about to happen.

'Please,' Edward spluttered. 'Please get Belle away from here. I cannot have her watch!'

The guards ignored his request. The heat from the sun fell on his back, and he remembered back to when he was a child; running through meadows, going horseback riding for the first time, playing hide and seek with the other children from the palace. Now, he was to meet his fate, and he didn't even get to say goodbye. Every regret, the poor princess he killed, the girl who he cursed to be a frog. Lori, Belle, every single one of the people he had hurt; it crippled him.

Remorse will not save you,
The truth will not help,
Sorcerers, the two of you
Will surely lose your heads

Snow sang under her breath as Edward was pulled over to the block. She wore black; not to mourn, but to show who she truly was. She had helped send two men to their deaths. Both of whom deserved it, but the cries from Belle and silence from James almost killed her inside. In doing this, she was hurting the people she loved.

James tried to comfort his mother, but she was frantic, screaming, trying to break free from the guards. Snow had asked for Belle not to see the execution, but Lori insisted.

Lori.

Snow vowed that one day Lori's head would be on that block. Chopped by the same executioner, she would have her head separated from her shoulders. Until that day, Snow had to play it safe.

Lori looked back onto the crowd and looked as Edward was dragged onto the board. Her heart sank slightly as she looked down at the man who she had once loved, once cherished. He looked up at her too, catching her gaze for only a second before turning back to the crowd. She could hear Belle's screaming; well, who couldn't? The screams were filled with so much anguish and pain that Lori wanted it just to be over and done with. The finale to the years of planning her revenge was not as satisfying as she had anticipated. She ran her finger along the wand's edge that she had taken from the dwarfs. She could use it to channel her power, to make it stronger.

The crowd fell silent as Edward was asked if he had any final words. He gulped and tried to hold back tears. 'I—' He started but stopped on meeting Belle's gaze. Tears patterned her cheeks. She looked like she hadn't slept in weeks. Her hair was limp, and nothing but sadness showed on her face. He shook his head and pressed his lips together. 'Get out of here, Belle.'

'Edward,' she cried. 'Please, someone, help him. He didn't do it.'

'I did,' Edward admitted. Belle gasped and fell to her knees. Edward felt the disappointment and hurt pierce through him. He looked down at Snow, who looked back at him with no compassion.

'You have been charged with the murder of Princess Mary. You have been sentenced to death by decapitation,' Snow said loudly.

'I'm sorry about your mother,' he whispered as his head was forced onto the block. Belle's screaming was drowned out by the chanting and jeering from the crowd. The sunlight highlighted the boards below him.

Snow pressed her lips together. She looked out at Edward as the sword swished through the air and prayed that her long, drawn-out plan would work.

This was going to be a painful yet rewarding journey.

Read on for an excerpt of Journey to Neverland
Book two in the Haunting Fairytales Series

journey to neverland

Peter sat on top of the tallest building in Santeria and looked out over the city. Chaos was breaking out, and it was all because of him. 'Brother,' he said to Pablo, who was sat next to him holding his wooden flute. 'You must now, brother; if not, *we* will burn.'

'*You* will burn,' Pablo replied, looking down at the angry mob circling their house. 'Mother and Father will die because of your stupidity. Why must you show your powers? They believe you to be a warlock!'

'Am I not?' Peter asked with a hint of a smile.

Pablo slammed his fist down on the block next to him. 'It is not funny, brother. You know they do not understand. Grandmother has told you to keep your magic hidden since you were a toddler. You have put us all at risk.'

Peter rolled his blue eyes. 'Brother.' He laughed, running his hand through his dirty blond hair. 'You are also magical; you play your flute with such enchantment …'

The Enchanted Kingdoms

'It is not magic!' Pablo shouted. They both ducked as some of the townspeople looked up. Pablo turned to Peter, who was a mirror image of him. 'I play well, but it does not make me a warlock,' he whispered.

Peter grinned broadly, showing off his pearly white teeth. 'Animals come to you when you play,' Peter said. 'You are magical, and that is fantastic. Don't you see? We are different, and that's the most brilliant.'

Pablo rolled his eyes at his brother's made-up word. 'You are to be married. You are nineteen, not nine. Forget these childish fantasies. Let them purge you of your demons and never use your powers again.'

Peter furrowed his brows. 'You'd have me be someone I am not?'

Pablo peeked down and saw that their house was alight with flames. 'For our family and futures, yes.'

Peter shook his head. 'I shall not. Sorry, brother.'

'Please, brother,' Pablo begged, but Peter sat cross-armed in defiance.

Pablo sighed and stood up. He pressed his lips to the top of the flute and played his music, letting the melody carry away his worries. He played more beautifully than he ever had; a tune of wonder and sadness mixed with anger and joy. 'It's working!' Peter exclaimed. They looked down, and the animals had come. Thousands of rats poured into the city. 'Do it,' Peter said.

Pablo continued to play, but this time, a different tune left the flute, influencing the rats to devour the townspeople. His stomach churned as screams filled his ears. His mother and father ran out of the house and climbed onto their roof to escape the flames.

The townspeople who had avoided the rats looked up at the building and saw Peter and Pablo. 'Demons!' they screamed as the small mob ran toward the building.

Tears trickled down their mother's cheeks as she looked at her sons. She climbed down the building, and slowly, the rats descended on her. Her husband jumped down and wrapped his arm around her stomach, hitting the rats off them both. She looked up at her husband and squeezed his hand then looked over at the townspeople. 'I called the rats here!' she screamed at the mob. 'Now, I wish for them to take me like they will take all of you! If you do not kill me, you will all die.'

'No,' Pablo called out, but it was too late. The townspeople turned on her and plunged a stake into her stomach. She fell to the ground, and the rats climbed her torso, devouring and tearing pieces of flesh. Their father lunged at the mob but was killed quickly.

'She lied to save us,' Pablo said with disbelief as tears streamed down his face.

Peter wiped away a tear and looked over the horizon. 'She gave us a distraction, so let's take it.'

They climbed down the wood ladder on the side of the building and took off toward the setting sun. They ran for miles without stopping. Years of toiling the fields had made them strong and fit. They ran until they reached the hills outside of the city. Ahead of them loomed a thousand trees.

'The Enchanted Forest,' Peter said with a mischievous grin.

'No,' Pablo warned, 'it is dangerous. Remember the stories we were told, of demons lurking in the trees and black magic?'

Peter waved his hand dismissively and walked into the forest like a moth drawn to a flame. Pablo looked back and heard the few townspeople who had escaped. He sighed and ran after Peter.

They walked through the thickening trees and over the uneven forest floor. Peter was entranced by fireflies and the blue and red flowers that somehow flourished beneath the thick canopy. He brushed his fingers along the petals and grinned broadly at his twin brother. 'Isn't it wonderful?'

'It's cold,' Pablo replied bluntly.

Peter rolled his eyes and skipped ahead. The tree trunks shimmered gold as darkness fell over the forest, and the wolves howled in the distance. 'Brother,' Peter said and placed his arm in front of his brother. 'Wolves everywhere.' Peter looked down at Pablo's pocket. 'Your flute, brother!'

Pablo snapped back to reality and slowly pulled his flute out of his pocket. The howling grew louder, followed by the sounds of crinkling leaves and snapping twigs. Several sets of eyes glowed yellow in the darkness, surrounding them both. Pablo placed his lips to the top of the flute, and the melody danced out of his flute and over to the wolves, who immediately whimpered and backed away.

Peter breathed a sigh of relief. 'Thank God I have you. What are you getting them to do?'

'Fear us,' Pablo said quickly and continued to play. The wolves left the clearing where they were stood, and Pablo put the flute back into his pocket. 'We should eat something.'

Peter nodded and lifted a hand into the air. A gush of wind knocked down a branch, and a startled squirrel tried to jump as it fell but missed its landing and fell with the branch. Peter picked up a large rock and walked over to the squirrel. He hit it and watched the light leave its eyes. 'We thank you for your sacrifice,' Peter said over its body then picked it up. 'Dinner,' he said brightly.

Pablo gathered several fallen branches and placed them above a small hole that Peter had dug. Peter used his powers and summoned fire. He looked down at the flames and smiled. 'I love magic.'

'That makes one of us.'

They cooked the squirrel and fell asleep next to the crackling fire.

***

Morning fell, leaving the forest covered in a dewy glow. Peter was up first and couldn't keep the smile off his face. This was the freest he had ever felt. He shook Pablo's shoulder. 'Come on, we should keep moving.'

Pablo rubbed his eyes and looked around groggily. 'I had hoped that this would have been all a dream.'

Peter pinched his arm. 'Nope, this is all very real. Come on, brother, it's like a dream, isn't it? We are in paradise.'

Pablo scoffed but said nothing and walked behind Peter. The blisters on his feet rubbed against his shoes. He took off a shoe to rub his aching feet, but his foot caught under a vine on the ground and he fell forward.

'Brother?' Peter turned back on hearing the skull-crushing thud. 'Pablo, can you hear me?' His hair was stained with crimson, which pooled on the jagged rock where Pablo lay unconscious.

Peter pushed his hands under Pablo's arms and dragged him along the forest floor. He could hear the steady trickling of a pool and dragged his brother towards the sound. The trees fell away and revealed a beautiful pool of shimmering water that glistened in the sunlight and flowers that wound their way up the rocks.

He pulled Pablo to the edge of the pool and laid him next to the water. Peter pulled off his brown top and submerged it in the water, which made his finger tingle on contact. He dabbed at the gash on Pablo's head with the wet top and watched as the gash healed over.

Pablo took in a deep breath and sat up. 'What happened?'

Peter looked at the water with awe. 'You hit your head, but brother …' He looked at Pablo wide-eyed. 'The water is magic.'

'How so?' Pablo looked down at the water with a frown. Magic was bad, it was demonised, and it was what got their parents killed and them in exile.

Peter took off his shoes and placed them on a rock then placed his feet into the water. 'Ah, I feel the pain from my ankles melt away. Brother, try it.'

Pablo pressed his lips together. 'I … I don't know.'

'Oh, come on,' Peter insisted. 'Stop being so fearful.'

Pablo cautiously dipped his foot into the pool and felt the pressure and pain leave his foot. The twins stripped and lowered themselves into the pool. 'Isn't this wonderful! We have found a pool of healing,' said Peter.

Pablo nodded in agreement and looked around the edges. 'It looks more like a fountain. Look.'

Peter looked around the edges; the rocks had formed a ridge, which wound around the circular pool, and in the ridge, the water waved down, connecting to a lower ridge until eventually, it hit the pool. 'It does look similar. It is a fountain of healing, a fountain of youth.'

'Yes. Peter …' He looked at his brother and sighed. 'We must talk about what happened.'

'Never,' Peter said. 'Never, never, never.'

'We must!' Pablo insisted. 'Mother and Father are dead. We killed an entire village through my music and …'

Peter slammed his hand down onto a rock next to him, and his expression darkened. 'We must never talk about it again. Think of this as a new start. This,' he said, spreading his arms, 'is Neverland. A new start where we will be happy and will never have to hide our powers again. Where magic is everything, and if people come, then they must love me for me and not expect me to be anyone else. A place where we don't have to grow up, where I will not be forced to marry or work. A place where our past will not be spoken, and we'll be free! Never growing up, never to speak of the past, never to be unhappy; Neverland.'

Pablo bit the inside of his cheek and nodded. There was no point in arguing. He knew once Peter got something in his head, nothing could deter him from it. 'We will need food,' Pablo pointed out.

Peter grinned. 'Glad to see you're on board, brother. We will sort out all the details. I'm going to grow my powers here. If I hurt myself as I have done before, I can heal myself with the fountain.'

Pablo nodded slowly. 'Suppose so.'

'And ...' Peter said excitedly. 'I can see how far I can stretch my powers. None of the Pan family have had the opportunity to see what they can do with the magic, but now, I can. *We* can.'

Pablo waded over to where his clothes were in a pile and reached into his pocket and pulled out his flute. Playing music was the only thing he loved to do. It carried him away to another world. He pressed the wood to his lips and held back a sob. The flute was crafted by his mother. He daresn't tell Peter he was sad, though. Peter was happy, Peter was carefree, and if Peter knew that Pablo was sad, he might leave him. He played his flute, and the sounds were more powerful than ever. It called deer to the pool and fairies, too. They both watched with fascination as the fairies danced on top of toadstools and rocks.

That evening, Peter danced with the fairies, made a campfire, hunted a deer, and laughed by the fire.

With each passing day, Peter's powers grew, and he forgot more and more about his past, his parents, and the city. Pablo watched cautiously as Peter grew more arrogant with it too. The forest changed around them. Everything was brighter, and the pool grew bigger. Peter laughed more than he ever had, and Pablo cried silently in the dead of night.

***

One morning, Pablo awoke to the sound of his flute playing. He shot up and looked around cautiously. He peered through two trees and saw Peter sigh and throw his flute to the ground. 'Why do you not play well with me, and you do for my brother? I am more powerful than he is!' Peter stomped off in frustration. When Peter was out of sight, Pablo grabbed his flute and sighed.

'He's growing too powerful,' a fairy said from behind him. He turned and looked at her face. She had nutmeg-coloured skin, a tuft of brown hair, a long face, and wide green eyes. 'You must stop him, Pablo.'

Pablo nodded; he had seen it over the past week. 'I will.'

Pablo practiced his flute all day and every night, growing his own powers, and each day, he felt more powerful than the last. The only way to stop Peter from growing too powerful or dangerous was by becoming powerful himself.

Peter saw the magic from the fountain dance into Pablo and watched on with greedy eyes. He wanted what Pablo had; after all, he was the more brilliant brother. Peter waited until Pablo was asleep later that night and snuck the flute from his grip. Placing it to his lips, he blew into it and wished for the forest to be his, for Neverland to be his. Slowly, the magic seeped out, and the water from the pool seeped into the ground and reached out to the edges of Santeria.

Most of the population of Santeria turned into mermaids through Peter's magic and fell into the ocean surrounding

The Enchanted Kingdoms

the huge island. The townspeople who had killed Peter's parents ran for their ship when they saw magic spreading through the land. They boarded their ship and tried to sail to another land, but it was as if an invisible barrier had surrounded the ocean a mile out from Santeria, preventing anyone from leaving. Instead, they settled on an island, which was a part of Santeria, and looked at Santeria across the short ocean separating them.

Peter walked out of the forest and looked around. The beach was beautiful—sand that shimmered like fairy dust, small pools of bright blue water, and the buildings had fallen down and were buried underneath the ground.

Peter turned to his brother. 'This is Neverland,' he said, his eyes flaming green. 'And I am its god!'

Pablo's smile turned into a hard line. 'God?'

Peter nodded. 'Yes.'

Peter left to dance around the campfire with the fairies and swim with the mermaids in the pools and ocean. Pablo settled into his new life begrudgingly but remained as content as he could. He noticed that the weather reflected his brother's mood and realised that Neverland was indeed Peter's, after all.

***

One evening at sundown, the sky flashed red and blue, and storm clouds shadowed the island. Peter stormed out from the forest and looked out at the ship by the island. 'They are hateful. They have been planning attacks to kill me! Nobody must be hateful, here. They are ruining everything!' Anger flashed across Peter's gaze. He walked into the ocean until the water was up to his waist and called the merpeople to him. They appeared, their heads surfacing from the water, and huddled around Peter.

Pablo looked at the ship nervously as the merpeople disappeared under the surface then reappeared by the ship. The men were once pirates and had gone back to their old ways. Pablo looked at the black and white flag grimly.

Peter raised his hands, and a mountainous wave loomed over the ship. Peter dropped his arms, and the wave crashed down onto the boat. Pablo watched as most of the crew were dragged into the murky depths by the merpeople. They tore the skin from the pirate's flesh and took the only woman on board, the captain's wife. Peter stopped, letting the rest go free, hoping he had taught them what would happen if they continued to try to fight them. The ocean was the only place untouched by the fountain and therefore, the only place in Neverland where one could die.

Peter smiled at Pablo as he passed him then walked back into the forest to the tree house he had built for them. Pablo looked down at his flute, and an idea popped into his head. If the flute gave Peter magic from the fountain, then surely, it could take it away, too. He pulled in a small canoe from one of the pools, pushed it out into the ocean, and climbed into it. He rowed over to the island, hoping Peter wouldn't come to the beach and see him, and nervously looked down at the water. A mermaid broke the surface and leaned on the side of the boat. 'What are you doing?'

Pablo pressed his lips together. 'To the island to punish the pirates more,' he lied.

The Enchanted Kingdoms

The mermaid seemed pleased with this and nodded before swimming away.

He reached the island and tied his canoe up. The pirates left on the ship had made a base on the island and were sat around a small fire. Pablo ducked behind the huge rocks and placed his lips to his flute. Slowly, the magic danced from the ground and flew into his flute. After fifteen minutes, he felt the last of the magic leave the ground and smiled.

'What yer doin'?' a gruff voice asked from behind him.

Pablo turned and jumped up. 'Look, I'm not your enemy nor your friend, but I do want to stop my brother's reign.'

The pirate narrowed his eyes. 'Why?'

'He's grown too powerful. He's dangerous,' Pablo admitted. 'Look, keep this to yourself. The island is free from Peter's power now.'

The pirate looked down. 'If yer lyin', I'll cut yer throat.'

'I'm not.'

The pirate laughed heartily and pulled out a dagger. Pablo backed away, but the pirate pushed the dagger against his own wrist. 'If there is not magic 'ere, then I will not heal?'

Pablo nodded and watched with horror as the pirate cut off his own hand. He screamed and fell to the ground as blood pooled into the dust. 'Told you,' Pablo said quickly and ran back to his canoe.

***

Peter shook Pablo awake the next evening and beckoned him to follow him down the clearing. Pablo sat next to Peter on a log and looked at the dancing flames of the fire.

'I know what you did,' Peter said darkly. 'You took power from the island. I tried to go there, and my powers did not work. Why would you do that to me, brother?'

Pablo gulped and lowered his gaze so as not to meet his twin's. 'I'm sorry, brother, but you have gone mad with power. You do not care who you hurt, and you will not talk about our parents ...'

'Enough,' Peter shouted. The sky above turned stormy, growling with impatience and flashing with reds and blues. 'You will hand me your flute.'

Pablo shook his head. 'It will not work for you properly. It is mine. Mother made it for me and ...'

'Give it to me!' Peter ordered. Slowly, large drops of rain crashed to the ground. Pablo jumped up. The fire extinguished, and they were left in the dark.

Pablo attempted to run. Vines from the ground chased him, attempting to capture him. Peter had every part of the forest ready to ensnare him, even the cobwebs dropped on him. Pablo panicked, headed into the thickest part of the forest—the bit that they called the woods due to its swamps, spaced-out, dead trees, and caves. Peter was close, and all the plants were swirling toward him. He quickly grabbed his flute and breathed in, taking the powers from the part of the woods he was in. Peter ran in and found Pablo. He was distraught to find that Pablo had taken power from the woods. He tried to fight him for the flute, but Pablo had always been the more athletic of the two.

Angry, Peter tricked Pablo one night, pretending to forgive him. 'Brother,' he said, smiling. 'It does not matter what happened. I miss you; come and eat with me.'

Pablo hesitantly walked out of the woods and back to the campfire. 'I called it Willow Woods,' Pablo said, 'after Mother. She has saved me more than once.'

Peter nodded, not letting his anger show through, and did a remarkable job at keeping calm enough that not even the weather changed. 'It's a wonderful tribute,' he lied.

Once outside the confines of the woods, Peter whistled, and hundreds of fairies appeared. 'Take him to the mountains!'

'Brother?'

Peter looked down. 'You are never to come back. You are banished to the mountains, and I will never let you leave there. If you do, I shall … I shall kill you.'

'Peter, no!' he screamed as he was pushed towards the mountains on the pirate's island. He tried to fight the fairies, but there were hundreds of them, all pulling at him. Peter used his powers to have vines wraps around Pablo's wrists and ankles. Once he was bound, they flew him up to the highest cave in the highest mountain and left him there.

***

Months turned into years, and Peter grew lonely without his brother. He walked down the beach and dipped his feet into the ocean. 'Why does no one venture here?'

A beautiful song filled his ears as three beautiful women swam over to him, their heads and chests bobbing about in the water. 'Hello, young man,' one said seductively. Peter gulped; they were the most beautiful women he had ever seen.

'Hi.'

They all smiled seductively and pushed out their heaving chests. 'I am Annora,' one said. She had gorgeous dark hair and olive skin with wide blue eyes.

The second spoke, her voice almost rang like bells. 'I am Ascilia.' She had dark blond hair, pale grey doe eyes, and thick lips.

The last had cinnamon skin, ebony black hair, and deep brown eyes. 'I am Avelina.'

'I'm Peter,' he replied, grinning. 'Welcome to Neverland.'

They all danced mesmerizingly in the water, stretching their arms out and making the water ripple over to Peter's feet. 'We heard this was the place where no one could die.'

He smiled. 'It is, it is.'

'We,' Avelina said, 'must eat souls to remain young, beautiful, and alive.'

Ascilia jumped in. 'But we would like to remain immortal forever.'

Peter raised his eyebrows. 'Of course, you can remain here with me.'

Annora pulled herself out of the water and climbed out onto the sand. Her tail melted away into the water. She kneeled on the hot sand and buried her fingers in the sand. 'I'd miss the water,' she admitted. She was the youngest of the three and the most free-spirited. 'We are sirens,' she explained, 'and we were cursed after we refused the advances of three warlocks. They had it so we could not

The Enchanted Kingdoms

love but only hunger for the flesh of men. To have to eat their flesh to survive. They didn't think we would do it.'

'But we did,' Avelina added. 'If only we could leave here and still be immortal. Perhaps you have magic that could help us?'

Ascilia smiled broadly. 'Please help us.'

Peter stood up. 'You can lure men?'

They all nodded.

'Then,' he said, smirking, 'lure men to Neverland, and I will give you water that will keep you immortal.'

The three sirens left and kept their end of the bargain; young men who passed through were lured into Neverland where Peter trapped them. Those who proved their allegiance stayed and were made into Lost Boys, and those who did not were banished to Willow Woods. One was turned into a fearsome giant who would eat anyone who went to Willow Woods.

Peter grew close to one fairy, Bell, and gave her the gift of some of his powers. She was able to jump between being a human and a fairy when she wanted, and she was Peter's most loyal subject.

However, Peter craved female company, and Bell was not enough. One night, he travelled until he found another world. He spent weeks in a strange city looking for a girl who he could bring to Neverland, who could be his queen. One night, he watched through a window as a plain looking blond girl read stories in her bed. He watched her night after night and realised she was lonelier than even he was.

Peter watched across the road, through the window, at the girl and her sister, whom he had heard call each other

Wendy and Alice. Peter flew over to the house, careful to stay out of sight, and floated next to the window, staying out of sight.

Alice looked out the window at the red skyline. Tears ran down her cheeks as she realised this would be the last time she looked out the window. Wendy started sobbing again behind her. Alice's stomach twisted uncomfortably. She turned and looked at her.

Wendy looked up with a face that almost mirrored Alice's. Heart-shaped, petite, and perfectly symmetrical with thin lips and glassy blue eyes. Alice swallowed, trying to move the lump in her throat, but it didn't work. She sat on the silk sheets and placed her hand on Wendy's. 'I'm leaving shortly.'

Wendy sat up straight and looked at Alice with wide eyes. 'I know we argue, but I—'

'I know.' Alice sniffed. 'I love you too. Even if you are a pain in the arse!' She giggled.

Wendy half smiled and looked at the open door. 'Mother's upset.'

'She always is about something,' Alice said, tight-lipped. 'It's not my fault if they won't accept me for me.'

Wendy nodded in acknowledgment.

Alice adjusted her cardigan. 'I'll come back for you one day.'

Wendy snorted. 'You'll forget all about me when you're off seeing the world.'

Alice shook her head. 'Never.' Alice grabbed a steel hairbrush from the dresser and brushed through Wendy's knotted hair. It was the same shade of ash blond like hers, but Wendy's was shorter, shoulder-length, whereas Alice's reached down her back. Not that it mattered as she always wore it in a ponytail with a blue ribbon anyway. 'Mother will have a heart attack if she sees your hair all knotted like this. Are you ready for the party tomorrow?'

She saw a glimmer of excitement in Wendy's eyes, but it disappeared as quickly as it came. 'It won't be the same without you,' Wendy admitted. 'Mother will be trying to set me up with Hugo.'

Alice smirked. 'Eww, not Hugo!'

Wendy scrunched her nose. 'I don't want to marry yet. I want to do what you do.'

'Two years,' Alice promised. 'Once you're nineteen, I will come for you, and we can travel together. Mother and Father can't stop you then.'

Wendy nodded slowly and bit her lip. 'I hope you find what you're looking for. I'll miss you.'

'Miss you too,' Alice said and turned. Tears crept out, but Alice didn't let Wendy see. She had spent years holding back tears to be the strong one.

Alice walked to the door and glanced to the left. 'Goodbye.'

Peter smiled as he watched Alice get into a car and leave. Wendy was alone and more vulnerable than ever.

***

Peter returned three days later and watched from a windowsill of a house across the road. Wendy sat by her window reading Alice's letter. She had arrived in Italy. Wendy felt jealousy bubble inside her and contemplated running away, as always. She felt completely and utterly alone. Daydreaming at the moon, she blinked rapidly as a shadow seemed to block the moon's shine to her window before flitting away. 'I must be tired.' She yawned and placed the letters on the desk next to her. The chimes from the clock sung in the background as she pulled on her nightdress and sighed. She knew so much more was out there than just attending engagements and marrying for money. So much more, maybe even magic.

Peter flew over and landed on the windowsill. Wendy gasped as she stared at the window and the boy behind it, his green eyes piercing into hers. Wendy jumped and knocked over her chair; she watched as the cat meowed and scrambled out of the room. 'Everything okay up there?' her mother called.

'Everything's fine,' she called back. It wasn't fine, but something told her that he was not a threat. The window slid up, and Wendy's heart pounded. 'My parents are downstairs,' she said quickly, just in case he got any ideas. 'How did you …? I am three stories up.'

Peter grinned as Wendy stuttered, and he lay on her bed, propping his feet up on the end. 'I flew.'

Wendy's eyes widened, and she took a step backward. 'People can't fly.'

He rolled his eyes. 'Sure, they can.' He jumped up and indeed flew in a swift, mesmerizing circle before landing back on her bed. 'Wendy,' the boy said with seriousness.

'How do you know my name?' Wendy didn't know what to do. She was sure that even Alice couldn't dream this up in her dizziest dreams. 'You can't be real.' He pinched her arm. 'Ouch,' she groaned, rubbing her arm.

The Enchanted Kingdoms

He smiled. 'Told you. I'm real. Look, I came here because I felt your young soul call out to me. You're lost, and I help those who are lost.'

She opened her mouth but quickly closed it. He was right.

He smiled warmly and leaned forward. 'I take lonely lost souls of the world to a home, one where they are never alone.'

Wendy gasped and jumped backward. 'Oh, my gosh! You're death, aren't you? Here to take me to heaven … or hell …' she said grimly.

He laughed boyishly. 'Of course, not. In Neverland, we would never grow old.'

She furrowed her brows. 'Sounds like death to me.'

He placed his hand on her shoulder, and she felt her worries melt away. 'You're just going to have to trust me. We're going to a magical place called Neverland. Pack some things; we leave now. You'll love it there.' He looked around. 'Unless you'd rather stay?'

Wendy had always been known for being the most sensible and cautious sister, yet Alice sprung to mind. What would Alice do? 'This is like an adventure, right?'

'Yes,' he said and smiled broadly.

'Okay,' she said excitedly. 'I'll pack. Give me ten minutes.' Grabbing a satchel, she only packed a few necessities, mainly dresses, and hung it on her shoulder then put on and fastened her coat. She shoved her feet into her shoes and ran into her father's study. She looked down at the beautiful rose necklace that she had been given for her birthday and dropped it into an envelope. She scrawled a quick letter detailing what had happened, Peter, and the magical world of Neverland. She addressed it to the last address where Alice had sent a letter from in Italy. Placing it between her father's outgoing post for the following day, she left a farewell note to her parents on her bed, saying she wasn't coming back, and leapt out of the window with Peter into the chilly night.

***

When they reached Neverland, Wendy squealed with delight. It was beautiful. She met the Lost Boys, who adored her, and met Bell, who flamed with jealousy. Wendy played and danced with Peter and the boys and, more importantly, explored.

'You must never go that island,' Peter warned her, pointing at the small island across the ocean.

'Why?'

He frowned. 'It is full of bad men.'

She nodded but continued to stare at the mountains. 'I'm going to swim with mermaids,' she said, smiling.

Peter grinned. 'Okay. I will see you for dinner.' He walked back into the forest, and she pulled a canoe into the ocean. She rowed over to the island and avoided being seen by the pirates who were in their camp. She could hear a beautiful melody dancing around the mountains and was lured by it. She ventured into a cave and met the dreaded Pied Piper who Peter had told her about. Peter had told her and the Lost Boys that he was a ferocious man who killed anyone on sight and lured them in with his nightmarish melodies.

'Who are you?' Pablo asked.

'Wendy,' she said shakily.

He smiled. 'I'm Pablo.'

'Peter said you're a murderer.'

He laughed. 'I have, indeed, murdered for my brother, but I promise you that I am the lesser of two evils.'

They sat in the cave and talked all night. Wendy left to go back to Peter but promised to return the following day, which she did. With each visit, she found herself falling in love with Pablo. He was kind, selfless, and caring.

One night, Wendy returned to the island and saw Peter standing by the forest with his arms crossed. 'Come with me,' he ordered.

She followed him to a desolate part of the forest. 'What are we doing here?' she asked, looking around at the dead leaves, aged trees, and dead animals. She eyed a cage which stood in a clearing. 'Peter?'

'You betrayed me!' he shouted and pushed her into the cage. 'You will not die, but you will starve; you will be in horrible pain like you caused me.'

'Peter …' she cried, 'it's not like that. I do love you, I do, but Pablo wants a future with me where we grow up …'

'Never,' Peter screamed. 'I will never grow up, he will never grow up, and you will never grow up!' He marched away, leaving her to rot. When he reached camp, he promised never to love again. Never ever.

The Lost Boys called him the King of Hearts; able to make everyone love him with his magnetic personality and wonder, yet never love them back.

Haunting Fairytales Series

R. l. Weeks lives in Bradworthy, a small, charming village in North Devon. When she's not writing, she's designing covers, shopping, or reading.

She writes paranormal and historical erotica's with K. L. Roth.

Her Haunting Fairytales Series, published by Vamptasy, was voted Best Fairytale Books 2016 by Reality Bites Magazine.

As well as writing Fairytales, R. l. Weeks enjoys writing horror. You can find her gripping horror stories on Kindle.

Want to find out more? Check out her website www.authorrlweeks.com

Printed in Great Britain
by Amazon